FLIGHT HOME

John Philip wearing a white flying suit in Egypt

FLIGHT HOME

VIVIEN GILLIARD

Flight Home
Vivien Gilliard

Published by Aspect Design 2014
Malvern, Worcestershire, United Kingdom.

Designed, printed and bound by Aspect Design
89 Newtown Road, Malvern, Worcs. WR14 1PD
United Kingdom
Tel: 01684 561567
E-mail: allan@aspect-design.net
Website: www.aspect-design.net

Original photographs Copyright © 2014 Vivien Gilliard

ISBN 978-1-908832-55-9

FOREWORD

This is my first book, which took me many years to research and to write.

I was given some inspiration initially when we visited the Airborne Museum in 1999 and met the late Dr Adrian Groeneweg OBE. When he came to stay with us in England, we discussed in detail the prelude to Market Garden and the Battle of Arnhem in Holland in September 1944. The following year he took us around the battle sites, and gave us detailed information. We were moved to see all the young school children in the Oosterbeek cemetery laying flowers on the graves to commemorate the events of 17–25 September 1944. My grateful thanks to Annelise, Coert, Robert and Tim who, like many other families in Holland, have placed flowers each year on the graves of fallen airmen and soldiers for decades. We met them there in 1999.

Adrian was also instrumental in my subsequent contact with the navigator on a Stirling aircraft, Reg Lawton. Unfortunately, Reg was unable to meet me, and was initially reluctant to talk about his World War Two experiences, but after our first conversation in November 1999, we had long discussions on the phone, and he sent me some copies from his log book, as well as considerable detail about flight operations with John Philip, and his own life during World War Two and after it. Reg seemed to be a warm and caring person, and although we never met he was always happy and ready to talk in great detail about any matters related to his own war experience, as well as current political events. I am indebted to him, and was sad to hear that he had passed away only a few years ago, well into his nineties. He regularly told me to 'hurry up and finish the book'.

I am grateful to Jeremy Matthews in Cornwall who gave me many interesting facts about village life there in the 1940s and certain events related to Emily's visits to her uncle and aunt.

My thanks to Valerie Hyman who read the whole of an early draft and encouraged me to persevere. Sylvia Shackleton helped by diligently typing certain archive letters. Also to Chris Shearer, who read one of the very first drafts and urged me on, despite its poor format. I attended two Arvon Foundation courses and I was guided by Sally Cline in the process of editing a part of my novel.

I would like to dedicate this to JDL. Throughout these long years, and many family and life events interruptions, I was given unstinting support, help and patience from him, and I believe I could not have completed this without his kindness and forbearance.

The book cover design was created with the help of Kerry Ellis from Texas, USA.

I am grateful to Daniel Smith at Aspect Design who has been aware of the importance of a publishing date for 2014 to coincide with the World War Two seventieth anniversary of the Arnhem battle, and the centenary of World War One.

HALE FAMILY TREE

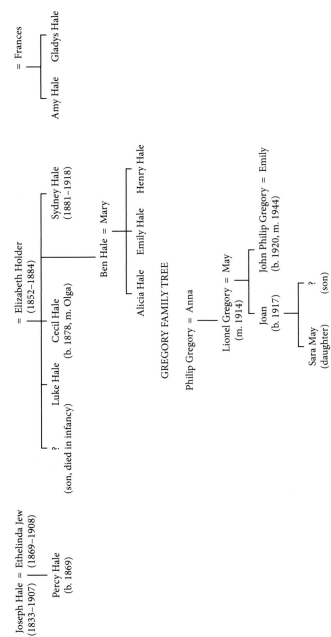

Joseph Hale = Ethelinda Jew
(1833–1907)   (1869–1908)

Percy Hale
(b. 1869)

= Elizabeth Holder
  (1852–1884)

? — (son, died in infancy)

Luke Hale
(b. 1878, m. Olga)

Cecil Hale

Sydney Hale
(1881–1918)

Ben Hale = Mary

Alicia Hale   Emily Hale   Henry Hale

= Frances

Amy Hale   Gladys Hale

GREGORY FAMILY TREE

Philip Gregory = Anna

Lionel Gregory = May
(m. 1914)

John Philip Gregory = Emily
(b. 1920, m. 1944)

Joan
(b. 1917)

Sara May
(daughter)

?
(son)

INTRODUCTION
DECEMBER 1998
THE HALE FAMILY

'Emily told me we should find everything about her past in a small leather suitcase, which she would leave under her bed.'

'How long ago was that?' his wife asked.

'At least ten years ago, I think. Here it is, just where she said; it is rather heavy.' David pulled it out and laid it on Emily's bed. They both touched it, carefully feeling the old soft leather exterior which was brown and water-stained in places. He unhooked the strap and opened the clasp.

'Look, it is full of letters, and photos.'

'And two old magazines. This one is dated 1942. I wonder why she kept it. There must be something in here that is important. Or interesting,' David said, as he flicked through the pages. Some typewritten sheets fell out onto the carpet. He picked them up. Emily must have typed these up on her portable typewriter, he thought. The pages were numbered, but the first page was missing. He looked gently inside the magazine, trying to retrieve the missing page. 'The spine is fragile. Maybe we should take it all downstairs and have a careful look.' As he spoke, he found the missing first page. Emily had folded it away inside an article in the magazine. Then he saw the black and white photograph of her with her pony and trap.

His wife was looking at a bundle of letters that were tied

together with some old string. She took out the top envelope, and carefully pulled out the letter.

'This is dated 1943.' She began to read it to herself, oblivious to David who silently read the article about his mother. When she finished reading, she looked at her husband and was about to tell him what she had read, but she saw that he was filled with his own emotional thoughts. She walked round to look at the old photograph in the magazine, and passed him the letter she had been reading.

'It's from Olga Hale,' he said, 'Uncle Cecil's wife.'

'Your great uncle Cecil, who lived at Mulberry House?'

'Yes.' There was a long pause, and he added, 'I wish I had known him, but he died not long after I was born. I did meet him, but I was a baby so I can't remember him, of course.'

'Perhaps you had better not read this letter yet.'

David seemed preoccupied by another photograph he had found, that had been folded into the same magazine. 'Look at this. That is Auntie Olga and my mother standing near the back door of Mulberry House with little Boxer, Olga's dog.'

They stood together inspecting each part of the little black and white photograph.

'Emily looks so young there. Do you think that was taken before the war?' his wife asked.

'I am guessing, but yes, I think it may have been. She told me she used to go down to Cornwall every year, and that Granny Mary went there with her and Alicia several times. It was a big house. Uncle Cecil was delighted to have them all to stay because he loved children, and Olga was too old to have a child when she married Cecil in the 1920s.'

'Is this Cecil?' She showed him a framed picture with a handsome man looking seriously at the photographer.

'Yes, that's him. Mother used to keep it on the mantelpiece downstairs,' David said, as he took several more photos out from under a bundle of letters. 'Look, this is Granny dressed up in her outfit for her part in the opera at Covent Garden before she got married.'

'She was beautiful.'

'Yes, we all thought so too. Certainly there were others who were attracted to her when she and Grandpa Ben lived in Nigeria.'

'What do you mean?'

'Well, there was a family rumour that she had had an affair.'

'There were many affairs, apparently, in those communities of ex-pats in the old British colonies!'

David wasn't listening to her, he had opened a magazine, dated 1941, where the page was folded over, and there was a tall man in a white flying suit, standing with others beside an aircraft in the desert. His wife looked at it over his shoulder.

'That's my father in his white desert flying suit,' said David.

'Let's take all this downstairs and study it more carefully with a cup of tea.'

'I think I'd like to read a few of the letters she kept in here,' David said quietly.

As he was closing the suitcase he saw a large envelope tucked inside the internal pocket, its fabric lining a faded red. He lifted it carefully out, and in bold black ink, he read out, 'My special brother, Percy.' The handwriting was the same as he had seen on old manuscripts, cursive, elegant and neat.

'What's in here?' he said to himself. He pulled out a pencil drawing on cartridge paper, which had not faded in any way, only the paper was yellowing slightly on the edges.

'That's a delicately beautiful drawing—who is that?'

'Maybe it is Cecil's brother. Mother told me he talked a few times about him when they stayed at Mulberry House, and that he still seemed sad when he remembered the old stories about Percy.'

'He's sitting on a horse here . . . do you think that could be his mother beside him, she looks so elegant in her long dress and hat?'

'Maybe, the artist captured something special about them. There are words underneath in tiny writing, I can't quite read them.'

'I can, the artist, or somebody, has written "Elizabeth with Percy on his horse."

The date looks like eighteen-seventy-something, is that an eight or a zero?'

PART ONE

CHAPTER ONE
OREDOWN, EAST SUSSEX, 1876

PERCY HALE'S VOICE

I struggled to climb up on to the seat of the pony and trap. At nine years old, I felt so grown up, but being short for my age, meant that it was difficult to get my foot up onto the step. I hesitated. When Father was in a hurry he would not wait for me to struggle up on my own, but would roughly lift me onto the seat. Father did not notice me for the rest of the day. He got onto the trap, quietened our pony, Alice, and waited. As soon as I was seated she trotted to the mill.

I looked at my father frequently. I knew he was irritable and preoccupied, but he looked different; his back was curved, his chin tucked toward his chest, eyes straight ahead. I had never seen his eyes red like that. He cleared his throat often, and stared into the distance, past the dark woods bordering the field to our house.

Not wishing to be a nuisance, and fearful of asking questions, I kept quiet, and let the thoughts pour in. The thoughts of the last few days would not stop travelling through my head. Baby Luke and my stepmother, Elizabeth, and the faces of those in the house. Luke was tiny the first time I saw him. Elizabeth held him close to her; breast feeding him. I had not seen that before. She looked down at him as he lay in her arms. I was startled when she spoke to me.

'Percy, he can't see me properly. Look at his eyes, they do not focus like ours.'

I remember coming closer to look into his face. He was smaller than anything I had ever seen.

'Yes,' I said. I saw how he looked at her, and that his dark blue eyes were different. I thought, he is looking at you, but I felt frightened to speak. I noticed the way she held him close. She had not held me that way during the four years she had lived with us. She had never talked to me, or even noticed me, before today. The skin on her face was smooth and rosy. When she smiled down at Luke she looked pretty. I had not thought she was even pretty before.

'Do you want to touch Luke's face? His skin feels like silk.'

I hesitated, afraid that she would get cross with me again if I did not touch Luke in the way she wanted me to. Her hand reached for mine and held mine. Looking at me, she put one of my fingers on his little cheek and I stroked him. He felt soft. Then he stopped suckling. I thought she would be angry with me. My baby brother's face moved towards the side where I had been touching his cheek. At that moment, I felt he was looking at me, and I could see how big his eyes were next to mine. I was closer to his face then, closer than she had been.

'Why can't he see me?'

'He can't until he grows bigger. His eyes will change, that's why.'

Maybe, again, she was cross with me. Luke looked at me, I was sure he did.

I remembered how he did that. Then I stood very still and watched her holding my baby brother. I wanted to stay close. She was kind to me that first day. And again the next day.

'Percy, go and find Nanny and bring her here.' Her voice was gentle in my ear, not like before. It was easy now to do what she asked. So I ran to get Nanny.

Quickly, because I wanted to be back before Luke stopped

feeding. Nanny followed me up the stairs. Slowly. Her feet heavy on each step, *thump, thump* and *thump* all the way up one flight. I got back to the room and told her Nanny was on the way, but she never looked at me again that day. At night I heard Luke crying all the time. Nanny didn't answer my questions the next day.

'Why was Luke crying?'

'Oh, no, he didn't cry much. You were asleep most of the night.'

'Was he sad?'

'Maybe hungry.'

'Why couldn't he eat then?'

'Oh, no, eating is not the only reason.'

Each answer started with the same 'oh no'. After three days, when Luke was nearly seven days old, I told her, laughing, 'Oh, no, Luke is crying such a lot again.'

I waited, expecting to hear 'oh no' back.

'He has a fever today.' Her mouth closed and her lips were pressed away.

'A fever, what is that?'

'Oh, no, dear, you don't need to know about that, Percy.'

'Please, tell me.'

She walked quickly out of the room. She left me to eat on my own, and without closing my door as she always told me to. The little hat on her head was crooked. I heard strange voices in the room below. Voices whispered. Later, the sound of horse's hooves clacked into the yard. I ran to the top of the stairs. I hid near the bannisters,by the large thick post, where I knew nobody could see me from downstairs. I saw two men with Father. One face had a big red nose, the other was pale, with curly grey hair, messy and wind-blown. I had not seen those two before. Father stared up. I ran to the play room. I wished very hard he had not seen me.

I heard Father coming up the stairs, and when he closed the door of Elizabeth's room, I crept out, as I knew he was still with her. My chest thumped. I tried to listen from outside, checking first left and right to make sure Nanny was not there. I could hear, 'No, oh, no,' and other mumbling. I felt frightened, and Luke was not crying. Somehow, when he had been crying, I had known that he was there too.

I wanted to ask somebody why I was not being told anything. I remember going to the kitchen, to see who was there—and ask them. I saw two glum faces looking at me when I walked in. They turned back and faced one another, and carried on peeling the potatoes. I heard a peeled potato drop into a pan of water. Splash!

'Go back to your room,' Elsie told me in her bossy high pitched voice.

'Where can I find Nanny?'

Silence. They did not look at me, but exchanged looks, one with eyebrows up.

'What is happening upstairs?'

They did not speak, or look at me, again. Katie shrugged.

'Can I have something to eat?'

'Wait until tea time.'

'So, tell me, where can I find Nanny, please?'

'Never. Ask Mr Joseph Hale, your father, tomorrow.'

'Tomorrow? Why tomorrow? I want to know now.' I remember feeling the tears coming, and trying to stop them, and not being able to. Just like when I was little.

They both worked away as if I was not there and had not spoken. After a time, in which nobody spoke, I felt so hot in that big dark kitchen that I turned and walked out, but I banged shut the door.

'Bang!' I shouted to them. I wanted to hear a noise.

I went outside to look at the horses. I knew the doctor's horse, he was black with a white line between his ears. I stood waiting for a long time before I heard Father's voice behind me and it made me want to run away.

'Why are you standing there? Go away and play, Percy,' he shouted.

As I ran up the stairs I could hear stepmother crying. Not crying the way I cry, but big breaths, and wailing. Nanny was talking loudly enough for me to hear.

'Oh, no, it will be all right, Mrs Hale. You'll see.'

She wailed with a huge sob. I felt frightened. I hadn't heard her cry before.

So many people to ask, but no one would talk to me. Maybe Father would come back and I could ask him, but I knew I would be too frightened to do that.

Father had not spoken to me for most of my life, and he only started to see me when Elizabeth came to our house, as my new mother, four years ago. Before that I had been told to keep out of his way.

'Your Father told us he wants you to be good and quiet.' Nanny had said to me.

Today she repeated it.

'I'm not disturbing him.' I looked at her, and wanted to yell loudly. Now I wanted to add, 'I could not help it that Mother died, I was little. As small as Luke.'

The house was too still. I ran up to my room and shut the door so quietly that I hoped nobody would know I was in there. I went to the window and searched for somebody I knew in the yard below. Only one dark brown mare was tethered there, and I had no idea who owned her. I saw a tall man come out of the house. He put on his top hat, and mounted the horse. He looked to me like a black witch from the story books, but the witches were usually women with large cloaks and full skirts. He wore a long black tail coat, and black trousers which stuck to his body. As he rode up the hill, I watched until he disappeared and became a long thin black line with dust rising behind him. Much later Nanny crept in with a tray of food.

'Here's your tea.'

'I am not hungry, Nanny.'

'Cook tells me you asked for food.'

'Where is Luke?'

She looked as if she was about to cry and her lip wobbled. She coughed, then turned her back to me and walked to the window. Her hands were red and she clasped and unclasped them behind her back.

'Are you going to tell me now?'

'You will see very soon.'

'What will I see? So . . . can I go and look at Luke again?'

'Oh, no, in good time you will.' She pulled at the hair that was falling over her left eye. She pushed it under her bonnet.

'What does that mean, Nanny?'

'Your Father is busy, and he will talk to you later.' She stared out through the window behind me, avoiding my eyes . . . then took out her handkerchief from the pocket of her white apron and wiped her eyes.

'Shall I go and see mother Elizabeth now?'

'Oh, no, she will not want to see you now. She wants to be on her own,' she whispered.

'Where is Luke then, is he with her now?'

She bit her top lip, coughed, and turned away back to the window. She told me that Father would be free soon, and he would call me and explain everything.

'Now be good and stop asking everyone questions. We can't tell you anything.'

'I don't feel hungry. You eat this.'

'Oh, no, I get my tea later with the others, in the kitchen.'

'Will you take me to see Luke?'

'Oh.' Then she paused, and I could see her face and eyes looking around as if she was trying to add something to her regular words, and that maybe she thought she could find them hiding somewhere in the room. I sensed my anger rising. Everyone in the house often told me to be good, or else this or that could happen. Being good was stuck on me with their glue, and now I no longer wanted anything that those around me wanted.

Good, yes, I am that, and it never gives me an answer.

I curled my two hands into a fist, and punched the desk where she had put the food. The tray bounced, and the crockery and cutlery made sounds so that she quickly came over to where I was standing, and kneeled beside me. For the first time in hours, I felt an arm around my shoulders and then she gave me a hug, just the way she used to when I was little.

'Oh, now you are a big boy, and Nanny doesn't hug you the way you needed me to when you were small. You will understand soon enough.' As she was getting back to her feet, we both heard the loud knock on the door, and suddenly Father appeared, holding the door wide open.

'Percy, come downstairs with me, now. I have to talk to you.'

I could feel myself blushing, and my heart thumping just as it did when I had been running fast, or riding hard. My feet felt heavy as I followed him down to his study. He pushed open the door, and once I walked in, I heard a sharp clack behind me. It startled me. I turned to see the big black latch falling closed. The old red rug muffled the sound of our steps. There he stood, facing me. The long burgundy curtains were pulled open, but it felt darker than last time I was in here. I must have been five or six then, and now its huge, tall, wood-panelled walls, book lined on the far side, looked unfamiliar. Father had his back to the tall window. His face was in shadow. He clasped his hands behind him, just like Nanny had earlier. I stood in front of him and tried to push my hands into my pockets, but my fists would not go in so I unclenched my hands, and waited.

'Sit down, Percy.'

I wondered whether to sit on the floor on the spot where I stood, or find a chair. He must have seen me hesitate.

'Sit there.'

He pointed to a large brown leather armchair in front of his huge desk. When I was seated, he looked at me, but did not speak. The longer I waited, the louder my heart seemed to beat. Could he hear it? I felt as if he was looking at every part of me for the first time. He looked at my feet, then my body, and finally my face. I looked away from his penetrating gaze, but when I looked back he was still staring at my face.

'You are beginning to resemble your mother.'

At that moment I longed to ask about her.

Could there be something about me that might at last make him want to know me?

I had other questions to ask. Only one fell out of my mouth, and once it was out I wanted to swallow it back again. Too late. I took my hands out of my pockets, and put them on my lap. Nanny always told me not to put them in my pockets, but I did. Especially when I was cold. I was cold now, and starting to get frightened. He did not answer me, and only after an uncomfortably long time, he went to sit on the chair by his desk, and turn again to face me.

'Your little brother, Luke, had a fever.'

'What is that?'

'His body got very hot, too hot.'

'Can we give him some cold water then?'

Again I felt as if I had asked the wrong question.

'No, there was nothing the doctor, or Elizabeth, could do,' he sighed. 'He has passed away.'

'Passed away? Does that mean "died", Father? Like our old dog?'

'Too many questions, Percy. Yes, yes and yes.'

Then warm tears ran down my face, and I could not control a big sob that escaped from my mouth. Now I was like mother Elizabeth. I wiped my face, but more tears came, then I sniffed and Father asked me to go and get a handkerchief. I could not move. The last thing I remember was that he put his hand on my shoulder and led me up the stairs.

PERCY'S VOICE

When my brother Cecil was born in 1878, Father had been at the mill all night after a flood. He returned at dawn. I had heard his horse in the lane and then in the yard below. I got out of bed quickly. I was familiar with these sounds because his horse trotted in a certain way. The hooves were strong and rhythmic, and when Father dismounted, Hastings did not stand still, he clicked his front hooves for several minutes in the yard, as if he was trying to dislodge some stones from his shoes. He always made the same movements, over and over, even after my father had gone inside.

'A robust little boy, Mr Hale,' Nanny had announced. 'Mrs Hale is waiting for you.' She must have heard Hastings arrive, as she had gone to the front door herself. I had been hiding behind the banister when he came in, and I saw him leave his brown hat on the hat stand, brush his jacket with his hands, and go to his study. I pictured him in there. Would he be long? I decided not to wait. Instead I went to look for Nanny in the kitchen. The door was ajar. I heard her telling Elsie that baby Cecil looked like his father, and was a big fellow.

'That will please Mr Hale. Now he has a second son, he will have one of the boys to take over the mill.'

I did not see Cecil until he was nearly ten days old. Nanny kept asking me to go in, but I decided it would be better if he was older before I got to know him. A year later, Ben was born. I found it easier to allow myself to play with them then. I remember thinking that if one died, there would still be one brother left. The memory of baby Luke's face still haunted me.

'Oh, Percy, come and hold Cecil's hand, while I put Ben in the chair for a walk.'

That was the first time we went out for a walk all together.

Father sent me away to boarding school when I was eleven, and my life changed. I had to learn subjects quickly that I had learnt in my own time at home. Boys were rough, and some were too ready for fights. Hitting and pushing, so I would hit back. Would I be able to cope, I wondered?

When I returned for the holidays my brothers were bigger. There they were, by the front door, racing one another to get to me first. It was the only time I got hugs and wet kisses. These were the moments that gave me courage to accept the time away from home.

'I am home,' I knew my shout would reverberate around the house, if I stood on the flagstones in the echoing hallway. It worked each time I did it, and somebody appeared, usually Cecil. Then they both stood behind the large dark brown wooden banister, at the top of the stairs, on the landing where I used to hide. I expect they thought I could not see them. I ran up the stairs two at a time. They giggled and ran into the nursery. I was faster, and caught Cecil and lifted him up, swung him over my shoulder before putting him down, while Ben had his arms in the air waiting for his turn.

'Ben, you're so big now.' I took him up and swung him round then tickled under his arm. Just then we all heard the bell for our tea. I led them downstairs. I could hear my insides rumbling, even though I had eaten a few apples from the orchard earlier.

'Who's hungry?'

'Me!' they answered together.

Old Nanny was waiting for us. Her hair was nearly all white now. It looked thin, and her white lace-edged bonnet was pulled hard down just above her ears. She handed us each our glass of milk, and passed round a plate of thick-sliced bread, generously spread with butter. A blue china bowl full of jam stood in the middle of the table. We were given two boiled eggs each. As I ate, I thought it comforting to be back in the old routine. I looked at my brothers, who were eating ravenously. I caught them shyly looking at me. When I had eaten my eggs, I spread the jam on my bread. They reached over for the bread and copied me.

'You are staring at me.' I wondered if I had changed much. I knew I was taller. I could tell that Cecil would grow taller than me. I looked at their bright blue eyes, smiled, and suggested we all explore the forest the next morning. 'Who wants to come?'

'Me.' Both waved their hands. Then silence.

'Please may I have another slice of bread, Nanny?'

She responded easily, and as she sat down again beside me, I noticed how awkwardly she bent herself into the chair. I had not noticed before, but today her back was hunched and her head was angled forward. The wisps of hair under her bonnet that kept escaping, she would push back in again each time. Could all these changes to my Nanny have happened during the ten weeks I had been away? It was easy to remember her as busy and active, but seeing her physical changes made me sad.

'Come with us tomorrow, will you, Nanny?' I asked, half in doubt, but wanting to believe that it could be like old times.

'Oh no, Percy, I walk too slowly for you young ones. Still it'd be best if you left Ben with me, then he can help me to play and soothe your new baby brother, Sydney.'

Ben started to cry. He was big, a chunky, broad-shouldered child, not tall and fine boned like Cecil. Even though a little boy and just out of babyhood, Ben's tears and sad face upset me.

'I'll take you with me the next day, Ben and we'll leave Cecil behind.'

His tears stopped, and he took another piece of bread.

'I will show you both my favourite tree. I used to try to climb it when I was ten, but I could only go half way up. I'm taller now, so I may be able to reach up further.

'Will you teach me?'

'Yes, Cecil, I will. Climbing's easy, you just need to remember to get a good place for your feet and hands. When you are thirteen you'll be as good as me. Then I will teach you, too, Ben.'

Cecil and Ben woke early, and came to get me up. We poured the water from the jug into the bowl, washed our faces with the flannel, then we dressed quickly and went to join the others for breakfast.

'You're lucky it's a clear bright day Cecil so we can go and find that oak tree.'

We went to the edge of the forest, which was near the manor house. Along the familiar track Cecil held my hand. He talked to me about other countries and how he was learning about different parts of the world. His excitement was infectious. In the 1870s ships and people were exploring different continents and oceans, and our old tutor had been teaching him because Cecil was interested in that subject.

'I am very big and what I want to do is sail on a huge ship and learn to be a sailor, like those lads we see in the harbour in Hastings.'

'What does Father say?'

'Oh, nothing.' I thought he sounded dismal, so I walked faster to get to our tree, and comforted him by explaining that if he worked hard he could still follow his wishes.

The sun was shining through the early fog, and burning off the low-lying mist. As I got to the group of oaks, I stopped.

'Are we here?'

'Yes, which tree do you think it is?'

Cecil looked about and up into the canopy.

The trees were still dormant. The tender, pale, small, green leaves would appear in March or April if it was not too cold. He turned to the west, and then back to where we had come from. After a long pause, he shook his head.

'Can't guess.'

I let go of his hand, and walked towards my tree. I was tall enough to stretch up and catch the lowest branch without having to leap up. Pulling myself up on it, I then stood there above him.

I could touch the next branch on my left and easily swing my feet up to the branch a few feet above.

'What about me?'

'I'll come and get you in a moment. Just watch me and see how easy it is once you know how, then I'll come and give you a hand and a push. I can get myself half way up.' I glanced down at him, and suddenly felt sad. I had been playing alone when I was young. My constant fear was that each baby would die before we could run around together. Losing Luke had left me with an aching sadness I could barely comprehend. Now I had Cecil. A happy time, I thought, as I looked down at him. Yet, it was not so long ago that Nanny was angry with me for not wanting to meet that new born baby.

'Mrs Hale is cross that you will not come and see the baby,' she had told me.

'I can't . . . I get butterflies in my tummy, when you ask me to go in there.'

When Luke died, they had left me with Auntie Jesse who worked at her embroidery all day and she had refused to speak to me.

'Hurry down, will you?' His loud voice pushed me back to the present.

Cecil was waiting and so I carefully angled my body around a branch, found my footing, and then sat on the first branch looking down at him.

'Now hold my hand tight, I will reach down, then pull you up so you can take hold of this branch.'

Before taking my hand he jumped up with his arms outstretched, and just caught the branch I was sitting on. I thought of him as my little brother, yet he could already reach up, because he was so tall, and we quickly went higher than half way. I showed him a strong branch that we could sit on together, which gave us a view of the deep blue stormy sea in the distance. He looked thrilled. Then we heard voices, and I put my hand to my mouth for him to be quiet. Below us, along the footpath came a small group of farm workers and children. Men wore brown woollen trousers and loose shirts, and the women had on long skirts. One was carrying a baby wrapped in a blanket, on her back. Another small child carried a dead black rabbit by the ears, as he ran to keep up with the others. He was followed by a man who held a bunch of rabbits. We could barely hear their words, but from the tone we knew they were local. An older man walked slowly some way behind that group. He held a worn old cap in his hand and we could see his white hair and long beard. When they were safely past us, I helped Cecil down from my oak tree.

'We can bring some bread and cheese next time, once Ben has learned to do this.'

'I'd like that.'

I did not know that there would be no more climbing for me. As Cecil and I walked back home, I remember how happy I had been that afternoon.

PART TWO

THE GREGORY FAMILY

CHAPTER TWO
France, Paris 1920
After the First World War

May woke and felt helpless and desperate. Lionel had screamed again in his sleep most of the night. She asked the doctor who lived in the building for help.

'Il souffre de sequelles dues aux gas employee par les Allemands pendant la guerre, Madame.' Dr Lefevre informed her that he suffered from the gas the Germans used during the war.

'Will he get better? Is there anything we can do?'

A little girl in the corner of the room started to cry before he could reply.

May picked up Joan and returned to the bedside. She stroked her face to soothe her, but Joan became fearful of the stranger beside her mother and cried louder.

'Madame, I am expected in the hospital. Give this for sleep, nothing more to be done. Bonjour.'

He handed her a small envelope full of a powder, and picked up his leather bag, saying abruptly he would see himself out. May heard footsteps hurrying down the stone staircase outside. She returned to soothing Joan, then looked in on Lionel who was now asleep. She could hardly bear to hear his laboured, painful breathing. Quietly, she walked away from his bed to her baby son, John Philip (JP). Joan followed. They both looked at the sleeping new born in his tiny basket. 'Shush, JP's sleeping now.' She gave Joan a gentle kiss on the cheek, and placed her index finger on her lips. Joan followed her to the far end of their room, where they were billeted with a French family on the first floor. The windows overlooked the street.

The peachy early morning light filtered in. It had been dark when she heard her husband's rasping breath. She had left their bed and lit a gas light. Waiting, listening, pacing, all of this while she could hear Lionel coughing and taking breaths in difficult gasps. Once he'd called to her for a brandy. His face had been red and wet.

Fear had enveloped her thoughts. 'Was it a fever?' He had taken the brandy and swallowed the large first measure in two gulps, then signalled for more. The gas lamp's cold, distorted, grey-blue light had made him almost ghost-like, even with the redness around his cheeks and swollen eyes.

'Have you sent for a doctor?' Lionel's words had sounded like a command barked at an army foot soldier.

'I have.'

May thought, 'He's had orders given to him for years . . . perhaps it has become his way of communicating now. I should forgive . . . yet he barked instructions at me. We can be together again. He will need me to help him recover . . . I remember our meeting in the station.'

She had not noticed him, and walked past him at the railway station.

'May, it's Lionel . . . ,' he spoke in a deep, grating voice she hadn't recognised.

She had tried to conceal her shock. His clothes had hung loosely from his frame. The jacket and his greatcoat looked much too large. His eyes were red and the skin on his face scarred and pock marked. He had written to her from hospital, but her expectations and hopes for a reunion were an awkward dream on that day. His nervousness, especially at anything sudden or noisy became unsettling. When John Philip suddenly started to cry, his father became anxious. He disliked to hear crying, and told her to calm their baby.

A loud cry drew her back into the present. Baby JP wanted a feed. Joan went to the cot to comfort her brother. May gazed lovingly at them. Both had their father's distinctive bright ginger hair. Joan's was a mass of long ginger curls. Her son was not comforted by the rocking, but then Joan put her index finger to her lips, saying 'shush' the same way as her mother had earlier. As she repeated this she rocked his basket. May went to them and gently lifted her son and put him to her breast. He suckled immediately. While he fed she stroked his head lovingly.

May mused, 'Only a few more months, and then I can wean John Philip. It will get easier when Lionel will be de-mobbed, and then we can sail back to England for Christmas. We'll return to live in north London with Lionel's father, Philip.'

While she fed JP her thoughts wandered, 'When he returned from the battles on the first visit he had not been my talkative old Lionel. Before going back to the front, he'd been morose, although he would go out each night drinking with other military men. I became sad at the thought of his departure and fearful that he might die. Then, after Armistice day, he was restless at night and rose at dawn each day. As well as the daylight agitations, his nights seem filled with nightmares. I'd wake to repetitive phrases shouted out, and limbs kicking. I ignored these early signs, then after a while I could not . . . The night terrors came again and again. Neither of us spoke about them.'

As time passed, he became more aloof, and silent a great deal of the day. At night he would go drinking with any other de-mobbed men.

May hoped Lionel would be happy to be free from the battles. She saw that he never held Joan or talked to her.

Suddenly, she saw Lionel in his uniform. He walked straight to the front entrance.

'He looks pale and yellow. Why has he got up?' But May did not ask him.

'I'm expected for duty today.'

With those few words, while he stood by the door, barely making eye contact with her, he marched out, carrying his hat.

May heard him walk briskly down the old stone stairs, and slam the external door of the building.

Lionel thought, 'It's hard to tell May the truth. I want to forget it, then we can start again. It should be obvious to her what our army suffered. My reality, my experiences . . . those years are continually around me. What I see in my world, she cannot know. Those who understand are the others who, like me, have survived. People only read about our war, and become confused by their illusions and misperceptions.[1] There should be a map . . . so they can know how it was there. I feel tired and ill. She has our John Philip and Joan to care for. Our life is not how it was. I am afraid . . . and I'm twenty-six. I must stop remembering. My children are the future now.' Lionel thought silently.

'You will all come to live with us,' Philip wrote with relief, to his son Lionel. Three of his neighbours never found their sons, or fathers, again.

Anna, Lionel's mother, had made space for them all in their small terraced house.

May quickly occupied herself and took in sewing. Nevertheless, the children soon needed larger clothes, and they were often short of money.

'JP cannot wear anything of Joan's!' May told Anna, trying to sound amusing.

Lionel left in the mornings to look for work, and returned at dusk. He never told his family that, like many others, he went to the soup kitchens set up for them by the British Legion.

From their terraced house, Philip would stand at the top floor window, where he was able to see the whole street, and look out for his son each evening.

'Well, son, anything for you?'

Philip had been a tall, muscular, strong man and had worked in constructing railways for years before the war. After an injury he had been given work as a clerk's assistant. He was fortunate that he could read and write and that he was numerate. He had known others hurt or disabled doing construction work who were dismissed and rarely found any other employment.

Begging on the streets was one option for the most unfortunate. Lionel looked at his father and wondered how to respond. Philip's grey hair was thinning and his upper body had shrunk.

'Nothing for any of us, Father, but . . .' his voice trailed off. He looked up at the ceiling. He wanted to tell him it seemed so hopeless, but he dared not. Father was kind, and always positive. They lived from his meagre income and the rent he got from a tenant in the basement.

'Where did you go this day?'

'Up by the docks and all around,' then slowly, and very quietly he added, 'too many of us, Father.'

Many evenings he had wanted to add that sad ending. He hadn't dared to. Lionel had tried the docks again that day, after not going near there for a while, but ended up sitting on the steps with other men, all desperate for work. They preferred to gather in groups with others like themselves, who had experience of the Great War. Nobody spoke much. It was a silent comradeship of mutual understanding about the trials and sufferings of their war. A group of sad, bereaved, and injured men.[2]

Your skin looks as if it clings to your bones, Lionel.' May had not wanted to say anything when he refused his dinner, but she could not stop herself. He had not eaten properly for several days. 'You are thinner now than when you left the army three years ago.'

Lionel thought angrily, 'I'll ignore what her criticisms imply.'

'Have you asked Father about using the lodger's room for your sewing?' he asked her instead. Father's lodger had left to go and live in Cornwall with his own family where he could work on the fishing boats. If she could take in more sewing, it would help them earn a few shillings towards their keep.

'Yes, I spoke to your father last night.'

Lionel took hold of her hand.

'He is happy to give me the extra space so I can take in as much as comes our way. If, after four weeks, I earn more than he'd get for renting it then we'll keep the arrangement.'

He kissed her hand. 'I am going out now, there is a man I met at the station who may have work for me.' May smiled at him and kissed his cheeks before he left. JP hugged his legs.

May thought to herself, 'In the weeks after our return from France, Lionel went out looking for work most days. Now I hope he finds some companionship in whatever he chooses. He looks sick. He has no interest in his appearance. His thick hair is matted and too long on the sides, though not touching his collar at the back, which looks better.'

A week ago, she had left the children, and followed Lionel, staying back at a safe distance. She knew he could not have seen her as she was far behind. There had been many men, as well as other people, walking around aimlessly. Some struggled on wooden crutches with only one leg. The roads had been full of people walking, as well as the horses and carts. She had followed for nearly an hour. At first he looked aimless, but then she noticed other men fall in with him, and his group gradually grew larger. When they all ended up sitting on the stairs of the old theatre, she waited and watched, and then seeing nothing going on, she turned back.

It had started to rain, lightly at first, then heavier drops, and she had begun to feel cold because she had stood still. She had not wanted to get soaked; but the rain settled on her clothes, then gradually it seeped into the fabric. Her pale green shirt began to look dark as it got wet. She shivered. She had felt hot from the long walk when she had followed Lionel to the steps, and had removed her jacket. But she put it on again as she hurried home. Joan and JP would need their tea. Once indoors, she left out her wet jacket to dry on the stand by the range.

May never asked Lionel again what he did, nor about his waiting with others on those steps. He regularly returned at tea time, and crept in quietly from the back entrance which was always latched. She kept busy with their children, as well as washing, sewing, collecting, and delivering her work. Nothing changed their routine for many weeks, but it became colder.

JP was a toddler, starting to say some words, and Joan was having her fifth birthday on the day that Lionel was too ill to get out of bed. His face was swollen and his skin became the colour of straw. Once again his breathing became heavy and rasping. May heard a new irregularity and became frightened. She ran upstairs to the third floor to call Philip.

'Father, come with me to Lionel, I do not like how he looks today.'

It was not the first time she had rushed to call him. He slowly lifted himself off his deep armchair, as he had done before, then followed her down the winding narrow stairs.

'Shush,' Joan said, and she put her index finger to her lips, when she saw them both walk in. Then she whispered, 'Daddy is quiet.' JP stood by his sister holding her hand.

May became alarmed, the rasping breathing, and groans of several minutes before were now but an empty silence. She looked at her pretty little daughter, her bright, happy, blue eyes.

'Joan, go and get some water now from the pitcher. Go quietly, no noise now, must stay very quiet, yes?'

With those instructions, the child obediently tiptoed out from the room and took her brother away. May looked at Philip, then went to Lionel. She hoped to hear something.

'He was on the bed.'

He followed her, and stood behind her when she stopped abruptly two steps into the room. Lionel lay on his side. He had always lain half sitting to get air to his lungs. She knew now. Father looked at her; they had come too late. May gently turned Lionel on his back, and his father put his hand to his son's face and shut his eyelids. May sensed the fear taking over her whole being. She stood up and turned to look at Philip, who was staring, unblinking, at his son, tears were filling his eyes and falling down his cheeks.

'The gas killed him, he'd suffered too much.'

Her body felt weak, her knees were shaking, she stretched towards him, and steadied herself by holding his arm. The room felt airless, then dark, very dark.

1918

A man had earlier stuck an injection into Lionel, then dabbed the place with iodine. 'That's tetanus,' he had said.

Lionel was not used to being informed. The mustard gas gave a burning feeling in his body, as if he was standing too near the fireplace, and the flames lapped at him. He took out his arms from under the cover to cool himself, but the movement caused more pain and he still felt hot and sick as pain flowed over him. It grew, stabbing at his chest, and restricted his breath. He felt his eyes streaming, burning sensations on his cheeks made worse by his tears. Lionel wanted to call out, but felt ashamed, thinking there were so many there worse than him.

Eventually, the wretchedness caused him to shout for help.

The shout did not leave his voice box. Hardly a mumble emerged. Trying to look around he realised, with terror, his vision was blurred. Is it the tears or the gas? He put his hands to his eyes, but his fingers were strangely heavy.

He felt the rising panic, as he thought he might go blind. No longer thinking of the shame of groaning, his muffled sounds pleaded for relief. He was not a large man, in height he was average, but he felt himself shrinking. The flames of the earlier fire inside were still raging, and his eyes oozed more than before. He did not know how much time passed and whether that feeling had been that day or the one before.

He drifted off into a restless sleep. He awoke, and remembered the feel and sounds of a train. He was unsure whether he had dreamt it. His ears worked alright, because he had heard the train tracks and felt the movement. Once again he had been lifted and moved. He dozed, though his body still felt burning sensations. Then, miraculously, he felt himself between cool sheets on another stretcher. Earlier, someone had placed a cool bandage on his eyes.

Time passed; he woke to find he had been laid in bed. His thoughts wandered. 'Am I in a hospital? Nurses talking . . . people still groaning all around me. One lad called for his mother. I wonder where Jacks is . . . I hoped he'd be nearby . . . I'll ask a nurse . . . but she changed my eye bandages and didn't hear me speak . . . ask about Jacks, no sounds, only my mouth opened . . . hard to talk, still difficult and painful to breathe. Where's Jacks? How to ask . . . I heard the doctors . . . men in the ward . . . casualties of a gas attack . . . I'm twenty-four, and I feel like forty.'

Occasionally there were empty beds in their ward. He heard the lads ask nurse about the person taken from a bed. Nurse said 'Oh, he was moved to be nearer to the doctor.' Or she would say he'd been taken to treat his wounds. After a while the men stopped asking. They had grown wise to the nurse's denials. Lionel thought about young Jacks often . . . only eighteen years old, nearly nineteen; his birthday had been Christmas Eve.

He never saw Jacks again, although at that time he still held a hope that he would come across him. Weeks later Lionel was sent to a convalescent camp. He wrote to May.

France, 27 April 1918

My dear May,

I am well. I have been kept in hospital to recuperate,

and I'll work here.

There are injured men coming and going each day, mostly they are sent back to the front lines when they recover. I am fortunate that they are giving me more time to get my strength back.

It has been very cold, but I am indoors most of the time, and I cannot help thinking about all the men who are still out on the front. The doctor said I shall stay here until I return to Paris. You will be glad to know it will not be long from now. I do not know whether it is for a visit or more permanent.

I have not heard from Father, but then he does not know where I am. Please give him this address which I shall write on the back of the envelope. It would be safer if you write to him as the post is slow here.

A hug for you and Joan.

Yours ever,

Lionel

After delivering and paying for the letter to be sent, he was confronted by an irritable officer.

'You work here for your keep.'

Lionel glared back.

The man's rank was below his. 'Clean up this area daily,' he ordered as he marched off.

A medical officer heard him coughing later, and noticed his streaming eyes. 'What are you doing here?'

Lionel was startled, but he tried to reply. To his astonishment, the officer, seeing Lionel confused put a hand on his shoulder.

'Stop what you are doing. Come with me.'

Lionel walked slowly. The man waited, then took him into a cubicle, and checked him carefully.

'You do not have to work here, you should rest.'

Lionel stared in disbelief.

As the days passed Lionel thought that work may have distracted him from the constant hunger. Only memories of May helped. Rations were meagre as he had no spare money, and no parcels from home. They relied on the Church charity. It had been a long time since he had received fresh socks and underwear, and his uniform was threadbare and not at all warm.

By Armistice day on 11 November 1918 none of that mattered. Lionel was sent back to Paris where May and his baby daughter Joan were billeted with a local family in a large room.

Lionel thought he would soon be back in his home again. 'I think I will be safer back home in England.[3] Familiar places, with Father and Mother nearby.'

CHAPTER THREE
Oredown, East Sussex
Ben Hale . . . a Fall

Ben's two older brothers, Percy and Cecil, gave him his earliest memories of feeling content and safe. Ben crawled after them before he learned to walk, and looked up into their faces often before responding to his mother, Elizabeth, or his Nanny. Especially if he fell over, or was reprimanded for touching something he was not meant to. He took his lead from his brothers, and his place with the boys. If they were not near when he woke each day, he went to find them, and would not speak until he was with Percy or Cecil. It was their names he uttered first. It was the same later in life when he had matured; he chose the Navy for his career, or it chose him because working and being with other men felt the natural place to be. His posture and his speech explained his passion for the sea and for the men under his command. He had a special talent for understanding the men he was with; it was an unspoken knowledge learned from observation and scrutinising the faces of those older than him as he matured. Along with his talent to read other men, and to communicate with those who picked up his signals, was also his total comprehension of what his superiors expected of him at sea. Once he was promoted he showed his ability, and strict control dominated his life.

Young Ben scrutinised Percy first, then Cecil. Ben was two years younger than Cecil, so he preferred to emulate Percy.

He craved his company. Percy was the only person he allowed to think for him, and who taught him about their world. He believed that Percy knew best. Percy cherished him, and in turn Percy was given Ben's love. Being loved unconditionally in that way was something Percy had not experienced, because his own mother, Ethelinda, had died a few days after his birth.

'Prr,' were Ben's first understandable sounds. Later it became 'Perri' until at age two he was able to say 'Percy'. The three boys became inseparable, until Percy was sent away to school. The two younger boys tried to fill the empty space left by Percy's departure. They waited for the spring and summer holidays when he returned, and looked forward to Christmas with him again when he came back home. Then, when Percy turned thirteen and they were still living at Lennox House in Oredown, Ben and his brother had to cope with their first misfortune.

'Ben is the healthy one of my children,' Joseph said to those who asked about his family. When there was mumps or chicken pox, or any other germs, he would catch them, but recover before anyone else.

'You are a good boy,' people said to him. So he did his utmost to live up to their expectations. That year though, was different. Ben was playing quietly when he heard Percy return home from his work at the mill. He ran to the largest pillar of the bannisters at the top of the stairs. He saw Percy below carrying a small case.

'Ben,' Percy called. Ben stood very still. Not knowing that Percy too used to hide there years ago. It was his turn to go to the forest, but he thought Percy had forgotten him. Percy casually walked up the stairs, pretending he could not see his brother, until he reached the last step.

'Boo!'

'I saw you,' Ben shrieked excitedly.

'I did first.'

'No, me, me! Let's go out, shall we Percy?'

'We shall. First, let's go and greet Mother and tell her where we are going.'

'Shall I come?'

'Yes, give me your hand.' They went together, and found her in her room, sitting quietly with baby brother Sydney beside the fireplace which glowed with the logs in the hearth.

'Hello, Mother, can I take Ben out with our pony?'

'Yes, but be home for tea. Your father does not like to wait.'

'I certainly shall.'

'Watch the sun.'

'I know, at four it is at the top of the old beech tree.' That was the one that was struck by the lightening, and survived, but only with a lumpy trunk and several small young branches which tried to grow. He waved to her, and Ben followed him out.

'Get your outdoor shoes on,' she called as they closed the door behind them. They both ran to the stairs.

'I'll race you out.'

'I'll be first.'

'Me, me,' he said laughing.

'Shoes first. I have mine on already.'

'Wait for me.'

He ran towards Percy and saw him pick up his riding crop. They walked to the field, opened the gate and put the reins on his pony. He had been used to riding bare back, but this time he had his little brother with him. He lifted Ben on to the saddle, and swung up behind him, holding Ben with the reins either side as he led the pony gently out, and left the wooden gate open. On the softer flatter ground, he nudged her into a gentle trot, then into a canter. He noticed Ben had gone very quiet and stopped laughing, and as they neared the woods, Percy reined her in, but at the same moment she saw a movement in the grass and reared up. He held Ben tight to break their fall and protect his little brother, but in doing that, Percy took a hard fall on his back, and hit his head. Ben leapt up. He expected Percy to do the same, but he lay on the ground, groaning.

'Are you hurt?' Several minutes passed before he got an answer.

'I cannot get up, my legs will not move. Wait.' Ben sat down beside him, then, he saw tears rolling down Percy's face. Ben got agitated, and had no idea what to do. He too began to cry. The pony walked over to them, and snuffled them both, and then stood waiting beside them. Percy asked Ben to hold his hand, which he did, but Ben saw his brother close his eyes and fall asleep. That was how they were both found hours later when they had not returned for tea. Both boys were shivering, and Percy's lips were nearly blue.

Joseph sent his fastest horse to urgently call for the doctor.

'He has injured his spine, Mr Hale.' Dr Brown said. He hoped the doctor could resolve the paralysis of the legs. 'Rest, let him rest, he may regain the strength in them in time, and keep him warm.' Joseph looked stunned, and was unable to respond, but his wife Elizabeth took the diagnosis more practically and asked questions.

'How can he be moved?'

'He is in too much pain to be moved, that is why I have given him a sleeping draft. You can arrange some wheels, but not immediately. Leave him to rest. Make him comfortable for now. He picked up his black leather bag and walked to the door, then turned and asked if he could look in again the next day.

'Yes, yes, of course,' Joseph answered quietly. Cecil and Ben appeared at the door when the doctor left. They had been waiting outside.

As days passed, then a whole fortnight, his family began to accept that he would remain paralysed. He talked, only when urged. One day he became withdrawn, and despite Ben and Cecil's stories and visits, he just turned away and closed his eyes. Spring was late, and that year a heavy cold passed round the household. Ben was first to get well, and Percy seemed to get worse just as everyone else was getting over it. Dr Brown was called again to use his skills for a fever that Percy hadn't shaken off.

The leeches were used, but that night Percy was delirious. Joseph sat helplessly with his son, hearing his rasping, shallow breathing, which became worse and more laboured. As the dawn broke, he heard the breathing become lighter and feint. Joseph was horrified to see him gently pass away. The death certificate signed by their doctor indicated pneumonia as the cause of death.

CECIL

Cecil had sat with Percy each day after the fall. He read to him and Ben. They refused to go to lessons. Elizabeth encouraged them to do whatever they wished. The three boys had meals together in Percy's room. The large window opposite his bed faced west, so he could see the evening sun. On a cloudless day his room turned from gloom to brightness in the sunshine. Ben was monosyllabic since the accident. Cecil tried to be brave, not to cry, and sought to behave like the eldest. Two nights before Percy died, Cecil crept in on his own, holding a candle to light his way, and whispered to Percy, 'Please don't leave us, we love you.'

He felt the absence of his older brother deep inside his body. His back hurt and his legs felt heavy before the death. Afterwards, he felt a dull ache in his upper body. Ben would sit with his arms wrapped around his lower chest, and rock. Cecil tried to comfort his little brother, but not knowing what to say or do he left him alone, and stared out of their big window into the distance. Mother stayed in her room except at meal times. Father left for the mill long before any of them woke up, and he only returned for supper. They ate in silence, and it was the sounds of cutlery and glass which broke the stillness at table. Nanny cried, or appeared with swollen red eyes.

'Control yourself, dear, you will upset the boys,' was all Elizabeth could say to her repeatedly.

Cecil and Ben were allowed in to the front parlour on the day of Percy's funeral. 'Go in very quietly and say your farewells to Percy,' they were told. They tiptoed in holding hands, and walked round the pale wooden coffin that had been set on two upholstered green chairs.

'I feel hot,' Ben said in a tiny voice.

Cecil looked at him, then gasped, as the emotion and fear, together with tears, flooded into him too.

Mother stood with them both, and when they started to sob, she kissed them each on the top of their head, and embraced them. 'Come, we must leave him now,' she whispered quietly.

Nanny took them by the hand, and they went out toward the stairs. Half way up they looked back, and saw mother putting on a black hat, and pulling the ribbon down and tying it in a bow under her chin. She put on her black gloves and then a large cape. Two men, also in black, carried the coffin out, followed by Joseph. By the time the front door closed, they were already in the room above looking out of their window into the yard. Mother looked up. She saw a tearful Cecil with his face pressed to the glass. Ben had covered his face with a handkerchief.

The empty feeling of loss Cecil felt sometimes, even as an older man, was eased by chewing on his pipe and distracting himself. He determined to study and leave home.

Ben stopped crying that year, and became bad and naughty. Cecil found Percy's riding crop hidden under Ben's bed, and Ben kept an old shirt of Percy's under his pillow.

'I can still smell something on his shirt that reminds me of him,' Ben told Cecil, and he screamed at Nanny, and refused to let her ever take it away to be washed.

Cecil was given Percy's signet ring to wear as he became the eldest in the family.

PART THREE

CHAPTER FOUR

A summer in Cornwall . . . 1926[4]

Cecil's voice

I recall I accompanied Father, in silence, to the mill each day. I was given the reins at thirteen and our horse, Alice, took us. She had trotted there over many years, so a blindfold would not have stopped her finding the way. Father raised his hat to greet people on our way and I learned to copy him. We steered through some water meadows, and I saw the changing seasons by observing the wild flowers and insects. On warm days I looked out for the fireflies if it was dark when we returned. He rarely spoke to me, and when he did it was about our customers. I watched everything and learnt by using my five senses, just like a young child.

'You will take over the mill when you come of age,' he had said this on our way back from church one day.

'No, Father, I shall go to sea like Ben. I want to work abroad.'

He seemed to expect my rejection, and no more was said. Ben had gone as a naval cadet, and he'd started his sail training on the *Herzogin Cecilie,* a four-mast barque.[5] My younger brother Sydney, I knew, would step into my place at our mill.

The broken family environment propelled me out of Oredown and Hastings and the stifling feeling I had of routine and village life. I felt my world had changed dramatically when the familiarity of my mother's love had suddenly gone forever. Mother had died at thirty-two, when I was nine. Then Father married again, for the third time. His new wife brought two daughters with her. Years of unease, mourning and a lack of novelty set me on a path of flight from home. Ben had easily found his niche and gone into the navy at fourteen. That had made me watchful for opportunities . . . I looked towards London which opened up the world outside my village. My inner darkness lifted. I knew and loved my countryside, but climbing a tree to look out of my pocket world no longer settled me. I had found home life difficult when Percy had gone.

I got my first post in Burma. Before I left, I had met the daughter of Frank Cooper, and I wanted to marry her, but Father was not happy to go below our status, as he called it, for me to marry a grocer's daughter. I became resentful, and was keen to leave home. Years later, it became clear to me that I had not had the intelligence to decide about marriage then. When I met Olga, after the Great War, I knew that she was the one for me, and realised that Father had been right about the person, but not the reason.

One Saturday morning, just as the dawn light grew, I walked through my garden in Cornwall. I took short lazy steps, and I stood motionless there, near the centre, listening to the birds, and around them a gently rising breeze was rustling the leaves of my precious Pittosporum plants. There was a scent about the place on these early summer days, musty, yet pure and fresh; then by sunrise it dissipated. The leaves would glisten, as the sun rose, on the small pale leaves, and silvery green splashes would flow on the breeze through the shrubs. In those moments I felt my whole being back in Burma, for I had worked strenuously in early daylight and I had matured there, modestly, and amongst the unpretentious, gentle, native-born folk. It had smelt of dusty earth after a rain shower there, and my clothes would be glued to my arms and chest in the humid heat, a thing I did not often

Cecil and Olga at Mulberry House, Cornwall, 1927

experience in my tiny village of Tremena. Now, all alone, in this special hidden garden, with Olga slumbering in the house, I felt connected . . . joined with her forever, in our own home. Still, I recalled my disbelief in her love for me.

I had worked for myself in a rubber plantation in Burma in order to have this estate back in England. Olga wrote me letters full of her news and hoped our love would sustain the long separations. Plans for our future together were merely words on a page; for marriage one day in the future. I doubted a gentle, beautiful woman could love me. I remember waiting two years for my holiday back to England. The long five to six weeks of the ship's journey back was a party. Then there she was in Chingford when I visited her, always arriving by horse drawn cab. She was lonely as so few men were left after the slaughter of the First World War, I thought. I confronted my own loneliness only when I returned to the Burmese plantations. The men, and our familiar routine, drove me on. Each year passed, then it became six, and seven more years. We were betrothed and eventually secured our wedding date with letters. We had met when Olga was young. My procrastination left us childless. She never spoke of it, and neither did I. Today I would see her glow when she welcomed and enjoyed the company of Ben's daughters. Our only surrogate family.

'Cecil,' she put her arm through mine, 'you woke early.'

I was astonished at how quietly Olga had crept up on me. I led her back through to the open French doors. Our breakfast table was crisply laid with the Fortnum and Mason blue china tea set Ben and Mary had sent as a wedding gift. Aligned, as she knew I liked things. I could smell the toast and bacon in the kitchen.

'I'll get the toast.' As she placed it between us she caressed my shoulders and told me the bed had felt cold when I left. I saw her scrutinising me, then in the vernacular, 'Why so early today?'

'I was thinking of Burma, how much I missed being with you then.'

'Are you reconsidering my journey there with you next year?'

'I only need to go back one last time, but I shall not go without you.'

'I want to see where and how you lived and worked, all those years without me.'

We heard Cathy, my factotum, coming in the kitchen side door. She was humming.

'We must leave in plenty of time for Penzance station,' Olga said as she went out to greet Cathy and plan the menu for the week.

When we both came to live in Cornwall after our wedding, I was relieved that Cathy took easily to Olga. Cathy had been running my home alone for years. Within a few days I found them together unpacking and organising all our wedding gifts from the crates, and animatedly talking about our wedding, and the guests, as well as plans for the house. My relief took the place of trepidation, but then the people who met my wife in our village easily warmed to her. Our wedding plans had kept me busy, but meals alone before she came, and a passionless and indifferent life did not fulfil me. I yearned for Olga and hungered for the loving which had been too brief.

Ben's two girls, Emily and Alicia, were coming for their summer holidays. A letter from Ben in Nigeria was on the hall table waiting for them. It had been there for a week.

'Olga, I will be in the music room when you are ready to leave, I must practice the piano. When you call, give me ten minutes to organise things before we go for the girls. Cathy, I can smell your baking—excellent.'

'Yes, I've two cakes baked ready to ice in the pantry and the scones and small cakes are in the oven. The chocolate cake is the one for Alicia's birthday tomorrow. I'll have that ready for you before I go.' Then she looked strangely at me. I knew she'd missed something I'd said. It was irksome for her not to be able to hear properly. Olga was more sensitive to that than I was. Cathy had had the measles before her elder brother Alois. She had told me that he had got it mildly, but she had been seriously unwell. I knew Olga would reply to any other questions. I left them and wandered through the open French doors, down the long garden to my music room. I opened the shutters to lighten the room enough to read the music sheet on the grand piano. It was Chopin's *Fantasy Impromptu*. That felt right for my mood, but first I'd move the boxes of greenery that were packed and ready to take to the station for the florist in London. They would go in the car later. I sat at the piano, on the stool with the colourfully flower-embroidered cover that Olga had sewn for me. As I played, I became submerged in the world of the music. Olga must have heard me from the house. I didn't see her enter. The moment I got up I saw her on the arm chair as I turned. I noticed a fleeting sadness on her face, so momentary that at first I felt maybe I had imagined it. She shivered.

'You play that with such sensitivity; it stirs me. Watching your strong hands expertly on the keys, I am reminded of how you were and the way I felt when we first met. It was so long ago. All my hopes and dreams, and now here we are.'

There was an intensity in her brown eyes. In that moment I still felt the vibrations of the music I had played, although it gently floated away. That artificial lift in her voice at the end, *and now here we are,* did she want to say, *without our child?* I longed to ask her because that had been in my thoughts as I played the Chopin piece.

'Come, darling,' I took her arm and put it through mine. 'It is nearly time for us to go to Penzance.'

We strolled back in silence, separated by our memories, not wanting to remember, yet our past was like a ghost around us.

I saw the gardener's jacket thrown by the plants. He had come in to load the boxes of cut greenery for me, but was now doing some essential pruning somewhere in the grounds.

'Cathy said she heard that we may have some rain showers later,' Olga said quietly, breaking our silence.

'That will not stop Emily and Alicia running about the place when they arrive. Their excitement at being back with us, and away from their boarding school is something they look forward to from the start of each term. It will be intriguing to see how they have grown up.'

CHAPTER FIVE

EMILY'S VOICE

My father, Ben, was fortunate. He missed the Great War. He had been in the navy where he was seconded to the Royal Engineers and in charge of inland waterways in Mesopotamia. He met my mother, Mary, when she had a small soprano part in Wagner's *Parsifal* and Heinrich Hensel was lead at the Royal Opera House in Covent Garden in 1914. She was friends with Claire Dux and kept autographs and photos of many of the cast.

Uncle Cecil missed the war too, as he became a planter and lived for many years in Burma. He laughed when he told us he returned for a holiday, or to try to get married. There were women who chased after the few men that remained unmarried. Sydney, his brother, died from the influenza that struck down many millions in 1918 all over the world at the end of the First World War.

Ben decided he wanted to marry Mary, but she preferred to continue her musical career; it was unheard of then. When she was not offered another singing part, she chose marriage. Uncle Cecil was not in Mother and Father's wedding photographs. Perhaps he was in Burma. Great grandpa Joseph died in 1907 when my father and Uncle Cecil were abroad, and telegrams were the fastest way to communicate. They saw his grave after the mill was sold.

When my sister and I spent summer with Olga and Uncle Cecil we felt like their own daughters. They had never had children. A great pity, as he was a good story teller and his musical knowledge and piano playing captivated us. I recall our arrival at Mulberry House from boarding school one summer. I suspect Uncle Cecil was excited to see us; he would not have used that word though. We were thrilled to be going there because there was no affection from anyone at school, and we knew he loved us. So did Olga.

We had not seen our parents for two years. Father worked in Nigeria and Mother loved that ex-pat world. She had already danced with HRH Edward the Prince of Wales when he was in Nigeria in the mid 1920s, and we would hear about it one day . . . and again rather often. She always brought out the dance card too, and the signed photograph the Prince had given her.

Uncle Cecil was obsessive about routine; I saw it daily. His day started with an amble down his big garden. The Pittosporum that he grew would be inspected, and two workers instructed. I have a clear picture of the huge house, with its leaded light windows and large oak beam porch. The heavy black front door led to a spacious, wood-lined hall and to the right was their wide, bright kitchen which faced west, so it got the afternoon sunshine. The large farmhouse table in the middle of the kitchen was loaded with food, or so it seemed to me, as I always felt hungry. There were oil lamps around when we were children, which we used most evenings. My second favourite person after Uncle was his housekeeper, Cathy. I especially loved Olga too. She was to be the kindest, most caring, and loving generous person I would ever know. She looked after me in my darkest hours as an adult.

On week days Cecil greeted Cathy in the kitchen after his tour of the garden. A gentle way of saying, I am ready for something to eat. She came in each day after picking up supplies from the butchers and other things from the general store. The blacksmith shop was run by Mr H. Grimes and it was nearly opposite us so

Edward VIII, Prince of Wales, gave my mother, Mary Hale,
a signed photograph when they were in Nigeria

they knew most things about the goings on at Mulberry House. On Friday, one of Cathy's brothers would collect fish and chips from a shop in the village, and Alicia and I would sit round the kitchen table to eat together before Cathy went home. I remember all the chatter and village stories everyone would tell, and because we knew most of the locals we just soaked it all up and waited for more the next week.

Uncle went regularly to the general store for the St Bruno tobacco for his pipe, and we'd get 1d to spend on sweets if we had been good. We always tried to go with him! There were no telephones at home, only the red phone kiosk by the store. Everyone knew about it if you went in there to make a telephone call. I suppose using the phone was only for urgent things. I went in to the shop for stamps and sweets, and I never used the phone outside.

I don't remember much about home in Essex when we were little, only one vivid memory looking out of our bedroom window in our own house, Highcombe, in Essex. That one memory was bathed in astonishment and fear. Once, Mother shouted at us to hurry upstairs fast. She had the bedroom windows wide open, and was pointing to a huge Zeppelin . . . then, as we were watching it, the Zeppelin was suddenly enveloped in flames and came down over Cuffley. None of us said much more that day.

In 1916 Mother took Father to see the house that would one day become our home. 'I don't like the house, but as it is next to the West Essex golf course, that will suit me splendidly,' was all he had said to her.

We heard our parents talking and whispering one evening and neither my sister, Alicia, nor I could understand what about, but I recall a deep feeling of foreboding enveloping me. In bed that night, I cried quietly. However, I had been heard.

'Why all those tears, dear, last night?' asked my mother.

I was silent and she did not press me, but my anxiety remained. Not long after, aged three, I was taken with my sister to

Miss Mulliner's boarding establishment. It was in Southsea overlooking the Solent and the common. I held Mother's hand and was terrified to let it go, as we were taken for a walk round Miss Mulliner's house. One room looked enormous, with high white ceilings and sounded hollow when you spoke in it. It was like a frightening fairy story. It felt freezing in there, as it was on the north side, and never got any sun. I remember feeling my heart thumping loudly while we were in that room and worrying that my mother might hear it.

That first day is distinct in my memory, with the musty smell of the place, the brown colour of Miss Mulliner's clothes, and a boned choker at her neck. When her skirt brushed against my cheek, I felt the rough dank wool of it. As I looked up at her, she towered over my mother, with that grey haired bun on her head. The skin on her face looked loose and flabby and she didn't seem to have eyelashes. Father did not come with us. I would see that long brown dress, and her grey bun, day after day after that.

She took us upstairs to see the Isle of Wight from the windows in the bedroom, then tried to distract me and take my hand, but I would not loosen my grip on Mother's hand. I cannot remember saying goodbye to my mother, and neither could Alicia who stood beside me. Nor how she left us alone that day; but I do still feel the agony of that separation and the tears and sobbing in bed that first night on my own. How I longed to be back home at Highcombe. I can still see the clothes on the chair beside my bed when I woke next morning . . . the same hand-knitted, dark blue jersey knicker-suit I had put on the day before, and wishing it was that day, and not this one, and I could be back at home with my mother.

Miss Mulliner coaxed us that first morning, 'Come along, dress up and after breakfast you will go and play with Joyce on the common. If you're good we will take you on the pony and trap. His name is Bobbie and he is stabled here behind Wyaston.'

I had my own pony and trap during the Second World War

and travelled each day to London to work at the BBC, but that was the future, and at five the little child in me found things like piano lessons, music and being top of the class helped me to cope somehow without my family. I remember my first piano lesson; the happiness that enveloped me as I found that learning to play the piano came so easily to me. My teacher's piano playing lifted me away from the sad thoughts of being without my parents. It must have been May or June as I remember looking at the elderflowers outside the window as I listened to her playing a new piece of music.

Uncle Cecil and I played duets when I went to Cornwall, and he encouraged my musical inclinations. So I learnt to bury my emotions. We all had to. Father had been posted to the Marine Department in Nigeria, which was run from the Colonial Office. Children were not taken there, so we had to be parked somewhere as Mother went with him. They travelled there by ship and Mother came home about once every eighteen months. Father came less often. We were told that they called it the white man's grave. I was eight when we went to Cornwall to be with Uncle Cecil and Olga. They both came to collect us from Penzance at the end of the summer term. It had just started to rain as we got off the train, and I can still sometimes smell that dusty fragrance, after a long dry spell, on the parched earth and ground. Each time I get that scent, I am filled with the old excitement at finding them waiting there for us.

We absorbed the gritty, sandy beaches we visited in an atmosphere of damp, salt-tasting happiness. The treasure trove of sea shells and unlimited rock pools were there for us to explore. The sun slid late into the horizon, and it felt hot most days. One stormy, very cool evening, we all sat curled up with Olga on the settee and Uncle Cecile read to us from his mother's diary about Percy and their escapades. We even had a coal fire one night.

Often we were alone on the beaches, which were unvisited by the numerous travellers, as they would be years later. We spent six weeks in a blur of joy that year, broken only by the dread of the final few days before we had to set off back to boarding school. Our last two nights in September at their house were agony for me as I was counting the time left with them before we returned, to be imprisoned, for it felt like it, for another long term with no break, and nobody to hug.

The maternal grandparents were in their seventies, so during certain school holidays we were sent to another coast. We went by paddle steamer across to Ryde, then on the train to Brading for a branch line to Bembridge on the Isle of Wight. We walked up the hill to Harbour Mount. Any baggage was brought up on a cart. Cousins came to stay from as far as Argentina and we were four girls in a double bed, two up and two down. There was always a family hut on the beach where we all kept our buckets and spades and bathing costumes. We walked down Ducie Avenue to get to the beach. In summer ten or more cousins would walk to Whitecliff Bay, taking a picnic lunch. There was a rusty old wreck in the middle of the bay. If we had been good we were allowed to stop at Mr McIver's tuck shop and buy 1d worth of sweets.

Grandpa Edward Matthews was a great preacher; there is a picture of him with Queen Mary in *Tatler,* at the opening of Jack's Palace in the East End of London in 1903. Grandpa was the local vicar in Bembridge.

Mother returned home for the birth of our brother, Henry Clifford, and she stayed for two years. We left Southsea, lived at home, and daily we cycled the few miles to Woodford High School. Our mother told us that the bicycles were given to us by her great friend in Nigeria. For her, there were many other presents inscribed by him 'to my darling little Mary'. I loved being home. The gas lights in the house were replaced by electricity that year, and we were very excited about the changes. We used to switch lights on and off such a lot. Mother acquired her first car—a 1926 Austin four-seater Tourer—and we all took

Grandpa Edward Matthews with Queen Mary
at Jacks Palace, London, 1923

day trips to Frinton whenever we could. Later she had a very early Peugeot, and I remember I had to help operate the wipers by hand. We went with her to St Osyth, where we hired a chalet on the beach. But two years later Mother returned to Nigeria to be with Father. Henry was left in the care of Mrs Oxley, who lived almost next door. Alicia and I were once again back in boarding school, at Maybury House, where I excelled. Then at fifteen I took University Entrance Exams for Cambridge and Bedford College, London. Both said they would have me at seventeen.

1933

I was very excited that on my seventeenth birthday I got my driving licence and Mother took us in her large Singer four-seater touring car to Cornwall, and I drove it too. No driving lessons then! I took turns with her to drive and our average touring speed was thirty miles an hour: we took two days over the journey, stopping at some of Mother's relations. My driving experience proved to be essential later in the Second World War. Mother and Henry stayed with Uncle Cecil and Olga. Alicia and I stayed in Pedn-Olva Hotel in St Ives, a lovely spot where we bathed from the rocks. I remember feeling so grown up, and we all felt life could not be better.

Later that year I needed Uncle Cecil's help:

Maybury House School, Woking

6 July 1933.

Dear Uncle,

I am leaving school this summer, and I would like you and Auntie Olga to give me much needed advice.

I talked briefly about my dilemma with you last year, but now I need to make a decision. Not to keep you on tenterhooks, it is to do with being accepted at university.

Sometimes I think I would like to work in London and earn my own money straight away. Then I argue with myself about not missing the opportunity to study. Once term ends I will go home for a few days and leave my trunk and everything. I'll take the usual train to Penzance on July 22nd. Please would you meet me off that train? I hope it will not inconvenience you. I would love to help like last year, with cutting and packing the pittosporum greenery. That will give you an extra pair of helping hands this summer, and it is work I like doing while I am with you both!

I will be coming on my own. I am so excited to see you and Auntie Olga again. I wish it was the end of term already.

Love from

Emily xx

CHAPTER SIX
CORNWALL, 1926

OLGA'S VOICE

I could hear Cecil playing Beethoven's Piano Sonata No. 8 or Sonata 'Pathétique', but only just, as I was still with Cathy in the kitchen.

Cathy said, 'It worries me to leave my little baby, and I am lucky to have this job, what with the General Strike and not many people working now.' She continued, 'Changing things at home will be easier next year, I hope.'

'Yes, you have a good deal of courage, raising a child the way you do, I admire that. Forgive me, Cathy, I must leave you, to remind my husband that we need to leave in time for the station. I must call him out from the music room. I'll see you before we go.'

I went to the back of the house. There was Cecil's pipe on the side table. I picked it up; it was still warm. I hesitated, should I take it to him I wondered, but then I left it exactly as he had, because he was so particular.

As I went out to the garden through the opened doors, I could hear Cathy humming, and I felt relieved as I thought that maybe I had been rather abrupt. Her life was a struggle, perhaps her mother's had been. I sensed my own anxiety rising, because of last night, as I slowly walked to join Cecil. My thoughts returned to our long separation, as well as his doubts, and mine.

I remembered how I had longed for his letters, and read them over again until the next one. We had met in 1919 at the Harvest Festival Ball. Mother had unkindly told me that I was a confirmed spinster because so many men had died in the First World War. My sister married a man twenty-eight years older than her that year, and Phoebe, my closest friend, was betrothed to an old man of fifty-five, because, at twenty-five, she did not want to remain unmarried. Cecil knew we were right for one another that first evening, but he was returning to Burma imminently, and he only confessed that feeling to me two years later when he returned home. I had felt reassured then, but he was still remote. Looking back twenty years to when I was still a young woman made me uncomfortable, but I could not help having these thoughts when my nieces were about to join us.

Our gardener interrupted my thoughts, 'Mrs Hale, I'll be near the mulberry tree if you need me before you go to the station.'

'Thank you,' I tried not to sound distant, but my thoughts were far away in time.

Later, I slid silently into our music room. It felt chilly. The July sun shone directly onto the piano and his hands passed expertly along the keys. Those familiar, strong, sensitive fingers played with an intensity that I loved. Just the way he had caressed me last night. He barely looked at the music sheet as he played Chopin's *Fantasy Impromptu*. When it ended, his hands lay on his lap and he was deep in thought. We heard Arthur open the door, Cecil looked at him and then saw me.

'I am taking these boxes to your car, sir.' Cecil nodded, then came to take my hand.

'My darling, you look radiant, I had not seen you come in.'

'You were deep in thought as you came to the end of that Chopin piece.'

I longed to hear his thoughts. Maybe he would talk when we were in the car, on our way to Penzance. Sadly, there were no words later. He pulled off the road, turned off the engine, took

Cecil Hale

me in his arms and we kissed hungrily the way we had all those years ago—and last night—unaware of the time.

Ben's girls spent the whole summer with us. The first night they arrived, when it was bed time, they bounced on their beds and giggled so much that Cecil said I should go up to quieten them, as those old springs on the beds would not cope. Next day, Alicia had her birthday. Cathy had made her favourite fudge and a cake, and I had bought her a flowery skirt and top which she wore as much as she could all that summer. Emily gathered lavender, and put it into a hand embroidered small pillow. Cecil bought her a set of Tennyson's poems with a lavender binding.

'Thank you!' Alicia said shyly and blushed when she unwrapped her gifts.

I gave her a big hug and told her our plan was to have a picnic at Godrevy beach, a swim if the tides were right, then back home for her birthday tea. They both smiled and I too started to feel excited. On our way to the beach, Cecil stopped the car to pick up the *British Gazette* and his St Bruno tobacco from our general store.

There were long walks together that summer, bathing off rocks, and we took picnics and explored the sandy and rocky beaches. Cathy cooked with them, and I found myself especially drawn to Emily, who was a bit of a tomboy—as I had been.

I caught Cecil looking at me often. 'You give me more than I could ever wish for,' he whispered when I was in his arms one night. There were stolen kisses, and we had our nights.

One day in early September, Alicia rushed downstairs, took my arm and pulled me upstairs. 'Emily isn't moving.' I ran back up with her.

I saw her pale face, and heard the laboured breathing. Instinctively, I knew she was having a nightmare. 'Shh, wait.' We both quietly watched.

She stared blindly at us when she woke. Later she described how she had felt drugged by deep sensations, and numbed by a cramp in her throat and chest. Emily felt the air had been sucked out of the place where she stood, but she was also moving, as if floating, from the terrace, right to the end of the garden underneath the huge mulberry tree to the furthest angle of the overgrown area; that wild part, past the Pittosporum plants, where the dark green shadow of the house lay for most of the day until early afternoon.

'I drifted to a place where I felt I could breathe, by the Mulberry tree, when it became cooler. My chest felt tight, and I could feel a dark sort of panic gripping me. Below me was a baby asleep, wrapped in a dark blanket. Where did it come from?'

She quickly went on. 'I looked up at the sky, it was a clear blue. I kept looking for something, but I also did not know what I was looking for and I felt frightened. There was nothing when I looked up, then suddenly I felt sad, the way I had felt when Mother left us. My limbs felt heavy, I could not move. There were squashed mulberry fruits on the ground that looked like drops of blood. I wish you had woken me, it was so scary, and it did not evaporate like other dreams have.'

I tried to comfort her, knowing from my own experience how a bad dream can linger. We did many energetic things that day. After that, she always wrote asking for advice whenever there were big decisions to be made in her life.

On Wednesdays I took our hen's eggs, home baked bread, fruit, and cakes to the village church where certain people came if they were finding it hard to feed the children in their family. Times were difficult for many in the late twenties, and especially after the General Strike.

'I am thirty-nine tomorrow!'

'Yes,' I know, Cecil had replied, 'I have not forgotten.' We were both awake in bed.

'It is too late for me.' I felt desperate.

'What do you mean?'

'To have your child.'

It was nearly dark, we had reduced the light from the oil lamps that Cathy prepared each day. I wanted something, words, contact, I did not know what, but he never moved. I knew that he also felt sad. Silence hung. Then I made the first move, because I knew I had caught him off guard and his old memories would come back. He had tried to forget them. I felt his sadness. We held one another and our passion was thirsty, as though it would be our last drink.

In 1933, my sister-in-law, Mary, came to stay and brought young Henry. She had a smart new car, and told us that Ben would be retiring and they would be back home for good. Emily and Alicia had grown up, but we were to see Emily back in Cornwall regularly. She had become close, and visited us in the next few years more than we had anticipated, and especially during the war. She wrote to us each month until March 1944.

PART FOUR

CHAPTER SEVEN
LONDON, 1927–1936

Two years after Lionel's heart gave up from the effects of mustard gas poisoning, May's routine changed. She took JP with her when the weather was good, and he felt happy to run errands and walk with her. The pavements were often crowded and his mother stopped frequently to talk with people she knew.

May found she was still affected by the men in the streets, who hung around, usually wearing their old great coats, or who wandered about aimlessly. Some sat on steps and pavements alone, or gathered in groups for warmth around a brazier on colder days.

I feel sorry for these lonely, helpless men, and I miss Lionel.

Some nights I still feel the pain when I think how much he suffered; the night panics and shouting out to the men as if he was still at war. These men can't work, and they don't seem to have a home. Lionel was angry, and disillusioned that our people were not told about the real war casualties. Too many were buried in France. Lionel felt ashamed and guilty when he came home.

One winter morning, May stopped sewing to go and buy new cotton reels and fabrics. Joan and JP were left with their grandparents. She hurriedly took off her half overall, put on her knitted, bright-green cardigan, and changed to her outdoor shoes. She took her black felt hat as she left. The children were playing dominoes, and looked engrossed.

'I'll not be long,' she called loudly as she latched the back door, particularly to stop JP from wandering off outside. He was still too short to reach the latch. May turned briskly toward the haberdashers. The wind felt icy and clouds darkened the sky. She pulled her hat down, and tied her scarf. She had tried to smarten the old hat with a ribbon and a flat bow. She thought it looked good, although May felt the hat was not sufficiently warm that day.

'We have to make do, everything is so dear now and the children will need winter woollies again soon,' she thought.

Stella, her neighbour, startled her when she was about to open the door to the shop.

'May, I wish I could sew like you!' she sighed.

'I always pass and look at all the ribbons, threads, and lace and want to sew, but there's never enough time in my day.'

They walked together round the shops.

'I'll return home taking another route, instead of the dull, easy walk back,' she told Stella. May wanted to have time alone to think about what Stella had told her.

In the distance, May saw a group of five men, some standing, others sitting, around a dark burning brazier for warmth. She smelt the cob nuts roasting on their fire.

From afar she could see that the man facing her looked weary, as well as disabled. The General Strike had affected too many workers, and there were unemployed men in London who lived rough. One man there had a leg missing and a wooden stub, like a broom handle, that protruded from a fold in his trouser leg, which, she assumed, covered the bit of his leg that remained. His face was brown from dirt and smoke, which accentuated the lines in his weathered face. His piercing blue eyes stared at her. May felt uneasy . . . she decided he must be another of the war wounded. As she crossed the road, she saw the head of a man who was sitting on the far pavement, and she felt her breath quicken. The mass of ginger red hair looked like Lionel when she had seen him at the railway station in Paris after he had been de-mobbed. May stopped and stared at the man opposite her. She knew it was not her husband, but for a moment, she could smell that railway station again as if it was 1918. 'It seems like Lionel's head,' she thought.

May did not know how long she had stood staring, a loud call to her from a man in the group startled her.

'I'm sorry,' she replied back with an awkward wave. After a moment, she gathered her courage and called back, 'I thought I saw a man I used to know.'

'Little lady, come and check, we'd like your company!' The big, tall man with wild, dark, greying hair laughed deeply as he spoke with a northern accent.

She blushed, and waved again, not knowing what else to do, and quickly turned to take her familiar route home. At the corner away from them, she felt weak and hot, and she leant against the side of a wall. May yearned to sit down, and looked up and down the street to see if there was anyone she knew. A couple walking towards her stared, but looked away when she caught their eye. She knew it would not take long to get back home, yet her legs felt weak. Thoughts raced. The mop of ginger hair took her back to not only to those years with Lionel after the war, but also their happy life together before 1914. She remembered again those haunted eyes that day at the station, when she had not recognised him.

'No, no, this is not the moment, I must not remember all this now. Later, tonight, when I am alone and the children are asleep, then I can think about the past, now I must forget,' she thought.

She shuddered, pushed herself away from the wall, and hurried back home. The sounds of the horses trotting in the street around her, the honking, and the trams helped her to slowly retreat from her past. When she opened the back door, she was relieved to smell the chicken soup that she had left simmering on the range.

'May,' Stella was about to confide something new, again.

May saw her mischievous expression. They were both waiting in a queue.

'A certain widowed gentleman noticed you buying bread last Friday.'

May knew of him only from what others had said, and most of that was to do with having money to purchase one of the few cars. May always dressed neatly, and because she made all her own clothes, she paid particular attention to details and styles, knowing that if she presented herself smartly she could get more work. Her suits and dresses were well cut, and the colours she wore, now that she had stopped wearing black, always made her peachy complexion attractive. She particularly liked to wear blue.

'Mr Powell is always polite and a real gentleman,' a woman told another in the queue at the bakery. 'He was saying he had to buy bread for Mr Webb who cannot get out.'

'Oh, he's always helping with something. Last week it was Mrs Philips' old man needing a ladder to help with a branch that had been torn in the high winds.

'Do you know, he took the ladder and a saw and went up there and cut it for them, easy as anything. Now, what do you think?'

As she heard the girls chatter on about customers, she paid, giving the correct coins. Next she went to the greengrocers for vegetables that they could not grow in their back yard, and Stella followed. She also picked up six eggs as most of their own hens had turned broody. 'Eggs are so dear,' she thought.

'Good afternoon, madam,' Martin greeted her. 'What will it be today?'

'Two pounds of onions and three of swede please.'

He weighed them, and put them in her basket, then threw in a parsnip and winked at her, as if to say not to tell the others. She'd got used to him doing that. She heard from Stella that he threw in something for her too. At the butchers, she was fifth in the queue, and could hear the two women ahead discussing Alec Powell, the widower again.

Stella was behind her and whispered that he had seen her walking the children in the local park. May thought it must have been the man with the smart black hat; he had stared at her.

Alec asked his neighbour, who played chess with Philip each week, to introduce him to the family. He wanted a formal introduction to May. He had tired of living alone.

His wife had been weak; physically shorter than the average thirteen-year-old, and very thin, but he had found that attractive.

Months passed before he met May. At first, they would meet in the company of her family. Later, they took walks in the park with her children. Strangely, she noticed that whenever she was out with the children, with Alec there, one or other of her children would make a big fuss about something that was trivial, and she would have to spend time to calm them. Or Joan would tease JP and annoy him so that he started to cry. Again, she would have to stop to sort out their problems, rather than listen to Alec Powell.

May had thought how well they both behaved at home, but how badly they would play up when this stranger was around. At first she could not make sense of it.

Two years after they met, he asked her to marry him and live in his house. JP was nearly twelve and active with local friends, and Joan had become a popular girl at school. Neither of them wanted to move away from their grandparents.

When May married Alec and moved to his house, it was JP who first went to live with them, but months later Joan did too. Each had been promised their own bedroom, and new books for JP and dresses and hats for Joan, who had begun to copy her mother's interest in clothes. Since May remarried she owned more new hats than anyone else Joan knew.

Both children would walk, or run away, back to their grandparents whenever there was trouble at the Powell's.

They also had their Uncle Michael, May's brother, who treated them as his own children, and lived three streets away. Joan frequently ran back to her 'home' as she called it, preferring to be there rather than to see her mother 'bossed around', by Alec. She did not like being told by both of them to call him Father, and she felt unsettled and unhappy with the new arrangements.

'Mother, I don't want to call him Father, because he's not.'

Joan began to learn from her mother about why her father had suddenly not been there . . . much later she learned that that meant he had died. She had not wanted to upset her mother by asking too much.

All she remembered was that one morning her father had been in the house, then after that, he was gone. Her mother had cried sometimes, and she had a memory of the front room being dark, and nobody being allowed in. She'd gone with JP to a neighbour that they hardly knew. At the end of that day Grandfather came for them. He had held her hand very tight all the way home, but when she talked he never answered her. JP ran to keep up because they walked too fast. When they got home, a cold supper was waiting for them on the kitchen table, and they were told to go upstairs to the room they shared when they had eaten everything up. Nobody answered her questions, and soon memories of her father faded. Once, she had run into her mother's bedroom and saw her folding up his few clothes and placing them into a box.

'What do you want Joan, you know you have to knock before I tell you to come in?'

The child stared at the box, and then at her mother, not knowing how to put the question into words. She went near the box and touched a threadbare grey jacket of her father's that was on the top. She could smell something of her father when she got near it.

'What is it?' Joan asked touching the box and the jacket.

'I am taking these away, they can't stay here anymore. Go and play now, and you can come with me for a walk later to choose sweets from the large jars in the sweetie shop.'

Joan had sat on the floor, and refused to move. She'd no idea why Mother wanted to put all the clothes her father used to wear in a box. So watching seemed the best way to try to understand what might be happening. It was years later that Joan was able to get some information about her father. By that time her own memory was shaded by other events, and her mother's memory had been influenced by her own emotions and the hardship of the years before he had died, as well as the struggles following his death. Everyone relied on May, because Philip became weaker after his son passed away. May took care of Lionel's parents and the children, as well as running the house and taking in sewing.

Many years later, when Joan matured and had a family of her own, she wondered whether her mother had married again more for financial support, than for love.

In 1934 Joan became a determined teenager. She rarely stayed in their new home. Alec, her stepfather, irritated her, and made her feel angry and embarrassed. When she was on her own she felt guilty about her behaviour, but her thoughts returned to the happier old days . . . Joan longed for life to be how it was before her father had died.

I remember the silence, and my feeling scared, and trying to comfort JP who moaned a lot. I kept wondering why nobody told me anything, why we had been left with that woman next door. I had asked at bedtime where they had taken Father, and unexpectedly Mummy burst into a flood of hysterical crying. I'd hugged her and cried with her that night. I was not sure whether I cried because Mother was crying, or because I felt sad, or because I'd been bewildered by the previous days. Seeing everyone wearing black and feeling sad, and looking at their sullen silent faces; nothing made any sense.

On Wednesday's Joan went straight from school to Grandfather's. She let herself in through the side door. One day, she unexpectedly found him asleep in the armchair of their front room. Usually, he would be looking out for her from the upstairs window. Joan noticed how pale his face looked. She sat beside him very quietly, not moving, and not daring to make a sound in case she woke him up. She was desperate to tell him her news, but anxious not to disturb him. Then she saw herself reflected in the glass window opposite. The door that she had left ajar, when she entered, threw the light in such a way that against the background of the room it seemed like a shadowy mirror.

She was not accustomed to looking at herself in the mirror. At first she had been taken aback by her own reflection. Her long curly hair caught the light around her oval face and on her rosy complexion, framing it. She secretly thought herself pretty for a moment.

Joan was physically more mature than other girls in her class, and school friends often mocked her because of her large breasts, while certain boys badgered her. Some people, usually men, looked at her in a certain way. She hated it when she went on Saturday to work in the shop. One evening she told her stepfather she would prefer not to work there anymore.

Alec had become threatening and angry, 'I have done so much for you and your mother. Don't I pay for everything in this house for you all? What thanks is there from you?'

'You did not hear me. I do not mind shop work. I just do not like the way some men leer at me there.'

His face turned red with fury 'You'll do what you have to, and pay for some of your keep here. You are not a child.'

She had felt frightened, and dared not answer back. Next time her stepfather asked for a share of her wages, she brazenly opened the door and walked out, then ran to her grandfather.

'Joan, my dear, how good to see you. I fell asleep. Is JP coming later?' Philip rubbed his eyes.

His deep, comforting voice cheered her up. She loved his company. She leaned towards him and put her hand on his and kissed his cheek. 'Can I stay longer today?' She did not want to talk about her brother.

'Of course, my dear. As you wish. Is there trouble with Alec again?'

'Oh, I have come to tell you, I got a job and lodgings with it too. I'll get training and my keep, and one day off a week, or two days every other weekend. They seem so nice.'

He saw her excitement. She was young and innocent, with her whole life ahead, and he wished he could protect her from the bruises she was bound to get as the years went by.

Did they not all get knocked by life events! She rushed on as he listened. He did not want to miss anything she might be saying that he could understand in a deeper way.

'I said yes, I would take the job, then I thought I best talk to you first. I can't tell Mother because she would tell Alec. She just cannot keep any secrets from him.'

'Did you tell them your age?'

'No, I lied. I told them I was nearly nineteen.' She looked down at his hands. Then she noticed how wrinkled they were.

'My dear, why have you lied?'

'I must leave there. You know, I often try not to argue with Alec. But I want to earn my own money, not work for free. I am sad to leave JP, but you are here for him.'

'Yes,' he turned away with a sigh. Then he tried to get up out of his chair. When she saw his difficulties she leapt up to help him.

'I'll make tea for you, Grandpa. You just stay here. I can bring it on the trolley, or a tray, just like the old times.'

Later, while they ate their tea together Joan talked with excitement about her work, the training, and plans for the future. He saw how animated she had become. He had not seen her so happy for some time. *It is best for her to experience and learn about life her own way. I have done as much as I can. I have tried to be a father . . . I missed my boy, but we had to get on with life. I see how she is bursting to start her new life, and that is best.*

Joan left home, but she wrote regularly to JP and asked him also to read her letters to Grandpa Philip. She hoped he would not mind, as she tried to save every penny she earned. The day after she had tea with her beloved grandfather, she packed her few belongings in a small holdall, and caught the train north. She had borrowed a few shillings to pay her fare, and promised to send a postal order to repay the loan.

'I am going to start work away from here,' she'd told JP, the night before she left.

They had whispered in their room because he had sensed that she was excited about something, and he wanted to know what it was. He had not expected her to say she was leaving him.

'I will write to you each week. Please don't say to Mother you know this until after I write to her, because I do not want her to get into trouble with Alec. He could also make trouble for you.' JP looked glum. He held back his tears.

Joan made sure nobody saw her leave. Two days later, her mother got a letter giving her new address and explaining her reasons. JP was told his sister had left home to go to work. A week later he got his first letter ever, in his own name, with a stamp on a clean white envelope. It was waiting for him on the mantlepiece when he returned from school.

He recognised her bold handwriting on the envelope. He treasured that letter for years. Nobody had ever sent him a letter before.

The Queens Fort, Durham
8 September 1935

Dear John Philip,

I am sorry I had to leave you and go away to work. I do like it here.

I share a room with three other girls and so far we get along quite well.

The train journey here was most interesting. I sat in a carriage with only two people at first, but then at each station we stopped at, more people got on the train, so that by the time I arrived our carriage was full. Most of them were reading something, but I had not brought a book so I just stared out of the window. I did not mind. The countryside is so beautiful.

We all help curl our hair and dress nicely in the uniform for work.

I think the others were also happy to leave home.

You will see my address at the back of the envelope, so please write to me and tell me what you are doing. Try to work hard at school so that you too can get a good job one day.

I send my love, and will write again in a few days, when there is more to write about. Please read this to Grandfather and Uncle Michael.

I hope Mother will manage without me. Sorry I had to leave you. I know you understand why.

Your loving sister,

Joan.

Some weeks after she had settled into her place of work, she got a letter from her mother.

Priory Road, Hampstead, London

5 November

Dear Joan,

Thank you for your last letter. It is always nice to have your news.

Grandfather fell over at home and I am staying with him for a few days in case he falls again. Anna sits with him. He asked about you. Please write to him and let us know how you are getting along.

I do get your news from letters you send to JP. He is doing well at school and he works very hard. I think he really misses you. He was very quiet for two weeks after you left home. I hope he is writing to you.

I started to make you a new dress for your birthday with a beautiful flowery black, red and green fabric from the market. They had just the right amount for a dress for you, with sleeves. It will be in the new style. I will have it finished soon, so write and let me know if you would like me to send it, or save it for you to see when you come back for a visit. I will post this on my way back, so you should get it tomorrow. Grandfather sends his love and Uncle Michael asked after you. He is often with us to help JP with homework if he needs it. JP is clever and has been given a very good report. He has won an apprenticeship.

Yours most affectionately,

from Mother.

Joan immediately wrote to her brother and to Grandfather promising to be there soon.

5 January 1936

Dear JP and Grandpa,

Thank you for always writing back soon.

Yes, I settled down quickly and the other girls are kind. Well, mostly. One of them is jealous and argues. I try to leave her alone.

I share a room with Susan, Mary and Alice. I have not told them my age. Please don't mention it in your letter in case somebody reads it. They are all so pretty and they know about many things. Susan has the nicest clothes and she makes them herself, just like Mother. We get our wages at the end of each week and I am trying to save so that I can get a new coat. It is much colder up here. The one I brought with me is getting rather short on my arms. I suppose I am still growing.

Yes, I do remember Father. You were only two when he died. Yes, his face was yellow because he was poisoned during the war, and his skin got damaged. There is one picture of him somewhere that Mother has. He was holding his horse.

No, as you ask, I think it is best you keep your own name. Alec never had children, and he wants you to have his name, but I don't think that is fair. Grandpa would not like it either, not just me. Grandpa told me that Alec's wife lost a baby boy when it was born. Then she died too from a fever. Still, if you want to be called Powell that is your decision.

You keep writing to say you and Alec have arguments. Talk to Mother and ask her yourself for advice. It is very hard to try to accept another man as a new father. We are not the only ones who lost a father from that war. Two girls here never even knew their own father and grew up with only women in their house. Anyway, I write what I think. I like my surname. So I will only change it when I marry. I hope to see you both soon.

Love from

Joan

7 February

Dear Joan,

Stepfather and I are not getting on at all now. Thank you for encouraging me to be calm and patient in your letter, which I got the next day. I spoke to Mother. I told her he was imposing rules and unnecessary regulations on me. I do not think Mother can help me.

I sometimes go and spend time with Uncle Michael. He is very kind. I feel that he really cares about you and me.

I am studying hard and my mathematics teacher told me I am doing well in the subject. I do not find it difficult at all. I also like English and Geography. I read a good deal during the holidays. I also help at the shop. Most of all I like to spend time with Uncle Michael. I am going there tomorrow to stay for a week.

Mother asked me to tell you Grandfather is not well. I spent some time there with him yesterday. He looks so old now. It was interesting talking to him and to learn about how it was hard to find good work when he was a young man. He worked because he could read and write.

Affectionately yours

JP.

Alec constantly encroached on JP's psychological space. JP became frustrated and angry. He tried to moderate his anger, but it felt hard to stay quiet. At other times he reacted only after reflection, and warily. Occasionally he would answer abruptly and this created trouble for his mother.

One evening, Alec passed by JP's bedroom, and seeing three books on the floor, he shouted at him.

'Your room is a mess. Pick those books up and put them on the shelf. They are precious and expensive,' he said critically, pointing his finger at the floor.

'I am using them for a composition. It is easier to keep them beside my table open on the pages I need.'

Alec disliked anyone who did not obey him instantly. 'Do not answer rudely. Do as I say.' He waited to be obeyed then slammed JP's door as he said, 'I shall come back and check on you again.'

JP thought, I missed Father when we were both young. I have felt his absence over the years, and when I saw my friends with their own fathers, going out, or in a shop, or even at home when I visited them, I felt his absence profoundly. Joan said Mother had been stoical when he died and never spoke to me about Father, and I felt too shy to ask her. I know Grandfather was trying to be a dad for us, and I loved his attention, but it was not the same; I have never known a father's love. I often think what it would have been like if Father had not left us.

The Queens Fort, Durham
1 August

Dear JP,

Thank you for your letter. I have been thinking about what you said before I left. Mother did tell me things about Father, but she said you were too young. This was how she told me about what he had said to her after I was born:

In the war, before it ended, she said, one day Father saw a man's face reflected in a puddle. He did not recognise himself with a weary face and hollow eyes. He talked to Mother about how there were thousands of casualties. A rumbling stomach, and the glances from the silent men around, kept him from bad thoughts when there was fierce fighting. He told Mother that it was for us that he kept going. He'd stare out beyond the trench, and imagine me starting to walk and Mother's tenderness and delicious food. Many months after you were born he told her more.

His small, wiry friend, Jacks, saved him once. Yet Jacks mumbled daily, especially during bombardment.

'Those shells from Jerry keep coming over, they are bound to kill us, we were here before Jerry struck with their artillery and we retreated.'

Maps showed which pieces of land they had won back.

They wore mud-caked clothes, and their boots were soaked; the leather never seemed to dry. She said Lionel felt comforted to know Jacks was still there because of the daily casualties.

He saved Father when he had been stuck in No Mans' Land. He'd heard him call out, and then wriggled to where Father lay and dragged him free. Nobody counted the dead. The men obeyed the officers' commands.

Once a deafening cacophony from the blasts made Jacks afraid, but Father was quiet.

When they were all relieved, they marched away from the firing zone. They longed to rest and eat, he'd told her.

In the villages people stared. Everyone seemed half starved; in torn or ragged clothes. A few old men had a rope or string to hold up their trousers. Men heard the rumble of guns . . . even in their sleep. They'd drink wine and stay in barns wearing great coats.

Of course, the officers had their own billets with their batmen. Father's officers spoke roughly to the men in lower ranks, with cast-iron discipline. Lionel saw that the Australian Officers treated men in all ranks equally, and they drank and ate together. Not like British officers. Some of them were tense, because the Australians refused to salute the British officers.

'You'll salute when you see me, or you'll get what for!' They heard shouts like that to junior rank, usually degrading and savage. Officers expected men to salute even off the battlefield.

When Jacks and Father returned with their company to front line duty, the line was where it had been four days before. They heard rumours that the last attempted push resulted in many deaths. None of them were told much.

Generals gave false promises, and he knew from experience that the Germans could retake their patch anytime. His men were sullen. Officers hardly spoke out.

When the Germans retreated they left all kinds of

poisonous germs like tetanus and typhus in the drinking wells, as well as planting booby traps and mines wherever they could. They left death traps for British troops and their allies.

When Jacks mumbled, Father could decipher those, 'I wish the shelling would stop,' words on Jacks's lips. After one heavy blast he saw terror in Jacks's eyes.

Then he told Mother the story of the worst part, even how Jacks stuttered. 'They m-move b-back, then they sh-shell the p-p-place they were dug in-n-n.' Showers of dirt, debris and mud fell on them often.

Then there was the time before he got sick; Jacks lit two cigarettes and passed one to our father. I suppose they were lucky to have each other. Suddenly, they heard the klaxon horn, and scrambled to find their own gas masks. The German gas bombardment started.

'Our new punishment for Jerry having to retreat.' Someone had shouted.

They saw a whitish mist growing heavy around them. Father remembered Jacks hated to wear his mask, so he stuck close by him, nudging him encouragingly, but he soon sensed his own fear; it was rising from below his belt and his breathing became shallow and short. He felt a brief panic. When the all clear signal finally sounded, everyone removed their gas masks and put them away.

Jacks told Father the mask had made him feel sick and sweaty, and he would not wear it.

'You'll be poisoned dead if not,' Father had said.

Thumps, screaming shells and pounding enveloped Jacks's next words and erased them. All he saw when he looked at him was his mouth moving. They all pushed forward again. Father felt his boots sticking in the mud. It was hard to lift each leg as he took a step; he walked and said he drifted into a trance. The world became blurred with muffled, elongated sounds. He felt some great shroud over him that separated his physical body from the outside world. His hands were numb and yet prickly from holding his bayonet tightly. He looked at Jacks and tried to speak. He realised nobody could hear him. He became silent for a few seconds, then abruptly reality hit. He'd heard shouting. A piercing scream to his left, where Jacks had been the last time he looked. Again, another scream, but now others were joining in and yelling.

'Back, go back.'

Men were turning to run.

An officer shouted, 'Stand your ground.'

Then a shell fell where they had been standing moments before. The officer's command blasted at them from their right. 'Anyone running away will be court-marshalled and shot.'

Father was relieved when he turned and heard a familiar grumbling voice beside him. Both waited for the next command. Lionel lit a cigarette and passed one to Jacks. Then the klaxon hooted for the second time that day. They too slowly replaced their masks, firstly stubbing out their cigarettes. Jacks struggled, but reluctantly covered his face. They heard the *plop* of the shells nearby . . . so close. When the next 'all clear' sounded, Father and Jacks started vomiting.

He said Jacks's face seemed yellow and dry. Suddenly, Jacks fell over retching. So he shouted for a stretcher. When it arrived he had fallen too, he'd been dizzy and weak.

'Lie still there, lie still,' the orderly told our father, but he could not control his legs.

'You've been gassed, don't move, it's a dose of mustard that's got you. Our lads got it last night . . . it'll get to your heart and stop you,' the Canadian orderly had said.

They were put on stretchers and carried to the First

Aid Post, until a medical officer whispered to get them into the next ambulance to the field hospital. Jacks had winked at Father, the old twinkle in his blue eyes was there and he shouted, 'I'm thirsty.'

Once in the ambulance with other injured men there was deathly silence, or crying and men groaning. The smell and warmth made our father feel sick. Father's thoughts were about being out . . . away from it all . . . noise, smell, death . . . wanting rest . . . sleep more . . . he'd see May . . . baby Joan, me . . . he wanted to look into Mother's loving hazel eyes . . . eat her food. He lay still, or slept.

Men were put in long lines wrapped in grey blankets. Each long line was a row of wounded men. There were too many lines to count, Father said. Lionel and Jacks were moved, but they became separated. After the noise and bombardment, he told her, the silence for our father was piercing.

You know, I asked Mother about our Father, but she did not want to tell me more. She said it was all in the past, and after somebody died, everyone had to get on with life in the best way they could. Talking would not bring him back, and would make us all sad. That was all. I tried to ask about the funeral, and about the family, but nobody wanted to tell me anything. Grandpa changed the subject. I asked him when I was older though.

When I was little, one day, Father was with us, then suddenly he was gone. My life changed and so did yours. You were so small. Now I do not know whether anybody could tell me where his grave is. Did you ever go to the grave with Mother or Grandpa?

I am happy to hear that you are doing well at school. It is the best way to help you change where you live. Work hard so you can get a good job. You can; because you are clever!

People here talk about many different things that happen on the farms, and in the forest. I listen to conversation and learn that way.

I am only allowed two days off this month.

I send love,

Joan.

Next morning Joan went to meet the postman, which was unusual because he often arrived too early for anybody to see him. That day she had heard the birds in the trees as the sun rose, and felt the warm air from her open window. She got up very quietly, not to wake the others, and quickly got dressed, so she could get a walk in before they were called for the days' work. On her way back she saw his bicycle against the small gate, and she ran to the door, and opened it. She rifled through the letters on the table, and found one for her, then went around to the back door where she knew the postman would stop to chat to the cook. Cook always seemed happy when she had been having a gossip with him, and news would get around to the others as to what he saw or heard on his delivery rounds. The letter Joan received looked too short. One page.

Her tummy churned from the fear of its contents. When she read it, her distress made her want to find a quiet place to sit alone.

Priory Road, London

15 August 1936

Dear Joan,

I am sorry to write bad news. Your Grandfather Philip died yesterday.

We are all shocked and very sad. It will be hard for all of us not to have him here.

The funeral will be next Thursday. I hope you will be able to come.

Love from Mother

CHAPTER EIGHT
FROM NIGERIA TO ESSEX

Commodore House, Lagos, Nigeria

October 1926

Dear Cecil,

We had a royal visit from HRH Edward Prince of Wales last year. There was a large party given by the Governor of Nigeria, Sir Hugh Clifford. Would you be astonished to hear that Mary and I were introduced to the Prince, and he asked her for more than one dance and it was marked by his aide on her dance card. He enjoyed his visit, and there are photographs which I am enclosing for you, Olga, Alicia, and Emily to see. All the ladies were most excited and are waving to him in one photograph.

Mary is expecting. She will return to have the baby. I can follow for my holiday in June. The Navy will not release me from duties earlier. When you go to London please find a day to visit them in Sewardstone Bury. Alicia and Emily will go to the local school. Perhaps we could all visit you in Cornwall next year.

It has been fearfully hot, but I do manage a few rounds of golf whenever I can. I will indulge when I am home, as the golf course is close.

Yours ever,

Ben

Mary arranged her return to Highcombe in England. They had bought the house in 1916. Her baby would be born there. Nigeria was known as the white man's grave because many white people got sick and died there. Ben had spent more time than previously at the golf club that year, and he had won several silver spoons.

'Another prize from our golf championship!' Ben held up the little silver spoon, when he saw Mary return from the Governor's house one afternoon.

'My prize is that I am to have a baby next year!'

'I had no idea you wanted another child,' he mumbled back, and hurried away making for the door.

'Don't go yet. Are you off to golf again?'

'Yes. Never wanted here. Always wrong.' He drove his car back to the club. 'Life is becoming complicated,' he grumbled to himself in the car.

Weeks passed; silent tensions grew.

'I intend to have the baby when I return to England. Please reserve a passage for me soon, so I can spend the holidays with Alicia and Emily over Christmas,' Mary asked Ben late one night.

'Hmm.'

'Was that monosyllabic grunt your agreement?'

Mary's slender figure had not changed, although her breasts looked larger. Only one other person knew. She needed to leave soon.

On her departure day, her substantial trunks and boxes were loaded. A porter took them directly to her cabin on the starboard side. By the time the ship sailed, and she had waved to her husband, and assorted friends at the quayside, the steward who would be looking after her, had already unpacked her outfits. The personal items she attended to herself later. Mary was excited about her two-weeks' voyage, and took a walk around the deck, but as the wind picked up she became anxious about her hairstyle and returned to the calm of her cabin.

Ben had been too jolly in front of the others, she thought. In the silence of her cabin, she decided to take a rest before dinner, to make sure that she would look her best later. The invitation card to dine at the captain's table had been waiting for her in her cabin. She hoped her secret would be safe, even though their intimate relationship had been the source of gossip in Lagos. Another person was travelling back, whom she guessed might be at the captain's table. She would need to be more aloof to those from her community, while in close company on board.

That evening, she chose her most alluring, silk, pale-blue chiffon, long dress, which was boned and fitted to the waist, with fine straps, the skirt hanging loosely in gentle pleats down to just above her ankles. Small white sequins were stitched around the bodice and straps. Her intention was to make a strong first impression. She wore her crystal necklace, picked up her stole and sequinned evening bag, and took another look in the long mirror.

As she entered the dining area alone, she felt others looking at her, and quickly made her way to the captain's table. Introductions were made, and she looked around to see if she knew anyone. Her eyes met the man opposite her, and they both looked away. The captain was attentive, but later when she was alone, she felt embarrassed that she had laughed too much.

'Please, let me know if there is anything you need that will make your journey more comfortable,' the captain had said when he accompanied her out at the end of dinner.

Mary sparkled in the social life on board. It was different from her social world in Africa. There were people returning home, and a brief stopover in Gibraltar, with snatched intimate moments. By the time her ship docked, she felt nothing in the future months could match the excitement of her journey, and she had made some new friends.

Cecil was there to meet her at the dockyard. He had driven his

Jaguar up from Cornwall especially to meet her, after receiving Ben's letter.

'When did you come up from Tremena?' She had not expected him, and became flustered.

'I have been in London for a week. Then I picked up your girls last Friday as it was the end of term. We met at Victoria station and I took them shopping as Ben instructed me in his last letter. They are at home, waiting for you, and are excited to see you.'

The winding roads towards Essex were an opportunity to talk. However, Cecil thought that Mary looked sullen that day, but he thought perhaps she was tired from the journey, and may have felt unwell during her trip.

'I have taken the liberty of appointing a maid-of-all-work, Annie is her name, and she seems to have made a good start. She cooks reasonably well which means you will not need to spend much time in the kitchen, Mary.'

'I am tired from the long journey, and we all had a late night yesterday. I was not well some of the time.'

'That's disappointing for you, I always understood that you had good sea legs.'

'Oh, I do, but it is different now. We have a small secret to announce.' Both waited silently for the other one to talk first.

'Your girls have grown quite tall!'

'Our third child is due early next year.'

He abruptly slowed the car to look at her, then his gaze returned to the road as he accelerated. 'I never expected this news,' he thought to himself. 'I wonder what Olga will feel.'

'That will be good news for your girls. You will be staying home longer than usual this time then?' Cecil tried to sound jolly. Mary didn't know how to reply at first.

They exchanged stories, and some comparisons of their colonial life; his in Burma, and Ben's in Africa. They agreed that their lives had not only been entertaining, but filled with recreations, and many pleasurable diversions.

Cecil drove up to the house, and as soon as he had pulled on the handbrake, the front door opened and Alicia ran out, followed by Emily. He noticed that they both wore the new dress he had bought for them in London. Their mother stepped carefully out of the car. Cecil closed the door for her. She leaned over and placed a kiss on the cheek of each girl. They shyly followed her into the house. Cecil went directly to the back of the house and found the gardener, Mr Collar. They carried in the boxes and trunks, as well as a small carved table, she had brought home.

Neither girl spoke. They sat together for a cup of tea. The girls were mesmerised by Mary's stories and experiences on board the ship. Her descriptions of the ports they had stopped at captivated their imagination. Later, after dinner, she described the colourful life of her adopted home in Nigeria. Knowing nothing at all of foreign places and cultures first hand, her daughters absorbed every detail. What they had learned from books at school was theory, and not as thrilling. Letters from her had been dull by comparison. When she described how she had danced with HRH Prince of Wales, and shown them his photograph, beside their car, her life seemed to epitomize another glamorous world separate from their own.

Bedtime came too soon, and Emily found it hard to fall asleep. They were over stimulated by their mother's extraordinary life far away from them. However, apart from whispers after lights were out, they had behaved impeccably. They wanted to show their mother how good they could be, especially because they wanted her to stay longer with them at home.

'When will you tell them about the baby?' Cecil asked her that evening.

'Oh, I expect they will notice sooner or later.'

Cecil was baffled. His tried to hide his dismay at her casual and indifferent manner.

'If you tell them it would give them time to understand their feelings. I believe they would get excited by the idea of a sibling.'

'Please, Cecil, pour me another glass of claret; that 1923 was really rather superb, don't you think?'

'I'll just open another. I thought that we would easily drink more than one this evening, and I left a 1925 on your sideboard.'

With a few more glasses of wine, conversation turned to politics, unemployment, and other world affairs, but not the General Strike of 1926. Cecil found that she was more interested in gossip about the aristocracy and royals, especially those surrounding the Prince of Wales, and social events of the season.

'I know little of these matters as we have become immersed in our village and rarely come to London, although we will be back for the wedding. I will be spending my last day in London tomorrow. I hope you will find time to visit us next summer. The girls are bound to tell you we have been exploring around most of the Cornish coast when they came for holidays. They are good company, and they love Tremena as much as we do now.'

'Yes, thank you. Once baby arrives, and Ben is back home, he will have to decide. We are due for another posting to Sierra Leone in 1928 maybe.'

When Emily was in her seventies she wrote:

> In 1926 my Mother came home to Highcombe where my brother was born.
>
> The last mile of the journey to school was along Woodford High Road, this must have been quite a risky venture as I was only ten years old, but the traffic was not as we think of it today. Our bicycles had been given to us by my mother's friend . . . with whom Mother must have had a fairly intimate relationship. A German nanny was engaged to look after Henry, and she was always comparing us to her previous charges, who must have been angels.

'I shall rise early tomorrow,' said Cecil. He ignored Mary's information about their new posting to Africa. 'You must be tired from your journey. It has been a long day for you, Mary.' He hoped she would make a move.

'Indeed.' She looked at him and smiled, but did not stir. Then she sipped the last of her wine and put the crystal glass down.

He waited.

'If I don't see you tomorrow morning, give my regards to Olga, please. I will see her at the wedding.' When he was by the door she added, 'Thank you for coming out to collect me and for keeping an eye on the girls. They have written telling me how much they enjoyed Cornwall, but also what fun they have had when they visited my mother and father at Bembridge during school holidays. I do not know how their grandparents manage to look after nine or ten grandchildren over at Harbour Mount. I expect they are quite strict.' Cecil held open the door as she rose, then followed her out.

Mary had a son. She named him Henry Clifford. [6]

Highcombe, Essex

31 July 1929

Dear Ben,

Now that little Henry is older, I have arranged with our neighbour that he will live with them. Mrs Oxley has become a good friend. Nigeria is not a place to bring him, and I believe he won't be distressed as he is now two. I have arranged for Emily and Alicia to go to a small independent girls' boarding school—at Maybury House in Woking. It is run by Miss Dow and Miss Popkin.

You wrote that in three years we may both return home, when you retire. I will come back here in a year to see Henry (and the girls) and give Mrs Oxley a break. There is a ship leaving in four weeks, and I will send you a telegram before

I board. It has been too quiet here, since you returned.

The girls have done well at school. Emily's piano playing has been most entertaining and she has passed Grade 5 with distinction. Her teacher sent a note telling me that she is talented. They have both cycled to Woodford High School daily.

Do you remember taking them to Connaught Waters where they learned to skate last winter? They still talk about it. They were taken to the fair last bank holiday on Chingford Plain, and both of them loved the swings and roundabouts, as well as the coconut shies.

Nearly all the gas lighting has gone here at home, and the electricity was installed. In the bathroom though there is still the bare fish-tale flame. The garage has been completed to the side of the house, and looks good.

My 1926 Austin 7 Tourer is going well. We have all gone to Frinton with it several times and enjoyed the beach.

Yours,

Mary

CHAPTER NINE
ESSEX AND CORNWALL, 1933–1939
LONDON, 1936 [7]

St Paul's School, Hampstead

June 1934

Dear Joan,

I got your letter last Monday. I am glad to hear you are still enjoying your work. The new clothes for the restaurant sound fancy.

Our history and English teachers at school have been talking to us about their career in the army during the last war. I asked if I could talk to them about the Air Force some time ago. One was most helpful, and gave me an address and person to write to for an application form. I am still too young, so I will accept the apprenticeship I have been offered and start there as a trainee engineer later this year at S. Smith and Sons. It is for four years. Then I can join the RAF. It will be nice to be a working man, even though I'm only fourteen. Were you fifteen when you started work?

I think that Moulton Grammar School was a good start for me, before we all came to live in London.

I talked to Uncle Michael last week. He said it was a good course for me, and a career choice in the Air Force later could work out well. I may not want to go, though, in two years' time. Do you remember how good he was to us when we used to run away from Stepfather? He still guides me. Mother was lucky to have her brother, Michael. And I to have you! Write back soon.

Love from,

John

Emily hoped to start her first job in January 1934 and was very excited about earning her own money for the first time.

Highcombe, Essex

20 September 1933

Dear Uncle Cecil

Thank you and Auntie Olga for a wonderfully happy holiday with you in Tremena. I had fun driving down and helping Mother drive the Singer touring-car. Now that I am seventeen it feels good to be able to drive. She also let me do most of the driving back home. Although it took us two days to get to you, and the same going home, it was exciting. We stopped in Wincanton at Mother's relations on the way back. I pushed the car to its maximum speed of thirty miles per hour!

I hope you will let me come again and help with cutting the pittosporum plants.

I'll write and tell you how I get on with my job interview. I am not sure about taking my place at university. Please tell Olga and Cathy I will write later this week, and give them more news about what is happening here.

Love Emily xxxo

Mulberry House, Tremena, Cornwall

24 September 1933

Dear Emily,

Thank you for your letter. I am writing back quickly as I hope you will try to think again about the offer of a university place at Cambridge and Bedford College. You are young, but if you work for a year you could still tell them you would take up the place later.

It is a wonderful opportunity for you and would make a difference in your chosen career in the future. You are sure to meet many interesting and clever people and it would broaden your view of the world.

Yours,

Uncle Cecil

Highcombe, Chingford, Essex

19 October 1933

Dear Uncle Cecil and Auntie Olga,

I wanted to tell you as soon as possible that I started my first job with the BBC as a trainee stenographer in the engineer department. I am earning £2 per week. It is all right. I just want to earn my own money. I sit in the general office of the engineering information department, answering letters of a technical nature from listeners to the Empire service from all over the world. The Director General, Sir John Reith, is my idol. The chief engineer is Sir Noel Ashbridge. In my lunch hours I walk down to Liberty's or along to the Times Bookshop in Wigmore Street. As I still lived at home, I am able to save enough to buy my first car, which is a Triumph open two-seater with a single seater dickie—I bought it at a party from a chap called John Marlowe who was going to China. It cost me less than a weeks' earnings—7/6d. and petrol, as you know, is only 1/3d. a gallon.

I joined all sorts of BBC clubs. I skate at Queens Club and I will learn to sail. Then there's the Motoring Club, which runs reliability trials as well as treasure hunts all over Surrey and Hertfordshire. So I'll become very active in that club. One day I will get a more reliable car. I have started to learn to do all sorts of repairs and wheel changes, of course. I've driven from home to the BBC each day, then to sporting events sometimes at Motspur Park, and across London back home to Essex late at night. There have been weekend trials in North Devon and weekend camping occasionally in places like Dartmoor. I expect I will do most things if I can.

Most of the people here are interesting, and we go out lunch time and wander around in London. I love going to Liberty on Regent Street, and looking at all their crafts.

I forgot to say, opposite the BBC are the stables. I do occasionally ride in with my pony, I return for her when the office day ends, and ride her home, using the trap. Mostly, I'll leave her at home and drive in with my car, as long as it is in good repair. I shall probably take the car on a tour of the Lake District with Doris next year, if we have saved enough money. I also go racing which I will tell you about next time I come. It is exciting.

Henry comes home from boarding school for the holidays and Father takes him around the golf course sometimes to keep him out of Mother's way, as he can be naughty. Please write whenever you have time. I hope I can come and see you again very soon.

Send love to Cathy too.

Love Emily

The Elm Park Hotel, Manchester

31 January 1936

Dear JP,

Now we have a new king!

What difference will that make to you and me?

I may be joining the Bluebell girls. We were told that we would go all over. We might even get to Paris.

Shall we meet up when I am in St John's Wood at Mother's in April?

One of the girls here, Susan, is getting married. I shared a room with her when I first came up here. Sometime last year she got rather too friendly with a man much older than her, and now they have to get married before it is too obvious that they are having a baby.

I am pleased to hear that you like your work and you are good at it. Your boss sounds nice. We never have anybody here who tells us how good or bad our work is, or how we could improve.

I am happy to be able to earn my keep and have some money to spend.

Mother wrote saying she was very pleased with your progress, so I am glad to know that you are writing to her. She is proud of your success, and believes you will do well. So do I. I know it was hard for her when we were very young, and I understand that more now. I have thought a lot about our life in London. It is so different here and there are many factories where people work long hours in dusty smelly places mostly. At least I can get outside during the day sometimes.

I have also learnt to cook some fancy food by watching in the kitchens and helping make the sauces. It would be fun to have our own shop one day, but it is probably a silly dream.

Write back soon.

Love from Joan.

Emily's car

Emily with the BBC dinghy sailing club, 1935

BBC

TELEVISION SERVICE

OPENING BY

HIS MAJESTY'S POSTMASTER-GENERAL

ALEXANDRA PALACE

2nd November 1936

Emily was involved with the BBC's first TV service, 1936

CHAPTER TEN
1938–1940[8]

Civil Flying School, White Waltham

2 April 1939

Dear Mother (and Joan),

I have now been at the Civil Flying School at White Waltham for almost a year. I was passed fit as a pilot last November, and I am getting on with flying duties. It has been confirmed this week that I am now a Pilot Officer.

I shall go back to St John's Wood for three days leave shortly. Tell me whether you want me to see you back at Priory Road, or whether you can meet me at my place in Alexandra Road. Write and let me know.

I have no address for Joan. Please, Mother, would you tell my sister?

Yours,

John P.

He posted the letter on his way to the officers' mess.

JP had found his home amongst other professional airmen like himself in the RAF. He rarely saw his mother, May.

In the officer's mess, the week of his promotion, he overheard the wing commander talking with a squadron leader.

'We have new lads, trained in Canada, joining our base

next week; and others from Australia and New Zealand who are being trained there, will join us next August.'

'By heavens, we could do with them now,' the other man said loudly, holding a pint in one hand and a cigarette in the other. 'Fully trained, sir?'

'Indeed.'

On his way to the mess he had passed new junior recruits; each one saluted him as they passed. It had taken JP by surprise when it happened the first time in the street or in the corridors.

He found a letter in his pigeon hole. Joan wrote to ask him to come and meet her with her baby daughter. He was asked to write back to her at Mother's as she would be moving by the time he received her letter. Once he knew his duty flying operations he wrote back.

Flying School, White Waltham

4 April 1939

Dear Joan,

Thank you for your letter. Yes, I would love to see you and my niece. It is difficult for any of us to arrange leave. If you are able to meet me nearer my base, we could have a little more time together. I have enclosed a map, and details below it of my days off.

If you can come, write back and give me the dates and times of the train, and I can meet you both off the train. Reply as soon as you can.

I look forward to seeing you both.

Yours,

JP

At the end of April there was occasional warmth in the sun and the trees began to change their wintery look, with a few ash trees showing bright green leaf buds. JP met his sister with her daughter off the train one icy cold, windy day.

'Joan,' he said as he hugged her warmly. 'It's been almost a year!'

'I heard from Mother the good news about your promotion.'

They walked away from the station as she spoke and JP sensed her excitement.

'I am a flying officer, that's all. I am pleased to meet your pretty Sara May.' JP smiled at her and stroked the child's cheek as he made funny clicking sounds at her. She smiled shyly back.

'Me too, I'm so happy to see you. It's been too long, and it looks like you're taller. Will you carry her for me?'

'Certainly. Tell me what you have been doing since we last met.'

'We have settled in the public house and I help Eric and the Watlings to run it. I have some other news for you too. We shall have another baby soon.'

'Congratulations, that is good news. It is comforting to know that you are settled. Shall we take a walk in the park, then we could have tea at a small shop in the high street?'

As they walked together in the local park, they shared memories and future plans.

'I am being sent away again,' John said suddenly.

She looked up at his face.

'You will understand that it is not possible for me to say exactly where, won't you, but it is very far away?'

'Yes, of course, but will you continue to write to us? Please keep in touch with Mother and Uncle Michael. He does worry about you so much.'

As brother and sister walked with the child, a few strangers stared at them in the village. They looked, people assumed, to be an attractive family. Both had bright ginger hair, and the little baby girl had curly red hair down to her shoulders.

'Where will you decide to live, Joan?'

'We are in the same place. I am living above the pub now. It is a fairly decent living most weeks, and the family help us to look after the little one.'

They talked as they roamed, but neither mentioned their fears that they might never meet again. She knew, as did he, that his work was dangerous. At the end of their visit, he walked them back to the station. His little niece had held his hand all the way, and she had been asking for attention in different ways. She did not always get the attention, but got some hugs as well as being carried. Sara May kissed JP goodbye after she saw her mother hug and kiss him, and he waved at Joan as she

John Philip, 1938 or 1939

hung out of the window on the train until it disappeared round a bend over the hill.

As he returned to the mess alone, his old, anxious feelings returned, and he briefly remembered the funeral of his grandfather, which still haunted him in small ways.

JP was posted to Port Said in Egypt. He needed to purchase all the appropriate uniforms for the extreme heat of that time of year from his own income. JP knew that he had grown another two inches since his seventeenth birthday almost two years previously. The white flying suit they found for him was the longest available at the uniform stores. He had said his farewells to his sister knowing that he was due to leave Liverpool with 216 Squadron within a week. The departure date was later set for 20 May 1939. He decided he would write home when he arrived at his base and settled to new flying duties in Egypt. Thoughts of going to an exotic country delighted him, as he had never imagined he could be selected for that kind of posting.

JP thought to himself, I had felt myself never quite as good or clever as my fellow officers, but perhaps I can measure up after all. I have managed to pass through it without any mistakes; flying is exciting too.

The posting was abruptly interrupted late in 1939 and JP was sent back to Britain once war was declared. He found a brief few hours to visit his mother in St John's Wood.

'I am disappointed not to see Joan and her children.'

'Of course you are, but she could not come at short notice, you have to understand that. It's a comfort to receive all your news whenever you write from Egypt. I know I should not ask, ignore me if you wish.'

May was eager for information, 'Do you know how long you will be posted there?'

'I cannot know, Mother.' He looked into the distance. 'RAF Command may know that one. The Germans already make life uncomfortable in North Africa.'

May found it hard to hide her emotions, as their time together ended. She had read the papers daily, and watched the *Movietone News*. The fighting and bombing raids seemed to get heavier as the months passed. He gave his mother a hug, promised to keep writing, and returned, walking briskly, to the station.

Once he had gone, May could not stop thinking about Lionel, how he had had a distorted sense of humour, and loved life before the war. He had been the one in any group who always found a joke to tell, and his conversations would hold everybody's interest, because he had read widely and done so many things with his father, Philip, as a boy.

Lionel had friends in his street who all had several sisters or brothers, or both, but he had the attention of both parents, and never had to share anything with siblings. She did not want her son to go through this war, and change, but she told herself this was not the time to remember the bad times. 'Forget it,' she repeated silently at each step back, 'forget it,' and she hurried to get back home before the blackout.

JP was given his airline ticket on Imperial Airways, and on 10 October 1939 [9] he flew from Hounslow to Alexandria, with several stops on the way. He was transferred to 216 Squadron on arrival in Egypt two days later.

JP and his squadron, flying bombers, were dispatched one night to strike specific targets. The crews had not had sufficient night flying experience, and it was a dark night. On their way, JP set course, but some time later he realized he and his crew were alone. The others were nowhere in sight. They completed over one hundred and fifty miles on course, without seeing a sign of any other aircraft or any of the shipping that they had set out to attack. Dawn was breaking, and he made the decision to head back. Moments later they saw the Italian ships below, having flown straight above them and no less than a mile from them, but across their bows.

He judged his aircraft had not been seen. They turned south-southwest so that they could make use of the darkness remaining, then turn back on course like a mirror image of where they had been. He sensed his own rising anticipation. The sound of the motors was incongruous in the stillness of the pale blue Mediterranean dawn. He approached his target at what he guessed to be a perfect angle on the starboard bow. The ship did not seem aware of his aircraft. When he was just a little more than a thousand yards from the leading ship he gave the command and they dropped the bomb. JP held his breath, wondering whether it would strike. As he glanced back he could see a column of water rise into the air and thick, blackish-grey smoke pour out of the ship. Soon the flames were thrown up into the air. The other ships were firing at his aircraft, and he banked steeply turning his aircraft for base. He saw the tracers missing the aircraft and hoped he would quickly be out of range.

At the moment of safety his thoughts turned back to where he had been some minutes before. He craned his neck and got another brief view of the ship they had wrecked, and he felt an emotion he had known at another time. Identifying with the enemy below was, in a minuscule proportion, part of what he knew other men may feel as they looked into the distance and fired . . . no face, no eyes, or human shape, just a target in the distance. Somebody would lose a son, husband, or father, a person who was meaningful to another, and their life ended. The sound of the engine as he returned carried with it his own inexpressible fears, but also his hopes that he would be able, always, to return from an operation, whatever feelings he had about it. It was a job he had done. He loved to fly from the first moment of learning, but this part of the work was different. It was time to forget.

During the flight back he remembered his training days and fellow pilots like Keith, Pitch and Peter. Keith was, he knew, on fighters back at home.

I will see Peter later, and perhaps if we have some free time, we will go on to the RAF station in Heliopolis, he thought.

Pitch had been killed in the Battle of Britain.

JP heard the other members of his crew cracking jokes and singing loudly. He was enjoying the view and the dawn breaking all around him. A hazy horizon with a pure blue-gold of sunlight was over the desert. His thoughts were targeted on bringing his men and aircraft home to base safely.

John Philip (highlighted) in flying kit at Flight Training School, England, 1938. Photograph from *The Bystander*, 20 July 1938.

CHAPTER ELEVEN
1939–1940
BRITAIN AT WAR WITH GERMANY AGAIN

Sunday 3 September 1939, at Mulberry House.

In their small village Cecil, Olga and Emily sat together in front of the wireless to hear the news.

Cecil said, 'There'll be no problems today with my accumulator batteries and we can leave the wireless on for as long as we need to.' He liked the old wireless and routinely used it.

'What a turbulent year,' he murmured as he sat in his favourite wing chair and refilled his pipe from the St Bruno pouch. Striking a match and putting the flame to his pipe, he slowly lit it, holding the match to the pipe until the moment when he could smoke it. All those around him would smell that sweetish particular tobacco scent. They knew when he had been in a room, the pipe odour lingered for hours.

Emily watched him silently. She felt lucky to have them around her because her aunt spoiled her with delicious pies, cakes, and kindness, and her uncle always made a fuss of her in an attentive, thoughtful way, which made her feel loved and cared about; and Cathy baked Cornish pasties for them all when they had a picnic.

Mulberry House had been one of the first to get electricity in Cornwall the year before. Nevertheless they still used the oil lamps to take from room to room most evenings, and for their personal use in the bedrooms; and Olga brought one with her to brighten the room that afternoon. She put it on the old oak table beside her husband.

As they sat waiting, he looked at the clock in the room. He leaned over and turned on his wireless. Within seconds the sound of the Big Ben chimes filled the room. Their clock also struck in small shrill chimes that were drowned out by the London sound on the wireless. They silently looked at it. He turned up the sound.

'Our clock keeps good time,' Olga said just before the chimes stopped.

Immediately on the chimes ending, the Prime Minister's voice began to tell the people what had been decided following Germany's invasion of Poland.

At the end of the broadcast, Cecil turned off the wireless, but tension still dominated the room. War had been declared. The thoughts of each person in the room were not only in the present, but in the past and on the future. Cecil remembered his own First World War experience, the death of his brother Sydney and his guilt when he returned in 1919 from Burma, because he had not done his share in the Great War. He had been safe from all the devastation. Cecil recalled that upon his return to Hastings, more than half his peers had been killed, and many were badly injured. Others had died on their way home by catching the 1918 Spanish flu which left some twenty million people worldwide dead.

Olga found herself thinking about Harry. They had wanted to get engaged just before the outbreak of the First World War, but her parents had disapproved of their daughter marrying a butcher's son. Not long after the war ended she had met Cecil. However, he seemed distant toward her, and told her that he had lost too many friends, as well as a much loved brother, Percy. Many of her friends remained unmarried because there were too few men left. Olga remembered the general feeling of despair in 1919. Many unemployed, and others who could not find work because of their serious injuries. They had felt lucky to have her brother Andrew alive, but when he came home he had changed. He was uncommunicative, morose, and drank heavily. Olga wondered how Alicia and Emily would fare during this war, and was fearful for their future. She carried on with the knitting that had lain on her lap during the broadcast.

Emily looked at her uncle and aunt. She sensed they were deep in their thoughts, remembering their previous war experiences. All she could remember was that when she was five in 1921 life was harder because of it. Nobody threw away anything that could be used. Food was precious. Making their way to Bembridge to stay with their grandparents on the Isle of Wight, many around Portsmouth port were in rags, trousers tattered and torn, and she had never forgotten those poor children in the back streets without shoes or decent clothes.

Emily saw Olga lay her knitting aside and leave the room. She went to find her, with only a brief glance back at her uncle. He did not see her leave. Olga was in the kitchen, where she had been working on the pastry before the broadcast. She looked up, then started kneading again, and waited for Emily to comment. The window behind Olga was wide open, and as the sunlight shone through it onto her back, her dark hair, greying a little now at the temples, looked as though there was a halo of light on it. Emily was extremely fond of her aunt, and wanted to ask many questions, but did not dare to, thinking it could upset her. Years later, she would recall that moment with Olga; her kindness and thoughtful words. In a few years' time Olga would help her make an important choice, but Emily did not know that then.

There was an easy silence between them. Emily listened to Olga when she eventually decided to comment on the broadcast.

'Cecil and I have great faith in Churchill,' Olga said without looking at Emily, and while beating the bread with her knuckles on the floured table.

'People I work with at the BBC speak highly of him too,' said Emily. 'A few, though, are critical.'

Cathy arrived at the usual time the next day. Emily had been

Emily, Olga and Boxer at Mulberry House, 1935

for an early walk in the woods with her uncle, and they were talking politics in the sitting room while drinking their cup of tea. Cathy could smell his pipe smoke from the kitchen corridor. She knocked lightly on the door, which was ajar, and greeted them. Emily smiled broadly when she saw her.

'Would you both like some fresh tea?' Cathy asked. Cecil nodded.

Emily returned to the kitchen with the tea pot as her Uncle liked his tea hot and it had cooled. She wanted to hear Cathy's views too, as she felt it was easier to talk to her about the good and bad things in the past, from the quiet of the kitchen.

'Did you hear the broadcast yesterday?' Emily asked.

'Oh, it's a phony war. It will be over by Christmas.'

'Do you think so? I do hope you're right. I have been reading about the First World War and the dreadful battles when some of those poor men were out in France. Then when they returned life for most of them was impossibly hard. Nobody wants another long war.'

At that moment Olga joined them. She looked jaded, and seemed in pain.

'Oh, you're both in conversation about the usual subject in everyone's thoughts.' She walked round to the range. 'Has this reached the right temperature now Cathy?' Olga held her open palm near the door.

'Yes, nearly, and we are stopping our gloomy talk now. Emily is coming in to Tremena with me later to get some groceries.'

'It's your last day tomorrow, dear, is there anything you would like to do before you return to London?' Olga asked.

'I have no plans, but shall we ask uncle?'

* * *

On 10 May 1940, when Neville Chamberlain had resigned, King George VI, who had succeeded his brother Edward after the abdication, sent for Winston Churchill and asked him to form a government. Winston Churchill set about the task of forming an all-party government. This he did in a day, knowing how grave things were. Then came the famous speech which has taken its place in the great quotes of British political history:

> I would say to this House, as I said to those who joined the Government, I have nothing to offer but blood, toil, tears and sweat . . . we have before us an ordeal of the most grievous kind . . . many long months of struggle and of suffering.
>
> You ask what is our policy? I will say: it is to wage war, by sea, land and air, with all our might and with all the strength that God can give us; to wage war against a monstrous tyranny, never surpassed in the dark lamentable catalogue of human crime. That, that is our policy . . .' [10]
>
> Guy Eden, *Portrait of Churchill*

Between 28 May and 4 June 1940 the British troops had been stranded in France at Dunkirk, and were withdrawing from every direction.

In the air, Air Chief Marshal Sir Hugh Dowding,[11] Commander-in-Chief of RAF Fighter Command, which was created in 1939, was mistakenly and partly blamed by the troops on the ground—the beaches in France—for not protecting them from the German bombers. This was due to his policy to intercept German bombers *before* they reached the beaches of Dunkirk, which were crowded with thousands of British men waiting for rescue . . . troops that were helpless and stranded on the French coast, marooned, with the Channel on one side and the Germans all around them on the other. The troops could not see the RAF attacking the German aircraft behind them. The German planes flying over the beaches were vicious and merciless in their attacks on the helpless soldiers. These soldiers expected, and looked for, RAF patrols overhead—they did not see them.

The RAF lost seventy-five pilots while trying to protect their troops below, but people believed the RAF had let down those troops at Dunkirk. Many returning soldiers were angry and bitter and unreservedly voicing their negative views of the RAF. In the cinemas, streets and pubs it became common to hear boos and hissing when the RAF was referred to.

'Unhappily the troops on the beaches saw very little of the epic conflict in the air, often miles away and above the clouds . . .' [12]

Resentment was very slow to dissipate even with the help of the BBC giving the details of numbers of enemy aircraft destroyed by the RAF.

After Dunkirk, which left the British Army dangerously low on munitions, there only remained the Air Force and Navy to defend the country against the advance of the Germans. France was over-run by Germans. A weak British Isles was left close to disaster. The Germans at that time were unaware of how bad it was in Britain. The campaign of words and bluff to protect Britain from 'grim disaster' had begun. There were fears that if Germany were to strike in the June of 1940, then all would be lost.

On 17 June 1940, France asked for an Armistice. Britain was then left to continue the war alone. Norway, Denmark, Belgium and Holland had been invaded by the Germans by the middle of 1940. Greece was invaded by the Italians, then later by the Germans, and the Greeks were on starvation rations. Malta was strategically important to the British, but the Maltese people were starving as German aircraft were bombing them and supplies were not getting through. The RAF was unable to operate adequately in Malta.

JP and his Squadron flying Bristol Bombay Bombers, or Vickers Valentia were dispatched from Egypt once again to strike the German ships and to protect the British convoys bringing food and fuel to Malta. They were striking successfully at fuel ships going to help Rommel's army. [13]

Tremena, Cornwall

28 July 1940

Dear Emily,

I am thinking of you and your sister, especially as it is her birthday this month. Life has changed here with the war, and we are all careful with the rations. The windows are all taped and we have blackouts just as you do in London. Your uncle has started keeping more chickens, so we are not so worried about the egg rationing as our hens lay quite well, and there is plenty of space for them to scratch around.

We have all had to change our ways, but never a week passes without your name being mentioned in—a good way! I don't suppose you have the time to play the piano anymore. I do remember what fun it was when you were here as young girls, and we all miss those days, but that time is past and we all have a lot to do for the war, and hope that it will turn out for the best for us all, without the numbers that were killed in the first war.

My family are all busy in their different ways with the war effort.

I think it is much harder for those who lived through 1914–18 because this time all their memories come back. I have heard your aunt and uncle talking about their old villages and they worry about your life in the Blitz in London. I am not at their house as much as I used to be before all this fighting. Most people here get on with their lives and wait to hear the news each day on the wireless or hear it at the pub.

Please keep writing. Sorry this is short, but I promise to write more of the village stories next time.

Take care of yourself, and keep away from danger if you can. I know you hate the Underground shelters, I would too if I lived there in London.

Love Cathy

CHAPTER TWELVE
1939—1940
A Visit

In Cornwall, Cecil became an ARP Warden along with Alfred Pellow. His wife Olga joined the British Red Cross along with Cathy. Police Sergeant Turner and Milton Nicholas got involved and the parish church hall became the place where the Home Guard were trained. On Sundays Cecil played the organ at the parish church of St Erth where he had his usual pew with his wife. The village became an even tighter community as the war progressed.

Cecil's music room was used to raise money in aid of the POW's comfort funds. Two of the operettas Olga and Cecil performed were well received by the people, and *The Rajah of Rajahpore* was particularly popular. Occasionally, at the village shop, there would be a heated discussion as to the merits of it compared to *The Legend of St Yvonne* which others preferred. As the funds grew, it was decided to save some of the money towards the building of a memorial hall. Several thousand pounds were put aside for this project.

Emily's job at the Ministry of Information (MIF) kept her in London, but in early summer she wrote to Uncle Cecil, inviting herself to Mulberry House again. She wanted to regain the family ties and get away from London.

22 Mecklenburgh Square, London

20 September 1940

Dear Uncle Cecil and Auntie Olga,

Four of us have been on loan from the BBC to the MIF.
I shall soon be back as secretary to John Snagge, the BBC's
Director of Presentation.

Once we have organized the work for a few weeks
ahead, I will ask him if I can take my holiday. I know he
will agree. Is it all right if I come and spend my holidays
with you? I could help with the work in the garden, it will
be a relief from all the gloom and blackouts in London.

Write when you can.

Yours,

Emily x

Her room-mate was envious of her relatives far from London,
but Emily brushed it off.

'You're very fortunate.'

'So are you. Just a few months until you are married, and then
I will need to find someone else to share with, or go back home
to Essex.'

At dawn one morning, she set off for Cornwall, in her car that
she had bought from a friend down the corridor at the BBC, for
7/6d. He had taught her the basics of car mechanics, and petrol
was only 1/3d. per gallon. The car was a Triumph open two-seater
with a single seater dickie. She had a flask of hot tea, a picnic and
a blanket in case she needed to stop for a nap on the way. This
was a journey she had never done alone. She hoped there would
not be any mechanical problems and took a number of tools and
a torch in case of an extended stop for repairs.

When Emily arrived in the village, she left her car and walked
across the bridge, and with her back to the rising sun went across
the meadows. An orange glow over the field of wild grasses
gave it an artificially burnished hue. The brilliance only lasted
briefly. The dog-rose in the hedgerow was in tumbling flower,
the arching stems spread widely with many flat, large, pale-pink-
petal flowers. As she walked, she remembered the names of the

Emily

wild flowers. Her teacher at Portsmouth had taught her them: over there was crested dog's tail, she caught sight of its long spike-like flower head; and then the triangular, purplish-green flower heads of Quaking grass, rattling as the breeze gently blew on them. Feeling exhilarated after her hour's walk, she returned and knocked gently on the door, knowing she would probably be in time for breakfast and to join Cecil and Olga for the Sunday church service later.

'Emily!' Olga said excitedly as she opened the door. 'We have been waiting for you since your letter.' Olga embraced her warmly and Emily followed her to the dining room where, upon seeing her, Cecil rose quickly and went across to give her a big hug and planted a kiss on each cheek.

'You look very healthy, your cheeks are rosy, did you take a walk?'

'Sorry, did I interrupt your breakfast? Yes, I had a beautiful walk as the sun was rising. It is years since I walked that way. I used to do it when we were very young with Alicia. Did you know she works in the WAAF now?'

'I'll pour you some tea. Stay and talk to Cecil while I put some eggs on for you. Would you like one or two?'

'Two please, I'm ravenous. Can you spare two eggs?'

'Good, yes, we can. I got plenty from the general store yesterday, they have their own hens, as do we. In most villages eggs are rationed, but for now we can get what we need.'

Ten minutes later she was back with the eggs, toast, her homemade strawberry jam, and a fresh pot of hot tea, laid out on a tray. Emily saw the familiar China tea pot. As Olga laid down the toast rack Emily said, 'Mmm, that bread smells delicious Auntie.'

'Our niece has been telling me about the blackouts in London and the general atmosphere,' said Cecil.

'I can't tell you how happy I am to be out of the city and back here. It always feels like home. Mother says I should spend more time with her, father and Henry. You know how much I prefer coming here though. Is that bad of me?'

'Well, we are delighted you choose us. It has been much too quiet here since you and your sister stopped coming as often as you used to. You are both working. We must all do what we can.'

'Anyway, I shall soon live back at Highcombe again because my London room-mate is getting married. I can't pay the rent there on my own.'

'Did you hear Churchill on the wireless again last week?'

'Oh, yes. Sometimes we get advance knowledge about his broadcasts at the BBC.'

'I suspected that,' Cecil said.

'Lord Beaverbrook has galvanized the aircraft industry to build one thousand four hundred fighters, and any damaged planes are quickly repaired.'

They chatted easily, until it was time to make their way to church where, as usual, Cecil would be expected to play the organ. Emily secretly hoped she would not be asked to play the piano later as she had not practiced for some time, and her uncle would be unhappy if she refused.

Olga reached out for the brown felt hat she wore to church, then collected her handbag. They waited while Cecil emptied his pipe; then he picked up his hat and walking stick, and went to get his jaguar. He left the engine running as he opened the door first for his wife, then for Emily. Once he was back at the steering wheel, he drove the short route to church.

That same afternoon they all sat by the radio after tea to hear the news. Emily tried to be discreet, but was studying her uncle's face, trying to read him. She also noticed that his hands seemed much more gnarled and the skin around his wrists was wrinkled and leathery brown. She wondered if he was doing more of the garden work alone now. When the news broadcast ended, Olga put down her knitting, and looked up at her husband. Both women seemed to be waiting for him to comment. He puffed at his pipe, silently, and looked out into the fields beyond the east side of the garden. After a few minutes Olga picked up her knitting again, and Emily carried on with the blue sweater she was knitting for herself, which had lain on her lap throughout the news broadcast. Her uncle, she thought, seemed in a sombre mood. He carried on smoking his pipe. Olga and Emily exchanged glances, because they had both noticed him staring out into the darkest part of the garden.

Suddenly, he leapt up, and snatched his binoculars off the window ledge. 'There,' he said in a loud voice. Looking in the same direction he muttered loudly, 'someone is creeping about amongst the pittosporum. I shall have to go out.'

Putting his binoculars around his neck, he briskly left the room and they saw him almost running down the side of the garden. They heard loud male voices, a sharp sound like a large clap or slap, then silence. When he did not return Olga and Emily decided to look for him. They followed each other down the garden searching amongst the greenery. Emily saw him behind the music barn near the old Mulberry tree, and beckoned her aunt.

'Cecil, darling, what happened just then?' Olga asked quietly.

'That little elf Eric was after my plants. I caught him with his shovel and clippers.'

'Where is he?'

'I sent him through that small hole in the fence. He told me he'd come in that way. He got quite a fright when he saw me towering over him. I caught him trying to dig up one of my ten new plants. See here's one laid out ready to take away. I took a lot of trouble planting these new ones.'

'Uncle Cecil, you're more than six feet tall; so Eric would have been terrified.'

'Well, he'd deserve it too. I took away his tools and sent him off, and I locked them away. I told him he can have them next Sunday, if he comes to church with his family.'

'Cecil, you know that family never come to church!'

'Well, we shall see what happens next week. I wager you they will all come, because they can't afford new ones, or those tools don't belong to him. So he would have to explain that away when he returns without plants or tools.'

'Oh, dear, there's often someone trying to cut or lift some of your precious greenery. Was it like that when you were in Burma?' Emily asked.

'Oh, no. That was different. The planters, and those who worked for us, or with us, had an interest in keeping everything there healthy. We all got economic benefit from it. Also, there were many like Eric who would be earning something, rather than stealing for a living. They were poor, too, but it was quite different, wasn't it Olga?'

'From what I saw when I came once with you, yes.' She nodded.

She turned away and made for the music barn. Emily followed her, and they quietly shut the door behind them when they saw that he did not follow.

The barn had a vaulted ceiling, with big, dark beams and cross beams handsomely arranged to support the huge roof. At one end was their gleaming grand piano with a music stool that had an attractive brown and flower embroidered petit point tapestry seat. Olga had worked on that embroidery. It had been a surprise Christmas present to Cecil. There were old Persian rugs covering the wooden floor. In particular one large beautiful one that Ben had brought him from Mesopotamia. Ben had expensive taste and Emily knew that rug must have been special. Mother had four beautiful silk Persians they had brought home after their posting abroad. Further back, arranged in rows, were the forty chairs, ready for their next music evening.

'When is your next concert?'

'We're doing *The Fisher Maiden* soon.'

'Will that be for the army boys' fund?'

'Yes, probably, the first of many events this season.'

This was the first indication to Emily that they expected the war to last a while.

'When do you think the fighting will slow down?'

At that moment Cecil joined them. 'It will get serious, I think, but then I'm not an optimist.' He glanced across at Emily, wondering, too late, if his comment had upset her. He made a mental note to be more restrained in future. However, he could not help thinking that there was little to be positive about. Europe was in turmoil, and Britain was alone in what seemed a sea of madness and destruction, and people were being made homeless, or killed, all over the eastern continent. She would know much of it anyway from working at the BBC.

Cecil took out Franz Schubert's *Impromptu* in A-flat, from inside the stool. Without looking at either of them he spoke softly, 'This damned war has hardly even started. After Dunkirk,' he spoke angrily, 'we were lucky to get so many of our boys back home, out of that hellish hole. That crazy Hitler is angry, he will be raining more bombs on us soon. A German punishment for escaping from their claws in France. Nobody took notice of Winston when he said we needed to build up our air force a few years ago. Now we all have to work like the devil to get our strength, and send our RAF boys up in the sky to fight back. It will be tough. We have no choice.'

'Do you think they are training enough men?' asked Emily.

'We are fortunate, young men are coming from Canada, Australia, New Zealand, and South Africa to support us and to train with the RAF. There is also a group from Poland.' Cecil paused, 'Winston said we are fighting to save the world from the pestilence of Nazi tyranny. But our men who fly up to protect us are being shot down, or killed, daily. This is a war to establish individual human rights, we are not in it to dominate another country.'

'It is grim, Emily, but we all have to be strong. The dangers are huge,' Olga added.

'We are fortunate to have Winston Churchill to lead us. Can you imagine Chamberlain in his place?'

'Yes, he has united everyone in this crisis.'

'Uncle, do you think they may invade one day?'

'We are all striving to prepare our country for such an ordeal. This is why young men and women are flooding in to the Navy, RAF and Army. Good old Winston urging us to prepare and protect. We are both nearly the same age you know!'

'No despondency is tolerated' Olga added. 'My cousin, who was rescued after his ship had been torpedoed, told us of the hundreds of Navy casualties in the Channel.'

'Father mentioned that too.'

'Ben wrote telling me the RAF lost twelve pilots in a day, all experienced and battle savvy no doubt. Although all the news reports announced was "heavy casualties",' said Olga.

'Some people,' Emily added, 'say they can identify German fighters in the skies. One chap in our office said he can recognize each different one—Stukas, and so on—of their aircraft.'

Before Emily returned to London the three of them heard the famous address together on the wireless, to spur the nation on and to instil courage:

> Should the invader come, there will be no . . . submission before him as we have seen—alas—in other countries. We shall defend every village, every town, and every city. The vast mass of London itself, fought street by street, could easily devour an entire hostile army, and we would rather see London laid in ruins and ashes than that it should be tamely and abjectly enslaved.

CHAPTER THIRTEEN
EMILY RETURNS HOME

'Time you found a bedsit again in London, dear. Years working at the BBC, you should have saved and been independent.'

'I will, Mother. We have had the first television outside broadcast for George V's funeral.'

'You were very secretive about that.'

'She told me,' Ben muttered as he walked to the door to collect his golf clubs.

'We were televising the procession as it passed Hyde Park corner. The announcers were Elizabeth Cowell, Jasmine Bligh and Leslie Mitchell. It was truly memorable, not only for me, but it is an enormous advance in a technical way.'

'That is marvelous, that you were involved in it, I wonder what new things that will bring us.'

'I have also taken down in shorthand, and typed up, Douglas Birkinshaw's definitive work, which describes the working of all the apparatus involved in the transmission of television from camera to aerial. It's called a "black book" now. I told Father about it as it is the engineers' bible.'

'She did,' Ben said to his wife.

'Mother, my friend has a bedsit at 22 Mecklenburgh Square, so I can go and share with her, if you feel it would be easier for me to leave home now.'

'When?'

Emily ignored her mother, and had turned away and continued explaining to her father more of the details she thought he would appreciate.

'Father, I am now attached to the War Office. Next door, for the Navy, are Taprell-Dorling and Bartimeous. Did you come across them?'

'I don't recall either name.'

'On the other side for the Foreign Office there's Osbert Lancaster, but I have no idea what he does. My task is to collect all the cables from Reuters and the other news agencies about the war—the Russians are fighting in Finland now—then I have to formulate them into a report, which the War Office then approves for the Press. The writers in the War Office are H. E. Bates, Warren Chetham-Strode and Spike Hughes. It works well for now. Somebody said these men are quite famous.'

'No doubt. There is a network of people who recommend each other, one can't be too careful these days who they might let in to the BBC or the Foreign Office. I suspect you were vetted before they let you loose in the War Office, my dear, although you may not have known it.'

Emily and her three friends rented a bedsit. They all worked at the Ministry of Information, and they became accustomed to the blackouts. They often heard the roar of aircraft and sirens in the night.

However, within six months, the BBC recalled Emily to be secretary to the Director of Presentation, John Snagge, because they were expanding their radio programs and news reports.

Emily could not face the Underground shelters during bombing raids, so they all stayed in their building during any air raids. [14] They criss-crossed sticky tape on the windows to stop flying glass. Later, after one girl married, the other three moved to 34 Manchester Street. That very week they saw that their previous bedsit got a direct hit. Every morning during the Blitz they looked around to see what buildings had gone, as they walked to work in silence. A scent of burning persisted all around. Rescuers were clearing homes and looking for survivors. People tried to get on with their routine, despite the destruction. Bruce Belfrage was reading the news when Broadcasting House got a direct hit. He was in the basement though, quite safe. There were a few casualties by the lift shaft not far from Emily.

Civilian petrol stopped altogether. Petrol was rationed throughout the country.

Emily bought a Dartmoor pony and trap . . . a little two-seater dog cart which she painted in yellow and black herself, the same week she brought it home. She returned to live with her parents again.

'I'm at peace to hear you are returning home, rather than continuing to live in London,' Ben told her.

Emily found herself reliant again on her parents, although she would have preferred not to be. That first evening she asked her father for help. 'I shall call my pony Nicolette; would you ask if I can keep her in the golf club paddock?'

'I am secretary at the golf club, so I see no problem with Nicolette staying in their paddock, I am certain nobody will say anything about it,' he said.

'Sixteen miles to London is not too far, and Mr Angell's stables are in Weymouth Mews just across Portland Place from Broadcasting House, it will be easy once she has done the journey a few times.'

'Try not to return too late, Emily,' her mother advised.

Emily drank up the tea her mother had made for her and in reply said, 'There was one evening when we were all invited to the Observer Corps party. I made a fool of myself telling the girls I knew the way in the black-out. I told them all to follow me, and a few yards on, I went smack into a wall. The bruise on my face lasted a week! I still get teased by everyone . . . they say, "Ask Emily, she'll tell you the way!" if ever there is any thing going on that we have to find. We still go to a few parties because everyone wants to keep their spirits up, and they are usually great fun.'

'You will have to leave very early to get to work from here with Nicolette,' said Ben.

'I did a run last Sunday, to see how she could negotiate bridges and transport noise. She was not bad, but very stubborn in places. The children loved patting her when we stopped.'

'She would like that,' he said.

'At first I will drive her up to London on Monday morning and back to Essex on Friday evenings. It is a long journey, but I have found places to stop for her to get a breather.

She will be stabled in Weymouth mews just across from Broadcasting House. I have spoken to Mr Angell. Just imagine, he's about eighty! He said his three sons have gone off to war in the Veterinary Corps. He told me he would stable her for nothing as long as I exercise his livery horses. That suits me rather well! I will ride one in the park before work each day.'

The pony was well known in London and filmed by *British Movietone News* in 1941. It was seen by her friend in India, who wrote to congratulate her. Emily had not known about it. She was invited to write an article in the *Riding* magazine of spring 1942 where the photograph of her with Nicolette was published.

Emily with her pony and trap, London.
From Riding and Driving, the Horselovers Magazine, spring 1942.
Caption read: 'Two small ladies—two great buses.'

CHAPTER FOURTEEN
1940–1943

In the morning after the first bombs fell on London, I awoke and thought about the places people were running to when the sirens sounded. We heard the rumble of aircraft each night. Some nights, we heard many German aircraft, but none of us said a word. For me it was a potent reminder of how fortunate we were to survive. The powerful sounds above and the explosions on the ground, I admit, were terrifying, but I was determined to keep my routine. I could not conceive of dying except outdoors. To be in a crowded stuffy tunnel underground all day, or night, was abhorrent to me. I found it hard to believe I was in danger, and refused to accept I would succumb to a bomb. Each day they fell on London, I would walk, like others, through or past the debris, smell the fires and dust, and sense the confusion and sadness all around. There were others like me, and many of us were determined that the Germans would not make us cower in fear. The bombing raids had created devastation in our city, but people remained courageous.

Hitler threatened us with destruction in 1940 if we did not surrender.[15] The German Luftwaffe had moved into positions in newly occupied countries, and they were merely an hours' flight from London. Other German airfields were thirty minutes flying time away.

In early July 1940, I knew from my job that there were three Air Fleets available to Goering (Commander of the German Air Force). One was based in Holland, Belgium, and northeast France; another was based in north and northwest France; and the last was in Norway and Denmark, whose countries had been conquered earlier. The Germans could muster over three thousand aircraft.

From various sources of information and the BBC, we knew that on the 10 August Fighter Command suffered serious losses among flight commanders, most of whom were in their twenties. Hitler continued to threaten Britain. He wanted us to surrender. That first week in August, the extremely heavy losses of Fighter Command made gloomy predictions for the RAF's survival. Winston Churchill galvanised production in the aircraft industry and within three months, between June and August, over one thousand four hundred fighters were built, and any damaged planes were hastily repaired and put back into operations. On Thursday 8 August, we heard Dowding proclaim the start of the Battle of Britain. He stated that, 'the fate of generations' lay in the hands of the RAF. That August they delivered the biggest German anti-convoy strike ever mounted.

We got a letter from our cousin on the Isle of Wight that year, which seemed to surprise Mother.

The Mount, Bembridge, Isle of Wight

15 August 1940

Dear Mary and Ben,

I thought you would like to hear our news. On 11 August a German armada [16] with probably seventy-five bombers and escorts of ninety single- and twin-engine fighters flew above us on the island. Yes, somebody here counted them! We were astounded, and fearful to look up and see such a large number of planes making their way towards our country. The roar of aircraft was terrifying. A gigantic operation seemed to be descending on us. We wondered if anyone along the British coast had been warned of the raid. Then, not long after, we saw a fierce dogfight above. Up in the skies, an even more ferocious fight must have been going on out of sight at great speed, because we saw three German fighters drop out in flames. We have sometimes seen dog fights several times a day. Once we saw a dog fight right above the Needles and another of their fighters plunge into the sea. What a relief it was not one of our boys.

We are all managing here, and we feel lucky that our hens still lay, so we don't have any problems with egg rationing. I have had to learn to drink tea without sugar now though.

Then we heard that on 12 August Portsmouth city and their docks had been bombed. Our friends were very upset to hear that an uncle and aunt in their family had been killed, as well as children playing in their street. It was even worse it seems in the dock area. We are all angry, and sad.

We are not alone though because we heard whispers that Liverpool had been bombed.

Everyone is doing what they can for the war effort. Write when you have time.

All the best to you, Emily and Alicia.

David

I remember walking from Regent Street through to Hyde Park towards Oxford Street. In Hyde Park furniture and possessions were piled up on the grass verge in places. They had been salvaged from bombed out homes or hotels for their owners to retrieve. Once treasured, all looked abandoned, small and large items that could lie there unclaimed. Our city smelt of fires. Each day we waited for the chimes of Big Ben before the news bulletins, and sat or stood round the wireless.

By September the crisis was that there were not enough RAF pilots—too many of them had died protecting our country. The Battle of Britain left countless bereaved families. My anger percolated into a determination to pursue whatever ends were needed to deliver our country from the consequences of those bombing raids. They would not possess us; we would overcome the dark and despairing times, and our strength of will grew. The Nazis would not decide our future, as they did in Europe.

There was virtually no civilian petrol and consequently not much traffic on the roads, so I made my way home each day . . . it was a long journey, but I used to stop the pony in a back street for her to rest. She was stabled free during the week. I would have to ride a fairly superior hack up and down Rotten Row, or around the inner circle of Regents Park, each morning before work. What a bargain! Sometimes it was a case of taking horses to Rotten Row for customers to ride—and I even got the odd tip.

I occasionally took the pony for an airing round London in the evening and got well known. That was how we were filmed. My journey back to Essex went through Camden Town and down the Seven Sisters Road. The worst part was getting under bridges when there were trains about. One Friday evening, as we went under a railway bridge, a train went over blaring its steam whistle, and the pony bolted. After about a mile of bouncing in and out of tramlines, a shaft broke, bringing the pony down. There I was, in the middle of Tottenham, with a pony, happily unhurt, and a broken trap with my weekend luggage on it. Some elderly men appeared. One said he had a stable not far away where I could put the pony. So I led her down a maze of back streets with him till we came to his home, which had a ramshackle shed at the back where he used to keep a pony for some business he had. I unharnessed my pony and put her in. Two young lads offered to help me find feed and bedding for her, and took me to collect it, so we were able to make her comfortable. Then back to the trap, which was being minded by an interested group of old men, who told me there was a wheelwright not half a mile away, so together we pushed it to him, but had to knock him up because he had closed for the evening. Luckily, he lived on the premises. Yes, he could fit me a new shaft by Monday morning and he would find me something to get the pony home next morning.

Then those splendid lads offered to drive me all the way home. They knew the way because they had been to a scout camp at Gilwell Park. I didn't ask where they got the petrol! On Saturday morning I made my way back by foot and bus to fetch the pony. She had not liked the stable and had broken out, but was all right. I led her to the wheelwright, who had borrowed for me a small four-wheeled cart exactly like the one we saw later in *Steptoe and Son*! I shall never forget how helpful all those people were, and the wonderful kindness and goodwill that can spring seemingly from nowhere when one is in trouble.

In the spring after Dunkirk, I decided to join the forces. A woman I knew was high up in the WRNS. She told me there was just the place for me. Wrens were being trained to use and service the new radar equipment. All highly secret. So I signed all the papers and resigned from the BBC. I found that many of those on the WRNS second course for females at Chelsea Polytechnic had come down from university with degrees in physics. They were housed and drilled at Westfield College in Hampstead and were taken by bus daily to Chelsea. After three months we took an exam in basic wireless. I passed, so I went on to Warrington, which was a former Butlins camp, to learn about radar. I managed to get top marks there, and got a plum job, so my friend Pam Morgan and I were sent to Defford which was an aerodrome working in conjunction with Malvern College where they did the radar research, the TRE, Telecommunications Research Establishment. We were attached to the Fleet Air Arm section, and we built and tested radar equipment under the direction of civilian scientist-boffins. The CO of the Naval Section was Commander Milward.[17]

Defford was mainly an RAF station. One of nearly every type of aircraft was there. In the Naval section we had mostly Swordfish, but also Wellingtons, a Martlet, a Lancaster, a Walrus and others. I had to go up with the pilots and always felt airsick. Here at Defford life was fun and eventful, and we seemed to be rather out of touch with the war, that is the bombing and fighting side of it. Defford was to be an eventful period of my life.

CHAPTER FIFTEEN
1939–42
JOHN PHILIP

JP was in the Middle East with 216 Squadron from the end of 1939, and they fitted bomb racks to their Bristol Bombay aircraft in order to launch bombing missions against enemy targets in Libya. Egypt was a British colony, and Libya remained the main theatre of war.

Malta's close proximity to Sicily led to pilot officers, like JP, watching Italian bombers leisurely cruising overhead. Once, they found some packing cases in the dockyard labeled 'Gladiators'. Inside were the parts of four of these fighters which were Fleet Air Arm reserve aircraft. They were quickly assembled, and after a few practice flights, they were up for dog fights the next time the Italian raiders came over Malta. When an Italian S79 came down in flames, it immediately lifted morale throughout the island, which had been bombed frequently and without mercy.[18]

JP became involved in the defence of Egypt and the Suez Canal area. Constant RAF attacks were made on aerodromes and bases such as Tobruk, and later Benghazi.

JP wrote to his mother from Egypt:

To May Powell
Priory Road, Hampstead, NW8
January 1942

Dear Mother,

I cannot give you my address for security reasons. I am well and taking interesting flying operations. You will be happy to hear that I was recently promoted to acting Squadron Leader.

We do also play hard, and there are good parties we go to occasionally in Cairo.

You would love to see the colourful clothes the girls wear, and even I can tell the fabric is superb and all beautifully made to a Paris standard. I remember the smart clothes you made for yourself and Joan. The girls often wear different outfits to each party, which seems to tell us there is no problem with rationing in this part of the world. How different it is back home, where you have to have coupons to buy any clothes. We get transport to Alexandria for the weekend about once a month. There are the races (horses or camels) at Heliopolis and other tracks. We lived up country in tents in the desert west of Alexandria, which were well equipped and comfortable despite little head room. Plenty of food too. Some popular local food is called 'fool' and made with black eye beans, and we add salads and creamed chick pea, which is delicious. They call it the poor man's meal, but we are not sure why it gets called that.

Some of the places we stay in Cairo and Alexandria are run by the Salvation Army. A few of our boys drink heavily when off duty and my lads get quite drunk, but they have had bad times, and lost friends. There are plenty of aircraft around now and they get us from the desert to Cairo, or Alexandria, on days off. Our lads get busy playing bridge nearly all day in their free time. I have played tennis at a club near Heliopolis and been promised another round of golf. The Officers' Mess library, Shallufa, has plenty of reading material, and currently I have Robin Fedden on *The Land of Egypt* which is quite interesting when I can find the time to read it.

We have recaptured Marsah Matruh from the Italians. (You would have heard this already in your newspapers.) There have been a few dust storms, called Khamsin, or hot sand wind. This has shut down our flying at times. It is troublesome, as it can extend to a considerable height and the sand can flow at 20 m.p.h. along large areas so that when we return to the airfield after a few hours, it can be blotted out by the sand and we cannot see where to land. There have also been clouds of locusts, but I have not come across any myself yet.

When I came out here from Liverpool on the SS *City of Hong Kong* on May 20th 1939, I could not tell you many details for security. Now I can. We got to Port Said. The ship went on to Port Sudan and then Bombay. Nearly all of us on the first leg of the journey were Pilot Officers, or Acting POs. I have kept the Ellerman's City and Hall Lines booklet to show you when I get back home, and I have some passenger autographs. It was an enjoyable trip at sea, especially for me as I saw different parts of the world, and met many other pilots. There was a judge on board too, I got his autograph. I was given a long list of clothes I had to purchase the day after I saw you, and I got most of them from the Army and Navy stores in London, before I left for Liverpool.

We keep up to date with all the world events, and like you, we see the *Movietone News,* and hear the Big Ben chimes before news broadcasts. When Germany invaded Poland in 1939, some of us realized that the reason we had been sent out here would get more interesting. We were not surprised by the decision that Germany would divide up Poland between herself and Russia, just to keep the Russians on their side. We were joined by a few Polish fighters, and they are extremely sad about what happened to their country, but happy that they got away, although some of them were distressed that they left wives and families back home in Poland. They told us that more than one thousand five hundred German aircraft crossed over into their country. With the German tanks and artillery their country was quickly overrun. Even so, France and Britain's ultimatum did nothing to frighten the Nazi Germans. The Poles we talk to think that many tens of thousands of their fellow countrymen and women have been killed by the Germans and Russians in September (1939) when they were fighting hard against them. Well, maybe you know most of this! Certainly one Polish young man that joined us is most capable, and learns fast, but there is the odd chap here who resents him, and I cannot understand why. They fought hard to protect their country, as we are doing now, but they lost their home, and are helping us, so it seems strange anyone would resent him. I like him. We are fortunate that people like him, as well as others from our colonies (Australia, New Zealand, South Africa and Canada) have joined us. When I was training in Canada people were friendly, and perhaps one day I may go back there. I would love to see more of the place.

We have been taken to Shepheard's in Cairo. It is always crowded with groups sitting together eating and drinking. I have heard many languages spoken there. Suffragis, or waiters, are experts at carrying loaded trays of drinks and delicious food. Again all the women are dressed for show, and most men are in uniform, like me.

I've been able to go to Luxor once with a girlfriend (not serious, sorry!). The Nile changes colour like the sky. Bright blue in daylight, and gold and rose in the sunset.

You'd love to see the herons sitting in the trees above the bank, and matchstick-legged white egrets stalk the banks. All around I saw figures working in the fields of sugar cane, or carpets of green vegetation. My friend called it 'beautiful scenery' but I kept thinking how short my time was there and I stupidly missed the pleasure of it all. The noise and bustle in Cairo is a contrast to how we live in the desert. People in Egypt seem happy, go to clubs, and some seem to ignore the war. I feel I have to be one person in the city, and sacrifice who I am, then another when I am working. I still don't know how, or who, my working 'me' should be. I do it the best way I can.

From your letters and news, I hear life is hard back home, and the rations are hardly sufficient. London has taken a huge bashing with the bombing raids, and we know that people, especially the women, back home are doing great things to keep up their spirits. I love the songs we hear on the wireless. This will make you smile, when you and Joan listen to 'We'll Meet Again' or that Ivor Novello one 'Keep the Home Fires Burning' then you know that is what I will be thinking too when I hear it, maybe at the same time as all of you! I will be home one day soon and surprise you, I hope.

Take care, Mother. It is good to hear your news, even if the letter takes a long while to get to me. I send you and Joan my love.

Yours,

John P.

* * *

In May 1942 an announcement was made regarding awards for the Distinguished Flying Cross (DFC).

Acting Squadron Leader JP Gregory of No. 38 Squadron . . . this officer has carried out many sorties both by day and by night. Whilst operating from Malta, Sqn. Ldr. Gregory has participated in attacks on shipping and other targets. On one occasion he attacked a large motor vessel in Tripoli harbour in the face of intense opposition and set it on fire. This officer has always pressed home his attacks, to the utmost limit. As flight commander he has displayed fine leadership and set a praiseworthy example.

Back in England, at an operations briefing in Defford in June 1942, each Wren was informed of their duty, 'Wren Emily Hale, you will go up with Squadron Leader Gregory at 09.30 in a Swordfish. He will brief you on the testing of radar.'

In another part of the Defford RAF station on the same day, JP was briefing his men for morning operations. Maps and boards around the room were marked with flags and coloured blocks. After the briefing they collected their apparel, warm jackets, and goggles before going out to their aircrafts.

Emily was dressed warmly and waiting beside the Swordfish when she saw a tall, slender, slightly-built young man, with a shock of neat ginger hair, come towards the machine, wearing a heavy leather flying jacket and carrying a leather helmet and goggles. She remembered what Pam had told her about him.

She saluted. She felt anxious as it was her first flight in a Swordfish.

He nodded, noticing her piercing blue eyes and genuine smile.

'Ready?' JP smiled back.

'Yes, sir.'

CHAPTER SIXTEEN
1940–1943
THE 'BOFFINS' WHO SAVED LIVES

'We seemed out of touch with the war in Defford.' Emily wrote in her diary many years later.

> I had a licence to drive Naval vehicles and often drove officers into Malvern. We had to cross the river at Upton. I remembered my first meeting with JP and hoped he would be on one of our trips, but I did not see him. The RAF officers had their own mess. I started to think that I had made a fool of myself on our trip in the Swordfish. When I thought back to it, I secretly blushed, so I tried not to think about it too often. He was doing the flying, and I was feeling rather sick, as I always seemed to be up in the air, so I asked him to fly "more steadily". I forget. He did not reply, but I noticed the plane did not rock too much. When we returned I felt so weak and queasy, that all I did was salute, and he said something which I could not hear because another noisy aircraft was landing. I was surprised at how often I thought of him, and looked out for that ginger crop of neatly combed head of hair. I think I saw him once in the distance looking dapper, and well turned out, but I could have been mistaken.
>
> Once, driving the big lorry which had a canvas cover supported by tubular steel bars, I forgot the height

and damaged it which made me unpopular with the maintenance crew. Another time I drove the lorry with considerable trepidation because it was loaded with a dozen or so sub-lieutenants who were fully trained and had just come to learn about radar; trained men who must have been about the most valuable commodity there was at that time in the war.'

Radar had an uneasy and complicated journey from 1940. It helped pilots to see through cloud, navigate to find targets more easily, as well as to return safely home, saving the lives of many aircrew, like JP, and putting a scowl on Hitler's face. However, sympathy for bombing German cities had almost evaporated, although Germans had bombed London, Coventry, Liverpool, Portsmouth, and other cities from 1940. Many boffins, scientists, and engineers were unable to talk about elementary radar then.

John Philip was an RAF pilot doing an easy stint at Defford after two tours of operations in Malta and the Western Desert of Egypt and Libya. Emily and her friend Pam Morgan went there from their radar training camp at Warrington. Under the direction of boffins they built and tested radar equipment. The RAF had used radar in Hamburg and that led to British shipping losses falling dramatically that summer.

'Did you see or hear from that Squadron Leader yet?' Pam asked Emily when they were alone.

'No, but I wish I knew what he had said to me after that flight.'

'There's a dance tomorrow, and I know some of the RAF officers will be there, shall we go?'

'You needn't ask, I love parties.'

'I have seen him in his little Morris 8 two-seater car.'

'Where, when?'

'Going to the mess. He had a little fawn puppy with him.'

'Right, you can help me spot him at the dance then!' Emily's voice sounded excited.

On a moonless night, Emily saw JP when she entered with Pam. He looked directly at her, as if he had been waiting, then whispered to the officer beside him, before going to her. She felt elated and did not wait; she went to him wondering at the same time what to say.

'I hoped I would find you here tonight,' he said, looking directly into her eyes.

'I couldn't hear what you said to me after our flight, and I felt rather sick, sorry.'

'I noticed you felt ill. It was noisy. Can I get you a drink?'

'Thank you, cider, please.'

They took their drinks out to the front of the building where others were standing around away from the band. JP felt tired, but the excitement of being beside her lifted him. She sensed it, and noticed her own tension. JP had heard that Emily was known as talkative and lively. He gathered in all he could see of her slender shape from the mess lights that fell on her. Only a few days since she had flown with him; and she had abruptly become tongue-tied. She waited. He held back, then took his pipe out of his pocket and paused as he was about to light it. 'Will you mind if I smoke?'

'No, I like it. My favourite uncle in Cornwall smokes a pipe and I have been used to that since I was seven.' She observed the familiar routine of lighting a pipe; then detected him relaxing. Emily wondered whether tonight would be the first of many reunions. Just then a flashing light illuminated them for an instant, and until the rumbling growl of the aircraft motors ceased any attempt at conversation was useless. She leant back against the wall and he turned from watching the aircraft, to face her, taking in her features. She seemed to him more lovely than he remembered. They stared at each other briefly. As his eyes adjusted to the gloom, he studied her face and eyes and she sensed a compassion, and a strange struggle or ache in him. He was in his early twenties, twenty-two she had heard, and already a Squadron Leader. He was taller than her, perhaps as tall as Uncle Cecil.

'I wanted to ask about your last tour in Africa, but perhaps you can't talk about that.'

'What would you like to know?'

'Life in Egypt, did you see the pyramids, bombing raids—anything at all.'

'Have you eaten?'

'Not much.' She had wanted to add that her agitation at the idea of seeing him again had spoilt her usually large appetite.

'Shall we go and eat, I can then answer some of your questions. Let's walk to the local pub. Are you alright with dogs—I have got a naughty puppy called Susan.'

'We never had pets as my parents were in Nigeria and we were at boarding school, but Uncle Cecil and Auntie Olga have a small dog, Boxer, who loves me.'

'Good, then let's take Susan with us.' He took her hand.

They made small talk at dinner. Rationing meant there were only sandwiches at the pub. JP spoke of life in a tent in the desert, the pitch black night skies with bright stars and the Milky Way, and playing golf in Alexandria. He steered all conversation away from anything that had to do with bombing raids over the Mediterranean.

'I'd be petrified up in the sky being shot at by anti-aircraft guns below,' Emily confessed, then wished she had not been so honest, feeling it was rather insensitive.

'Many of us are fearful, but we cannot, and would not, admit to it because it is a job that has to be done. As to being fired at, nothing before or since has been a patch on the flak in Benghazi. We all got through that! Now tell me, are you a boffin?'

'No probably more a "puffin", it is the RAF that describes engineers and scientists as boffins. The Baffin torpedo bomber, as you know, was retired just before the war. Do I look like an eccentric and inventive scientist or engineer?'

'I'll tell you one day, I don't want you to blush, or frighten you away!'

A whining under the table distracted him. JP lifted up his four-month-old golden Labrador on to his lap, 'Do you need a drink, or to go out, now?' She jumped up and licked his face. 'Come on, let's go back along the perimeter, it is a route that is familiar to her.'

They walked silently, hand in hand. They could see dim outlines of wide buildings, and a soft wind blew around them. He tightened his hold on her hand, and only let it go to relight his pipe.

'I don't want to cause you any pain,' he said suddenly.

She glanced at him, then looked straight ahead remembering how a friend lost her husband to a bombing raid. She could not answer, and wondered whether he expected a reply. She kept her hand in his and pressed her thumb harder on his hand. Much later she said, 'It was pretty frightful when my friend got a telegram, but she's back now, after a week with her parents, and trying to get on with her duties. She doesn't talk much, I expect she tries to forget it.'

'No . . . I mean yes. I find the hardest part is writing letters to the parents, wives, or families, and I have had to do too many of those,' said JP.

Emily replied, 'I can't think how one can avoid those horrible thoughts, but if I wallow in them my life would petrify. My uncle says he is a pessimist these days, but I feel I am an optimist.' Her voice was steady.

'One day this war will all be in the past. May, my mother, repeats that each time I see her. She hated what the First World War did and the aftermath. I can't remember my father—he died after the end of the war from the effects of gas poisoning; he had clung to life, but his body could not.

'So sad. It was auspicious that Father and Uncle Cecil were abroad and away from the Great War. Now let's chase away these black thoughts. I pray that all those I love will get through it with me.' She stood on her tip toes in front of him and kissed him lightly on the lips.

He put both hands on her waist and pulled her closer and whispered, 'I wanted so much to find you and to know you.'

'Me too, and we can't fight it.' They held one another until JP shivered from the cold wind and tiredness that had begun to overwhelm him. 'I must get some sleep, I have lost too many hours this week, forgive me,' he told her gently.

'Yes . . . and I am too awake for sleep, but I know you must go.' She bent down to stroke Susan who jumped around excitedly. 'Where does she go when you are flying?'

'There are many officers around who like to keep an eye on her. She's pretty spoilt.'

As they parted he arranged to meet her on his next free day.

'We can take a walk along the river,' he suggested.

'I'll bring a picnic, which we can eat in your car if it is raining.'

'How do you know about my car?'

'Pam saw you!'

'There are no clouds predicted,' he laughed, but he had another operation for dawn the next day and hoped that their next meeting would give them more time together.

'He's long overdue, Pam,' Emily said, looking anxiously at her friend, when JP did not show up.

Pam put her arm round Emily and sighed. 'Just wait, be patient . . . tell me what he was like.'

'What do you mean *was*?'

'I meant, what was he like when you were together. You haven't told me anything, and I don't think he is dead, Emily!'

'Yes, I did want to tell you, but there were so many thoughts engulfing me after that night, that it has been hard for me to concentrate on their meaning. He said so much, but at times he didn't say more than a few words, but even those few carried emotion and could be understood several ways. I'm a bit older than him, but he is more mature. He has seen and done so much, and some things he hates to recall.'

'Are you in love?'

'Oh, you know, tall, dark and handsome . . . maybe I am! We talked such a lot, and I felt very comfortable with him.'

Pam shouted, 'Listen!' They heard the low rumbling of the familiar aircraft sounds of landings and take-offs. They ran outside to watch which ones were there.

'Maybe he's with that Lysander,' Pam offered, and they both looked up to the sky to see whether any others were coming in. The dark clouds gradually closed over the remnants of the blue sky, and no more aircraft appeared. Emily turned back indoors to take up her knitting which she expertly worked while reading a book. Pam felt helpless.

A faint knock on their door later, and an envelope was pushed under it. Emily didn't move, but her friend rushed to pick it up.

'It's for you.'

'Open it, please, could you?'

'No, here, you open it,' and she put it into Emily's hand.

Emily suddenly felt cold, and shivered, but she tore open the envelope. Pam saw her face turn pale.

> RAF Officers' Mess, Defford.
>
> Dear Emily,
>
> We got delayed on an operation. Can't be helped. Can we meet outside the officers' mess at 1230 hours?
>
> Yours
>
> John (JP)

She stared at his handwriting. Then she jumped up and down, and handed the letter to her friend, who noticed the colour was back in Emily's cheeks.

CHAPTER SEVENTEEN
1942–43
NAVIGATING THROUGH FAMILY

RAF Station, Defford, Worcestershire

30 March 1943

Dear Auntie Olga and Uncle Cecil,

Thank you for your letters. I should have replied sooner. There are so many things going on here, which I will tell you about when we meet. I cannot say too much in letters. I am one of the WRENS here, and because I know how to drive I get some interesting duties. I did mess up once though. I forgot the height of a big lorry I was driving, and when I stopped outside a theatre in Worcester there was an overhanging canopy across the pathway, and the whole of the cover was bent backwards. The maintenance crew were furious with me. Another time I was given the duty to drive the lorry carefully because it was loaded with sub-lieutenants, who were fully trained in our new equipment . . . they could have been the most important people in the war that week.

I recently went up in a Swordfish aeroplane with an RAF pilot who was decorated for duties in Africa. Unfortunately, I was pretty airsick, but I did manage to do what I had been trained to do by talking with him down a rubber speaking tube! The reason I tell you all this is that, since then, we have been seeing each other and I would love to bring him to meet you, but I do not want you to say anything to the family at Highcombe, or anyone else. We may not know if we can get a week's leave together until a day or two before, because of some secret operations. How does that suit your plans? Can we both stay with you for about eight days? I hope you will like him, I do think you will, but most of all I want him to meet you first. He has a Labrador, Susan, so please write and tell me if she can come too.

That is all for now. I'll wait for your reply before we make our plans.

Love Emily xo

Mulberry House, Tremena, Cornwall
12 April 1943

My dear Emily,

We were so delighted to read your letter and your news. You can come any time you wish, we are always here, and the only visit I have to make from time to time is to my mother. Write to us once you have a date. Let us know if you want us to collect you from Penzance station.

We look forward to seeing you both. You forgot to tell us his name!

Love Auntie Olga

Olga sealed the envelope with Cecil's red wax, stamped the wax seal with his signet ready to post later, and left it on the hall table. When she returned to the sitting room, Cecil was dozing. She took up her knitting and her thoughts wandered to the first time Emily and her sister Alicia came to stay, then wistfully, another holiday she recalled vividly just before Alicia's birthday.

Mulberry House was the largest in Tremena and Cecil had wanted a permanent home when he returned from Burma. He had told her that Cornwall's mellow weather would suit him best, and the large garden could produce an income from growing greenery for the florists in London. The house had been empty and damp, and he had relished the hope that one day, when they lived there, he could nurture it back into a family home with a few children, and some extended family nearby, or coming to stay for long periods. She remembered the first time he had brought her to see it, and her feeling straight away when she walked through the huge, studded, old oak door, that it felt like a home that she could love for them together. 'It feels right for us,' she remembered telling him.

She recalled how Cecil had encouraged Emily's skill at the piano during their holidays, and had practiced with her nearly every day; the two of them often competed and played duets. Each time they visited he noticed how much she had improved, and the attention he lavished on her gave her more confidence. Emily seemed to thrive in Cornwall, and she had a close bond with her uncle, which Olga liked, because her husband was much more like the young man she had first met when he was with Emily.

It had been a hot, sunny, dry week, and Cecil had been glad to hear the first drops of rain at the end of July when Emily and Alicia were coming from boarding school. The sky was dark and the expected rain clouds swept through, to his great relief. He had left his Jaguar outside Penzance station, and as he and Olga walked towards the platform they heard the London train pulling in. They saw both girls jump off the train, as the rain got heavier. Emily, half Cecil's height, ran to her uncle and aunt.

'Oh, Uncle Cecil.' She hugged them both. 'I love this dusty, earthy smell of the first rain after hot days. It reminds me of Cornwall. I am so happy to be back. Has it been very hot here?'

Before he could reply, Alicia was there, followed by the porter pushing their two trunks.

'Auntie Olga.' She reached up to kiss her first, then her uncle.

'Let's make our way to the Jaguar. Porter, see the trunks are safely in, it's the black Jaguar parked outside.'

'What a delicious scent in the air,' Alicia said, looking up at her uncle.

They had all followed the porter arm-in-arm, but both girls were running to keep up with Cecil's large strides. By the time they returned to the house a July sun was strong and still high. The sandy, delicious smell lingered. The side door had been open, and there stood Cathy, eager to greet them. The two girls ran about the house.

Olga recalled being as excited as they were, even at age thirty-nine. She had followed the girls around while they reminded themselves of the layout of each room. They bounced on the bed in their room. Giggles and squeals of happy laughter were heard by their uncle below.

'Auntie Olga, I am so excited,' Alicia had screeched. Olga remembered leaving them to re-join her husband in the garden room.

'I expect they may be too excited to sleep tonight.'

It was Alicia's birthday and they had all planned a special day for the start of her teens. She found little presents at the dinner table. Each little parcel was carefully wrapped.

'When I woke up today I felt so thrilled to be coming here. For some moments I dared not move.' Alicia whispered. 'I still can't believe it. I remembered I would have a lovely bed and eiderdown on me here.' Her gush of words had made them all laugh, as she rarely said much.

'Can I open my presents now, please?' she asked, but tore open the paper without waiting for a reply.

'We thought that if the weather permitted tomorrow, we would all take a picnic to a beach in the north that you have not been to before.'

Olga thought back to how they would be standing talking to her all morning, or following her around the house, especially

Emily. They both wanted attention and love, and she knew they had missed their parents. They hadn't known a regular family life. She had remarked to Cecil how they looked for letters and postcards from Africa each day when the postman arrived.

'Time goes so fast, slow down the hours!' Emily had said with a laugh as they packed up everything into the car for a picnic the week after they had arrived. Cecil had stopped at the general store to pick up the *British Gazette*. He made a phone call from the red telephone box outside the post office. Emily had asked her aunt who he had been talking to on the phone.

Their summer rolled over six weeks with memorable days out, or at home in the garden with their aunt and uncle. Cooking with Olga, walks, and visits to people in the village. By the time September came, when most of their holiday in Cornwall was over, the girls became subdued. That last week, they woke at dawn to make the most of each remaining hour.

One day, Emily had a nightmare about the dark mulberry tree in the garden. She had a panic attack in the dream; she told Olga she had wanted to run away from something, but could not. They had had to shake her awake: 'It is late, wake up.' She had been relieved to find herself in that bed, but remained disturbed by her dream.

On their last evening both girls stayed up. After supper they all sat in the garden room. Cecil closed the French doors as it had begun to feel chilly. The pinkish sunlight soaked into the room, colouring the walls.

'Shall we light the fire for their last evening, and have some stories, Cecil?'

'Oh, yes please . . . tell us about when you were a boy again and about your brother Percy'.

'Oh, you've heard that before.'

'No, no, I'd like the stories again, Uncle,' Emily pleaded. Olga pictured the scene as if looking at an old photo album.

Cecil took out his pipe, and went through his routine,

knocking out the old tobacco, cleaning with a pipe cleaner, and then putting in fresh tobacco from the St Bruno tin. Lighting, then drawing the air into his pipe. Soon the sweet tobacco scent was in the whole room. While concentrating on the task, he had been thoughtful. The frown seemed to tell Olga his thoughts needed more of his energy.

'Uncle, would you tell us again about your big brother, Percy?'

'Yes, Emily, in a moment.'

Olga detected a glimmer of sadness in his voice, so minute, that maybe she had imagined it. They all sat facing Cecil on the long settee. Emily slipped off her sandals and snuggled closer to Olga with her arms clasped round her knees. It was still bright in the room, but the daylight was starting to fade, and beside Olga, resting on the old oak table, was one of the oil lamps ready to light when dusk closed in. Cecil used the match he had used for his pipe to light the paper in the grate. Soon the flames were flowing under the kindling, and the sounds of sparks and crackling wood were the only noises in the room. He seemed to be waiting for the fire to take hold and the warmth to permeate the room. Nobody spoke. He leaned back deeply into his armchair, sucking on his pipe.

'Ah, Percy,' he sighed quietly.

The flames now caught the wood and coals, and an orange-red glow reflected on the shiny brass surround. The smell of the coal fire seeped into the room. At first all eyes looked at the flames. There was a gentle, easy silence for many minutes. Cecil was facing his wife and the two girls. He spoke slowly at first.

'My father, Joseph, and my mother, Elizabeth, were only together for nine years you see . . . she was his second wife.'

'Why was it so short?' Olga asked Cecil.

'That is a long story, probably easier if I tell you why and how my father came to marry my mother.'

'I feel, at fifty-seven, suddenly quite old, too many years have passed since I played with my older brother, Percy,' thought Cecil; 'I hear murmurs of our past.'

The thoughts took him back and back.

It was so long ago. Cecil was not sure whether his memory was clear. Sometimes he remembered some things Percy had told him, or shown him, so was it Percy's memory or his? It was hard to untangle. He experienced a rush of those old, empty, uncomfortable feelings which he never knew what to do with. Percy's face was like a photograph in front of him, but not like his own, chocolate-coloured wedding photo.

Percy's face was bright, with big blue eyes and straight blonde hair, almost too long below his ears. Percy used to hold his hand and take him everywhere as soon as he could walk. Percy read stories to him and they played, and laughed often; at times he had soothed away his tears. 'Be brave,' he had said.

'Father, Joseph, was tall, dark and handsome, and most sociable.' Cecil began.

They all laughed.

'Was he like Cyrano de Bergerac then?' Emily asked.

'Oh, yes, I know it is amusing, but that is what everyone thought of him. They all said he was very good-looking. He loved to look at the pretty girls, it seems, and most of all a beautiful woman. They searched him out, too. Their parents always invited him to social events. Percy told me he looked very handsome on his grey horse. It seems father was most attached to that stallion. Eventually, at thirty-three, he fell for a woman called Ethelinda. Father married without the usual fanfare from his family, and against his father's wish. My father had not known her long. So there was a good deal of whispering going on about babies and so on in the village. The story I was told by our nanny, when I was much older, was that Ethelinda and father had a little boy, Percy, only six months after they were married. Of course, everyone was delighted they had an heir and father celebrated by having a huge party.'

Cecil's voice trailed into silence. He sat smoking his pipe quietly. He pushed more tobacco in and relit. The coals in the grate were a deep red. Cecil picked up the brass shovel, scooped up more coals and poured them slowly into the grate.

Olga looked at the girls who both stared at her husband, waiting. Now they all knew he was preparing for a long story.

'Ethelinda, father's first wife, died only a week after the party.' He heard the girls gasp, but he carried on. 'They had tried everything to save her. Nanny described to me the overwhelming grief that enveloped the household.'

'Emily, dear, would you light the lamps in here please?' Olga asked. 'There are some more matches in the drawer beside Cecil.'

'Olga, my dear, I'll do that, I have some matches here in my pocket.' He struck the match and went over to light the oil lamp beside his wife and both his nieces. Before returning to his armchair he very carefully opened the side panel of his desk, and removed a large sheet of folded paper from an envelope. They could all see the beautiful, elegant black ink handwriting as he lifted each page of the papers. The glow from the oil lamp gave the sheets of paper in his hands an amber hue. As the light from the lamps brightened, the room at first took on a yellowish tinge, then, after several minutes, a brighter, clearer light glowed from the lamps. They were all warmed by the coals in the grate. Each person in the room was either facing the light of the lamp or the light from the coals in the grate, and each face had a different share of light and shade. The moving colours tinted their expressions. Cecil looked at the women in front of him individually, then together. It was a calamitous story he was telling, and their expressions became fixed in his mind. Outside, the sky was dark grey with heavy rain clouds. It grew quiet, the silence only interrupted by the wind blowing the trees and the vegetation, as well as the crackling sounds in the fireplace. He decided to cut back the family story, and glanced at each face as if to make sure nothing had changed. His face was inscrutable to his wife, who was aware that he was clever at hiding his own feelings.

'I'll tell you what father told me when he was only two years older than I am now. He showed me this diary, this family tree. It did help me to understand Percy, and the family's life from a distance of time.' He held it up. 'This was mother's—Elizabeth's.'

Again Cecil got up. This time he went to the French doors and stood, with his back to the room, looking out as he spoke. They could hear him, but not as well as before. It was hard to breathe too loudly in case one missed a word he was saying. He never looked at them, as the monologue developed and grew. His hands were clasped behind his back. The right hand twitched in a certain way when he said something emotional. He put one hand in his pocket to finger something.

'Can I tell them all how hard it was for me, too?' Cecil wondered. 'Percy had been a tiny baby when *his* mother died, so he never knew her. And he had father and Nanny. I was only eight, poor Ben was six, when my mother died. She was too young when she left us all.'

'It was a tragedy for us that my mother died at thirty-two. We had to get used to a stepmother a year later. That was common then,' Cecil added. 'People never talked to us about anything. All we ever heard were whispers, or loud voices behind closed doors. They did not want us to know something was amiss, but, of course, we could feel that sadness all around us. They thought talking about it would upset us, but not talking to us made us feel even worse!'

Nobody spoke.

Cecil went on to describe in detail their village life, and the favourable, but hard work at the mill.

'When did Percy start his riding lessons?' Olga tried to draw Cecil away from his maudlin mood, and for a while she succeeded. He returned to his leather chair. His expression changed from sadness and anger to a happier one as he continued.

'Percy told me he took riding lessons aged five. Father was very proud of him, saying he was a natural. We had some fun with him when we were older and could get around. We explored the fields and sea shore, and we rode bare back. I was taught how to climb trees, and we took food up into the trees and watched the world go by.'

'I love riding, too,' Emily said, jumping up to go to the gas lamp, and brighten the room.

'Time for bed,' Olga announced.

'Oh, no, not yet!' Emily exclaimed. Alicia repeated it.

Later, Cecil could hear voices and laughter above, and he was relieved he had not made them miserable. Olga remembered how low he seemed that evening, but suspected it had more to do with the end of the girls' holiday than Percy. The following day Cecil was troubled because they had gone back to school, but that evening the wine glasses clinked and he became mischievous.

He lifted me up to dance and held me close, and I could hear his heart racing as he kissed my neck and cheeks, 'Let's go to bed,' he had whispered, pulling me by the hand. Midnight brought us beautiful moments and the fulfilment of his desires—and mine. I felt renewed. 'Never go away too far,' he had murmured, as he drew me again toward him that dawn.

'Have you written back to Emily yet?' Cecil asked when he woke from his snooze.

'Yes, as we discussed.' Olga hesitated briefly as she returned to him from her daydream, then she added, 'It is such agreeable news in these difficult times. I hope she will bring this young man to meet us soon.'

JP and his crew had to deliver two more SOE agents into France.[19] Then he would be free to arrange a holiday. Secret missions were weather dependent. All Emily knew was that he had to fly off somewhere for two further operations, and that these could be days apart, or weeks away. The SOE agent would parachute out of the plane, but on rare occasions JP might land the Lysander following a prearranged signal.

JP became more attentive and Emily looked out for him each day, but their relationship was coloured by the effects of the war. If Emily did not see him for several days, she would become anxious, and then silent when he appeared again . . . almost as if she was angry with him, but she knew it was more likely that she was angry with herself for being too possessive.

CHAPTER EIGHTEEN
1943
ENCOUNTER

Over the next few weeks JP felt perturbed by a restlessness he had not experienced before. Emily knew something disturbed her, but because she also felt happy, she tried to ignore those feelings. JP had left her with a strong impression and she was not used to her moods which now swung from elation, to fear and anxiety. She was often more anxious than she wished to admit. When she or Pam heard that an aircraft crashed or went missing, they would hurry away to investigate the details together. Both were attached to someone on regular operations, and they were not the only ones who kept alert to the goings on in Defford. Most days brought gloomy news; yet everyone seemed to be looking out for one another, and there was no hostility or jealousies amongst the small population on the base.

When JP set out to find Emily, he was single-minded; he was not a man of casual impulses. He loved her piercing blue eyes and beautiful features, and needed to feel the sensation of her in his arms. He longed to be with her, more than he had wanted any woman before. JP sensed, from her manner, that she too wished to share his free time. After one late night flight, that ended on his return to base at dawn, he felt reassured when he found a letter from her at the officer's mess. The white envelope had his name on it, and was marked 'private and personal'. Her handwriting was slanting and bold. He took the letter to his office, and quickly slit the envelope with a small knife.

Defford

20 March '43

Dear John,

I want you to get this when you return.

If you are not exhausted, meet me this evening where most of the WRNS and some officers go for a drink, to hear music, sing and maybe dance. Quite a few people play the piano—I do—and we often sing songs together. Don't miss your rest if you need it. I'll be there with Pam, so if you can't come I will understand .

Emily

The first evening he saw her at the barn he made sure she did not see him. Emily had her back to him; her light-brown curly hair bounced as she played confidently on the piano. The lilac, short-sleeved bodice blouse clung to her shapely figure. JP observed those around her singing, and all of them were engrossed by the rhythms she played expertly. Her touch on the piano was light and sharp.

Daisy, Daisy, give me your answer, do.
I'm half-crazy all for the love of you,
It won't be a stylish marriage,
I can't afford a carriage;
But you'll look sweet upon the seat of a bicycle built for two.

Henry, Henry, this is my answer true
I'm not crazy over the likes of you.
If you can't afford a carriage
Forget about the marriage;
I won't be jammed

I won't be crammed
On a bicycle built for two.

When her turn ended a younger pilot officer took her place
and he started the familiar, 'Pack up your troubles in your old kit
bag, and smile, smile smile . . .'

JP saw Emily scan the room, and knew he could not keep
himself hidden for long.

He had wanted to reassure himself she would be looking for
him. Her face was flushed. The moment he moved Emily saw his
unmistakable tall frame. She smiled broadly and put up her hand
in a shy little wave. He took a deep breath to steady himself from
the familiar powerful sensations. As she came towards him, her
eyes sparkled and were accentuated by the colour she wore. Her
straight uniform skirt clung to her slender hips. He thought he
could see her breasts through her blouse, and he blushed. She
stopped beside him and spoke. The singing was loud and others
near him were drunk. People shouted, 'Smile, smile, smile . . . '
the sounds reverberated and bounced off the thin walls and he
could not hear what she said. JP quickly took her hand and led
her outside.

She heard his breath shorten, and wondered why. He wanted
to hold her again, hear her voice and laughter as well as her
gentle teasing. When they got to his car, he opened the door for
her, but then pulled her towards him. As she started to speak he
kissed her on the neck and mouth, and held her closer. She felt
bewildered, then easily reached up to kiss him back. He did not
want her to be another fleeting romance; he felt a need to possess
her, to know everything he could about her past life and to share
his with her.

'I want to be alone with you all night,' he said in a hushed
voice she barely recognised. He could not draw away from her.

Emily clung to him and felt his hands exploring under her
blouse. The touch excited her and a wave of agitation warmed her

as she reciprocated each embrace and kiss. When he remembered those moments on a flight home days later, he understood that his personal life had changed. Perhaps she felt that too?

Later, they took his puppy, Susan, for a walk around the fenced area. It was a black, clear, cold night. He lit his pipe then pulled Emily to him again, wrapping her inside his coat.

Pointing at the sky with his pipe, he said, 'Do you see those three stars together in a line?'

'Yes, I do.'

'That's the belt of Orion.'

'Hmm.'

'That points in a southerly direction towards Sirius—it's the brightest star in the northern hemisphere. There!'

'I never knew. So what is that cluster of stars?'

'That's known as the Seven Sisters. I learnt about stars for my navigation course. A planet like Venus is brighter than a star and it is just above the horizon, over there. Too late to see it now, but next time you can look out for it. Just imagine it for us.'

'What do you mean?'

'Symbolic for love,' he whispered. After a silence neither dared to break, he added, 'When we fly home and the skies are clear like tonight, seeing the stars is uplifting. The crew always chatter, mostly nonsense, and they tell silly jokes because it gives them some relief from the work we have had to do. But I'm quiet.'

'How high do you fly?'

'Different heights, between ten thousand feet and above, but it varies. Why do you ask?' He carried on without waiting for her reply. 'It's cold up there; we dress to keep warm. But we all feel the cold. It can drop to anything below 22 °F which feels freezing. When I am at the controls nobody can walk around. The gunner on my aircraft, though, is in the coldest place, and he's also the most vulnerable, poor blighter. We do get a thermos of hot tea each, big sandwiches, and usually a Mars bar to sustain us on the flight home.'

'Do you always fly with the same people?'

'Crew, you mean. Yes, mostly, unless something happens.'

'I'd be sick again up there.' She laughed.

'You could get used to it. The sunrise and sunsets can be wonderful.'

'That helps. I'd be terrified though.' He hugged her closer.

'When we were in Egypt the African sky in the desert seemed blacker than here. Many nights were silent. Occasionally, I'd see a shooting star. When I started my apprenticeship at fourteen, I always hoped to reach this level. My stepfather was critical of everything I did, so when I spoke about my training later, May, my mother, encouraged me. I was glad to leave home. I worked hard and I was determined to succeed.'

'Do you remember your father?'

'No.'

'Does Joan?'

'Yes, but she never said much to me. She did once tell me some things about him in a letter, but she was also young when he died, and I will never know whether her story was accurate.'

After a short silence he added, 'Now, we do not know where she is.'

'Since when?'

'The letter from May said she has not heard from Joan since the Germans bombed Manchester and Coventry. She only told me, once I got back from Egypt. I am going to meet Mother when I have a few days free. I would like her to meet you, but not this time.'

'She must be worried. Were your nephew and niece alright?'

'We hope so . . . I'll show you a photograph of her and her children that I keep in my desk.'

'Yes, and I'd like you to meet Uncle Cecil and Auntie Olga. I've written to ask them already.'

'That tells me a good deal.' He smiled broadly, but she could not see it in the darkness.

'I give myself away, but I feel each day is precious and I always felt closer to them than to my mother and father, who were in places like Nigeria during my youth. Would you like to visit Cornwall, we could stay with them and take your puppy? They have a small dog, Boxer, who is sweet and good.'

He was silent when she had hoped for an enthusiastic reply; then he suddenly put his arms around her and kissed her on the lips. He breathed in her scent and told her softly she would be in his thoughts when he went away the next night.

'I was hoping you'd say that.' She laughed nervously. He felt comforted and took his pipe again from his pocket. In the darkness he held out the matches he used to light the tobacco. She blew out the flame, so that for an instant he glanced at her expression. Her lipstick had gone and she wore no other makeup. Hers was a simple beauty, with long lashes accentuated by dark eyebrows and clear rosy skin. He stroked her face and neck.

His face in the glow from the matches as he relit his pipe was framed by darkness. She held that in her memory, reawakening it in later years as if she had switched on a light to brighten a room.

'I shall remember your face in this match-light each night when you are not with me before I sleep.' She shivered suddenly as if a freezing breeze passed over her, and because they stood close, he removed his scarf and put it around her.

'Do you suppose we can share a room when we go to Cornwall?'

'I didn't ask them that!' She laughed, shyly.

'I'll try to arrange to have a stay away together soon. I can't set a bad example and bring you back to my room in the officer's quarters.'

'I know that, but we can still make plans to be alone together. It's such fun having you here and I look out for you.'

'Shall we go back and warm up with a dance, they sounded very jolly over there?'

'I'd like that,' Emily replied.

By the time they got back it was a slow foxtrot, and JP held her in his arms as closely as he dared in front of other officers.

It was dawn when they separated. He stood and watched her familiar figure disappear as she walked back, then he emptied his pipe and returned to the officer's mess for an early breakfast. There were letters to write and other ground duties before he could rest and prepare for the night flight—if the weather was clear, and if conditions were acceptable to drop another SOE agent in France.[20]

Hampstead

My dear Emily,

I came to London immediately after our last flight. I found Mother well, but distressed that there had been no word from Joan. As you would understand, all the family here is upset too, but Uncle Michael is confident she will reappear because once before she failed to communicate with the family. She may not be aware of how fearful we all are. There's a family from Canada lodging here. Their son joined the RAF at the start of the war, but he was killed last winter on a mission, although the navigator did parachute out and survived. They are hoping to meet him. I have found time to speak to Mother about you. I didn't say much because we were not alone too often. Stepfather retired and is home most days. She said she hopes to be able to meet you next time, and that I should bring you. She knows we're planning a holiday in Cornwall. I will see you when I am back at Defford next week.

Yours ever,

John

Two months passed and Emily felt the need to return to her Uncle Cecil. JP was uncertain. She set a date, bought her ticket, and sent them a telegram. The war had claimed the lives of close friends, and Pam had been posted to Anglesey. There were whispers that she too would be posted there soon. She wanted to get away for her holiday, and knew that a trip to Tremena from Anglesey would be complicated.

'I understand you want to go, and I'll follow if I can,' JP had said.

'Do you? I'm disappointed, I want to travel there with you.'

'I will come. There's information I cannot discuss now—it is unlikely to alter much.'

Emily's eyes looked sad and troubled, for she much preferred their original plan.

'I'm going next Wednesday, but if your plans change, I will be very happy. I've written everything here,' she passed him a folded piece of paper. 'In case they can manage to give you the time off, all the details are there.' She knew it was not in his control, but she had begun to feel sad about it, although she tried not to show it.

It was summer 1943.

TREMENA, SUMMER 1943

EMILY'S VOICE

Our days in Cornwall with Uncle Cecil and Auntie Olga had a relaxed, rhythmic routine, even though we would be there for only fourteen days. John had not been due to join me until the middle of the second week due to flight duties. So I bought my train ticket and set off, reluctantly, though a part of me was also excited to see them both again. I had wanted John to travel with me. It had not felt right leaving without him, especially as the evening before my departure he had not returned from operations to France. I guessed it was France, although he had never said exactly where it was.

John never gave any information. Squadron leaders remained silent about their secret operations. I had shared my concern with him, but it was out of our hands.

Pam's fiancée, a navigator, had not returned one night—none of their crew came back to base. She immediately had expected the worst, and became withdrawn and distressed. Her pain and silence were hard to bear for the rest of us, yet each day, or each week, there had been unhappy news from somewhere and we all developed an emotional shield and got on with duties, and that in itself had a measure of distraction. None of us spoke about the disasters. We immersed ourselves in our various daily routines in the war effort. Everyone had their part to play, and each side of the puzzle was connected. So we tried to forget, got busy, then played hard and had fun when we were off duty. I knew some boys, well men, who thought they could be dead any day. Most were in their early twenties and some were twenty-one or younger. We became a close-knit, large group. Then, nearly a fortnight after Pam's fiancée disappeared, the crew returned to base quite unexpectedly late at night. Their Lancaster had been shot to pieces, but the crew had parachuted out and were subsequently rescued and brought back to base, except one lad, the young gunner, who had broken both his legs.

Once I got my seat on the train to Penzance, I took out my knitting and my book. My thoughts repeatedly intruded, usually negative, but then I was delighted to be returning to a place I loved. The long train journey was one I had always enjoyed, especially the views. Reading, I decided, was the most successful distraction, as I could immerse myself in the story and try to escape the present. It worked rather well, so that as the doors to my carriage—which I shared with others—opened and closed I never bothered to look up. Until, suddenly, I heard my name.

'Emily.' It was a familiar, quiet, but deep, loving voice. I caught my breath. I coughed.

Then I looked up. There stood John. He had dark circles

under his eyes, and he was unshaven, but looked smart in his uniform, with his pipe in his hand. He smiled. A smile I had fallen in love with.

'I had begun to think I was on the wrong train, and on the wrong day!' he said as he held open his arms. I went to him eagerly. I felt the panic and anxiety about his safety drop away. Neither of us felt embarrassed by the people in our carriage, who stared at us.

He held my hand and shoulder, gently sitting me down, then he lifted a bag and golf clubs on to the rack above, and sat heavily beside me. His body looked thin. Later he moved opposite me.

'I do not usually travel facing backwards!' He winked at me. 'I'll just get a small nap, if you will forgive me . . .' Within moments I could see that he was in a deep sleep, his head leaning on the corner by the door. I suspected he had missed a nights' sleep. For the first time I could study him, in the daylight, unselfconsciously and for as long as I wanted, because he was fast asleep . . . something I had never seen. Leaning his head in a relaxed way, his long legs slightly splayed in front of me.

John was twenty-three then, I was twenty-seven. On rare occasions I had noticed his boyishness, but our life left little room for that. He had developed smile lines and fine wrinkles around his eyes, and a frown line between his bushy eyebrows. I wondered if that was the result of hours of deep concentration on flights. He told me that his crew were the best, and they all had their own life stories to tell when they were flying home over England. He listened, but never spoke to them about his own. I always believed that they were all enormously respectful towards him, and liked him. His responsibility, and that of the navigator, was to fly them all back to base. John slept during most of the train journey, and I was glad of it. I hoped he would feel refreshed when we got through to Penzance.

When he woke he was apologetic, saying he had neglected me. It had been the first time John and I had spent so much time together at one stretch, even though he had been asleep during all but the last hour of our train journey. Uncle Cecil came to the station for me. I had written to say I would be alone, and I said that I would explain once we were together. Both of them greeted us, and I was so excited I forgot to introduce John politely.

'Emily wrote in March telling us she'd be coming with you, but she forgot to tell us your name!' Auntie Olga said as she had held out her hand which he shook strongly saying, 'It's John Philip'.

Then Uncle turned to him after giving me a large hug, 'I'm Cecil Hale.' He continued, 'Emily wrote she'd be alone, so we're delighted you could make it. I see you brought your golf clubs, Emily must have told you we both play.'

Auntie added, 'We often compete on a golf round, and others around here join in, we are very competitive—in a friendly way of course!' They took us back along the scenic route.

I was once again transported, along with a man I loved and my favourite loving relatives, to a home that had given me the best of all I needed in my youth.

I had wished for Uncle and Auntie to get to know John. That had been my hope, and within it a complex set of decisions, which eventually resolved. That first night we were allocated separate rooms at Mulberry House, and so we quickly learnt to find which of the creaking floor boards to avoid between my room and John's. I think Auntie Olga must have known we were tucked up together most nights after they were both asleep.

I sensed their happiness at having us there. So meal times, golf, and outings to many different beaches, felt special; more importantly because I could share with John those childhood memories of places in Cornwall that I had been to, but that were new to him. Uncle Cecil and Auntie Olga must have used up all their meat and egg rations for us. They seemed to want to feed us up. I could tell she wanted to fatten John up, for he looked so thin. Still, food was rationed for the whole country, although the airmen got a huge cooked breakfast before or after a flight, or both, because they worked hard. When we returned to Defford I received two letters, which helped me to consider John's marriage proposal.

Our days in Cornwall had been a source of great happiness and comfort then, and I recalled them regularly with joy in later turbulent times. Yet, after the war, I had to suddenly understand a situation that taxed my memory and comprehension, even decades later.

CHAPTER NINETEEN
AUGUST 1943
THE GUEST AT MULBERRY HOUSE

Cecil was sitting with his papers on his lap smoking his pipe. Olga smiled to herself as she remembered one particular moment of John's visit. She leaned back while knitting, looking into the distance. Cecil looked up when she spoke.

'One day I observed Emily, without her noticing, as she only had eyes for John. She was wearing a grey, simple skirt, loose fitting on her small hips, not quite straight down to her knees, but with enough fabric that showed not only her small waist and hips, but her long, slender legs. The loving way John looked at her that day was a surprise!'

'His eyes were on her even while they swam,' Cecil added. 'I recognised how closely she resembles her mother, Mary, but while Mary was a beautiful woman with strong features, her daughter has a more gentle, arresting beauty. Emily is totally unaware of her warmth, whereas her mother was coquettish; her seductiveness drew men towards her plainly without any effort. Mary boasted about her flirtations with HRH Prince of Wales to anyone who would listen!'

'I hope they will return soon,' Olga mused, 'it seems to me they had a good rest and some fun together, without the burdens of responsibility.'

'The war will dictate when they can return. John is perfect for her at this time of her life.'

'How do you mean?'

'People have intense relationships during a war because they don't know how long they have left to live.'

'I forget. I thought perhaps you were talking about how it was for us in the early 1920s.'

'Yes, that too. It was harder for you than for me. My trouble was I had lost many close friends in the First World War, and Percy before that. It felt hard to try to get close to anyone again.'

'You've said that before, but perhaps the long separations helped you to change.'

'John goes out each day or week, and Emily has no idea if he will return. The RAF has lost thousands of men already. I think it is something neither of them talk about.'

Emily had returned to Defford for eight weeks, before being posted to Anglesey to join Pam and others who had been with her that year. John was sent to another base.

RAF Station, Fairford
(after Saturday)

My darling Emily,

Sweet of you to write such a lovely long letter with all the news of your doings and I always enjoy reading your news.

The road journey to North Wales sounds wonderful—I have always wanted to go there having flown over it so many times. It is one of the many things we must do together in the future. No, I did not go to the rugger match. I had to fly. I also was not feeling so good . . . if I had gone I should have met a crowd of people who were at the party and as sure as eggs, there would have been another party that night.

I am living in luxury at the moment; my commanding officer is living out with his wife for a week or more, and I am staying in his room in the group captain's house. His own sprung bed, real white blankets and a wireless set. A nice little sitting room with an open brick fireplace, and a bathroom next door, and, the CO's bottle of whisky always filled and always there. A cup of tea in bed, a batman, the whole works, and only twenty yards from the mess. Some people can get organised! I had a very pleasant evening by the fire sipping the odd wine with GC and listening to GC's adventures at Casablanca, Washington, and many other places his tour visited recently with the PM.

I occasionally shot lines about my days in darkest Africa, but preferred to listen as he is a very interesting speaker.

Haven't been doing too much else of interest. I've done a little flying, but I am quite busy arranging the programme for the chaps. It's quite a change from Defford where most pilots are fairly old sweats, and get on with it. Here, they have to be breastfed for every single flight and every detail has to be explained from the time they leave the flight office to the time they get back to the mess. Although they are all good types, they are rather inclined to think that the flight commander is a nursemaid.

Darling, I haven't written to you since that lovely weekend, to say how much I loved it and how you looked more beautiful than ever.

You didn't say how your mother and father took the news about our engagement. Hope the telephone didn't keep ringing too long.

I should be leaving here on Saturday so please ring me up at 2000 hours on Friday and tell me if you will be back at Defford by then. I could probably wangle a couple of nights, but I rather think you said you were going to be there for ten days, in which case if you write don't forget the new address (Tel: Tharonby 431, Officers' Mess).

I will certainly try and arrange leave on the fifth,

sweetest, but I'm afraid I can't promise. If you stay somewhere near I could come home for nights.

I haven't said any of the things I intended to say in this letter.

Longing to see you again, and I hope you are leading a quieter life now than the hectic time you seem to have been having at Defford at the White Line . . .

Until as soon as possible,

Every atom of love,

John

RAF Leicester East
Sunday

My darling sweetheart,

I am writing this at 0200 hours having just come back from a session of night flying.

I wasn't flying myself, but my flight was in good strength for the first time, and believe me it was a nerve-racking experience, and I feel worn out, but wide awake. Luckily, the worst damage was a burst tyre, but very nearly something else.

Thanks so much, darling, for your lovely letters. I think you may be over doing it with the driving. There are too few women drivers, so, of course, they will need you, but take good care.

The party was quite good, but I got rather drunk and was one of the very few to get back unassisted and into the right bed. I am definitely going to give it up, I just can't take it.

I flew to Fairford today and did a circuit over Aylton and Defford. It was a beautiful afternoon and I was thinking of you travelling in a nasty train somewhere. Bredon looked lovely and so did the Malverns. The view from the air in that region is one of the prettiest in the world. I felt homesick and secretly would have liked to land and have tea with the chaps and then call in to the Wrennery and go for a ride with a very sweet naughty (you) and sit on top of Bredon until it got dark and later pop in to the New Inn and have one for the road. While thinking of these things, I suddenly discovered I was supposed to be map reading, as I had handed over controls to the navigator and I wasn't sure where I was and couldn't for the life of me decide whether we were over Coventry or Leicester.

I dreamed of you last night, although it wasn't a very nice dream, but you came in and pulled me out of one of those strange moments you get into in dreams, and however much you try to hold on to things they slip away. It's the first time I've had a dream for ages. Do you dream? I've never thought to ask you before. I am getting sleepier and sleepier and I don't think I can write much more.

I haven't been in to Leicester since you were here last, but hope to pop in one day this week and see what the shops are like.

I hope to be able to get to Defford on the way down next weekend, that's, of course, if you can be there, but I'm afraid I can't say definitely. I will certainly try and fix the leave. We must think of somewhere to go. What about near where you are now? It should be nice up there and we could go for walks and drinks (and things) if it's not too cold. If it is, I can warm you up.

Darling, I'm beginning to fade so I will write again tomorrow, and apologise for this nonsense if I don't make it.

Stacks of love, be good and take care.

Love John

Emily re-read John's last three letters, then took out a letter she had folded safely away. It was on blue writing paper, with Olga's address embossed in the top left. A long letter from her Aunt that she had received on 2 September and Emily read it again, hoping to find guidance.

Mulberry House

Tremena, near Hayle, Cornwall

31 August 1943

My dearest Emily,

The plums were marvellous—and all with the fresh bloom still on them—but thank you so much, it is good of you to send them. Am afraid I stuck to more than my share, but CB's eyes nearly popped out when he thought I was sending too many up the hill! Greedy guts!

Perhaps some time you will send me the name of the shop where you got them, for the future purchasing . . . for the packing, etc. was perfect and even if you might still be at Defford next year or nearby—it would save you endless trouble if I could write direct to the place, so do that will you?

We missed you sadly, both of you. Can't think it is only a week since you went back. One looks forward to these visits so much and they are gone in a flash. We are both happy you came to us.

Beryl comes tomorrow for I think, I hope, ten days—she is a pet really.

The weather still patchy—I haven't bathed since you went back.

Eric is still home, and we are taking the kids for a 'cruise' when the day is suitable. Tell John that I played CB golf the other day—level from the mens' tees and beat him on the last green. And wasn't I pleased about it! The match became so keen we were hardly speaking towards the end—concentration quite intense.

Don't think, Emily dear, that either of us have mentioned your John to Highcombe—it's the last thing either of us would do.

I can't tell you how the people he met liked him here—such as Sue and Bob who were at the Tregambo on Sunday for Lillian's sixtieth birthday. Bob said, 'I liked that Jonny fella Emily brought along—he looks you straight in the eye and he's got some manners about him, not like many of the youngsters nowadays.' He continued, 'I'm not a bad judge of a man!' So you see, we all think about you. I'll tell John one day.

In fact you are both lucky young things you have met—perhaps John is the luckier of the two.

I wonder what your plans are, though I'm not inquisitive to know really! I'll tell you this, Emily, I was much younger than you when the last war came, but gosh how it mucked up the lives of most of us. Looking back now—my advice to you is if you are hesitating about getting married during the war days—why wait, after the war things will be just as uncertain with regard to the future for a good many years. It will not be easy to slip into civilian life with wonderful prospects straight away, and so the years go on, and you would both miss so much fun and happiness that you could share together.

Nothing will be so easy after the war—of that I am sure. The war may be over in a matter of months—but it may not. Even then the strength of the forces must be maintained far longer than before, and again I say, so the years go on.

You are the sort to know your own mind and to have your own plans. Bad as your upbringing may have been—at least it was not a bad upbringing, but you girls missed the love you should have had in your early youth and at that impressionable age—maybe the fact that you had that upbringing will help you now to decide what is the biggest decision of your young life.

Supposing you marry, and supposing you have a baby,

or two, if you cannot cope you can always send them to Auntie and I could love yours as much as I might have loved my own if that last war had not intervened.

I wonder if I am leading you astray.

My fond love always,

Olga

Emily tucked it away in her bag until she read it again ten years later. The letter was still amongst her papers in 1998.

Leading Wren E. Hale

Bishops Palace, Glyngarth, Merian Bridge, Anglesey

30 November 1943

Darling John,

We must meet very soon as I have something important to tell you which I think you will be happy to hear. Not to do with work or home. Ring if you can and we can arrange to talk about it when we will get some leave together.

I can't wait to see you again.

It seems like ages since we were together.

All my love,

Emily xxx

PART FIVE

CHAPTER TWENTY

Emily's Voice

During the winter of 1943, John managed to find time to be with me for longer as he had been posted earlier that year to the Air Ministry. We had fun, and explored each other passionately, as he called it, as well as some special weekends together, which led to the inevitable situation that I wrote to him about in November. I had not been worried at first, because missing my monthly cycle was common, but then I felt something in me had changed, and I knew it was time to share my suspicions with John.

I realised I was already pregnant when I went on a trip with another Wren, Eleanor, to Anglesey. I had begun to feel sleepy sometimes during the afternoon, which was not at all like me. I also felt a little sick in the early morning, although it passed once she encouraged me to eat a small breakfast. One day I had felt tearful about a little thing that would never have troubled me before, and I talked about that to Eleanor, because she had been telling me about her own experience of pregnancy.

I drove a small Bedford truck up there to Anglesey, loaded with radar equipment which we were to install in a Catalina Flying Boat. We were lodged in the Bishop's Palace, which was being used as some sort of hostel, and we walked each day along the cliff path of the Saunders Roe works which had moved up there during the war. Flying in the Catalina to test the gear was one of my most exciting experiences in flying—one of the few times that I was not sick—and the take-off from the water sitting in the nacelle which bulged out at the rear was marvellous. On the return trip the van was loaded with late hydrangeas as they were growing and flowering in abundance all up the hill behind the Bishop's Palace. The Palace lawn, which sloped down to the Menai Straits, was a beautiful place for a picnic. I imagined John and I sitting there, with no cares about anything except one another!

Eleanor told me she had been pregnant the year before. All the details a mother may have discussed with her daughter, she helped me to reveal to her, by gently asking the right questions and listening to me. Such conversations had never been possible with my mother. If Olga had had children, and been nearer, I would have confided in her.

It was not something I would have put into a letter, even though there were moments when I started writing things down that I would have liked to tell Auntie Olga, but then when I read them the next day, or hours later, I would think myself self -indulgent, and tear up my notes. I began to think that maybe I should tell John what I was thinking and feeling, but in so many ways it was hard for me to do that because our time together was often too short, and I never felt I should worry him because I knew he had so much to deal with in his new job with the Air Ministry.

One weekend, John came to see me and we talked about what we should do about the pregnancy. We were already engaged, although John had not yet found the time to choose a ring, which he felt embarrassed about, but he wanted to go only to Mappin and Webb in London. It had been hard to find the time for us to coordinate going together during the war.

After I got Auntie Olga's first letter, it had been easy to decide to accept John's marriage proposal. I respected her thoughts, and

I also understood that her reasons for encouraging me, were as much to do with her own experiences of waiting for Cecil, as wanting me to have happiness for myself.

She had an altogether different experience because of the 1914–18 war, and her age when they married. I was certain they must have tried to have a child, even though she was in her late thirties, but it never succeeded for her, and I had an inkling she had been sad about that for many years.

The words in her letter to me confirmed my suspicions.

Olga wrote again in the late autumn. Her timing was impeccable.

Trenithan, Carbis Bay, Cornwall

Dear Emily,

How kind of you to keep writing when you have such a lot on your mind.

How about your John—what a grand man, and may I say that to us it would be a happy and glorious thing if you are going to be married.

I do hope so Emily, take it from me—who married late—that you'll regret it if you don't take your happiness now while you've got it. Get married and go through all the trials that you may get together. You may have some difficulty with jobs and money (everyone has!) but if you are together, the worries are shared and halved—then if you have a family your happiness will be complete.

My dear, don't wait. I know every man likes to feel sure of himself, financially, and in the right job, but how can a man who is in the RAF, possibly feel sure of such a secure position—that kind of sure marriage went with the war!

All this may sound cheek from me—but Emily, I'm too fond of you to see you waiting for something that you should have now, and keep, when you've got the chance of happiness. I've got everything my dear, and I'd love to see you the same.

Yours ever

Olga

Before Christmas in 1943 John arranged for us to have an evening out together.

Afterwards, he presented me with a beautiful solitaire diamond ring, which I wore for some time, and treasured, until a burglar stole it years later.

It was during one winter leave in 1943 that we were married by my Uncle Frank Gillingham at his church, St Michael's, in Chester Square, London.[21]

There was a small reception at a hotel. We spent a week's honeymoon at The Lygon Arms, in Broadway. I had borrowed a wedding dress from a friend that I shared a bedsit with when we were both in London during the blitz, because my coupons did not stretch to expensive clothes. It fitted me perfectly, and the only two people who knew it was borrowed were my mother and Olga. Then back to work, and now that we were married, we lived at a farmhouse on the perimeter of the aerodrome, enjoying nights in a big double feather bed, and breakfast with farm food by a log fire. I was eating for two and John had a healthy appetite now that we were together.

John had a little Morris 8 two-seater car in which he would go off to the officers' mess, but I was only a leading Wren and went on my bicycle.

He still had his Labrador, Susan, and she lived with us, and slept at the foot of our bed at night. All the Wrens were issued with bicycles for getting about the aerodrome, and there were no Wren officers on the station, although later on qualified radar mechanics, like me, were made into officers. Soon after this, I came out of the Wrens as an expectant mother. My discharge report said, 'Suitable for re-engagement.' I went home to Essex for a short time and started knitting. Then John was posted to

Fairford, and we lodged with the delightful Atkinson family in Fairford village. They had three Jersey cows called Melody, Harmony, and Symphony—one of the daughters was studying music—and they made their own butter, cheese, and so on. John was now flying Stirlings, a four-engined RAF Bomber, and they were used for troop-carrying, towing gliders, and supply-dropping, which included the odd spy dressed up as a parson, into occupied France. Then, about eight weeks before the baby was born, I went down to stay with Cecil and Olga, who were delighted to have me there. I booked a fortnight in a nursing home in Penzance. John decided it would be easier for him to 'fly home' to see me in Cornwall. That suited me perfectly because the war seemed far away from Tremena, and I always felt much happier when I returned to live at Mulberry House.

Mother and Father were pleased that we would be away from the doodle bugs (V1 buzz bombs) that had been fired from Germany, and started to hit London in June 1944. They started falling on London a week after D-day . . . it was like a second blitz. Two thousand hit London during 1944 and over six thousand Londoners were killed. Some called it 'the doodle bug summer'. Over a million people left London, and thousands of others left from Kent, Surrey, and Sussex; the railway stations were chaotic.

CHAPTER TWENTY-ONE

190 Squadron

RAF Station, Fairford, Glocs.

7 June 1944

My darling sweetheart,

I am terribly sorry to hear that you had to have another dose of those beastly tablets, but do hope you are well on the way to recovery. I received your lovely letter. I'm glad you are getting some attention as your husband is doing little for you. Awfully sweet of Mother's friend to be looking after you, too.

Yes, darling, D-day is over and it was very exciting and I expect you are reading all the important bits in the papers. I should love to tell you all about it. We shall have to wait.

I am thinking of you all the time and I have your little photo. Everything has gone very well from this end and all under control.

The crew gave a running commentary about the great events on D-day, as I flew over Malvern. I expect Uncle George was on the beaches, but I didn't see him! I feel as fit as two fleas, but I am hoping to have a good snooze this afternoon. I'm longing to drive (fly) and see my wonderful good girl and give her bigger kisses than ever.

Hood has been a perfect brick and has given me a pint

of tea and a paper each morning. I shot a hell of a line to
him. I expect this letter will be late arriving, but no fault of
mine. I hope to pop down any moment to see you.
    All my love my beautiful, soon be with you.
    John

As he sealed the envelope, he wondered whether his duties
could allow him a visit to Cornwall that week. Life had turned
brittle in a repetition of 1942. The war precipitated bombing
raids, night flights, and scrambles. His squadron met each duty
fastidiously, with little time to look at the scenery.

CORNWALL, 18 JULY 1944

Early in July, Emily had returned to stay with her uncle, while
she waited for her baby. She had written to ask them, even though
Olga had suggested it when she told them about the baby. Olga
had been delighted, but Cecil carried that responsibility with
some disquiet, in case JP should die.

Emily looked up at the blue sky, which was sprinkled with
fluffs of grey-white clouds.

She was relieved the clouds were sparse. John had telephoned
Mulberry House the night before and told her to go outside the
next morning at 11.50 to look for his aircraft.

It had been a brief call which Olga answered. She ran to
find Emily who stood beside a pile of cut up Pittosporum in the
garden.

'There will be a surprise for you, but you must look above the
house at 11.50,' John had told her. 'I would have written to you,
but I only decided an hour ago; the weather forecast is good for
a flight to Cornwall tomorrow from Fairford.'

'What am I looking for?'

'A Stirling aircraft, which I hope you'd recognise!'

'Will you come here to see me?' Emily asked hesitantly.

'Perhaps,' he joked.

'How long do I wait?'

'If I am not there, you will know by 1215 hours.'

'I'll hardly sleep from excitement.'

'Sweetheart, you must get your rest. If I don't make it, I shall try again the next day.'

'Will you telephone again?'

'No, if you see the aircraft, it will be me if I flip the wings gently, like a wave!'

'Oh!'

'Take the car to Portreath base. I'll land and wait for you to collect me.'

'I got your last letter, you've worked hard.'

'No more talk now, we'll do that soon. You have all my love, take care, g'bye darling.'

The line went dead. She held the phone. Her face flushed. She knew she would have to compose herself. Cecil hurried toward her as she returned to the garden.

'I have to search above this house tomorrow. John says he is flying down to Cornwall.'

'What a surprise for you!'

The evening dragged. Her apprehension caused the baby to kick more. Emily went to bed early with a book. She sensed the tension in the house. By eleven, she had read three pages in an hour without taking in the narrative, and switched off her light. The windows were wide open; the fresh air cooled her. The night sky was like evenings in Defford star gazing, holding one another, and talking. John had often had to send her away because he had felt sleepy. Flight duties had priority.

Emily heard the aircraft before she saw it. The wings flipped from side to side high above the house. She was thrilled and ran to the car. Being eight months pregnant, her run became a fast walk. She called to Cathy who waved from the kitchen, 'Tell

Auntie and Uncle I'm off to Portreath, and we'll see them later.'

'Will you be home for lunch?'

'Yes, Cathy, but late.'

John's old car started immediately. She raced to where he would be landing. He was with his navigator, Reg Lawton, who would wait in the mess for his squadron leader. John, in full RAF uniform, waved. Emily had their puppy in the car. She barked, and jumped, and leapt about. Emily glowed excitedly when she met him, but was undemonstrative. Once away from the base, they got out of the car and held and caressed one another with a frantic urgency. They had eight hours together.

RAF Station, Fairford, Gloucs.

24 July 1944

My darling Emily,

I'm sorry I have not written for so long; no real excuse, but I have had a lot of standing by to do, and yet nothing actually comes off which is the worst part of operations, and the most tiring. All arrangements have to be made. Flight plans, briefing, time off, etc. loading, crews and what not, and then at the very end, usually at about 2300 hours the whole lot is postponed, or cancelled, and everyone concerned has to be informed, with the resultant fraying of tempers and cursing.

I have only flown once since I saw you last.

Thanks for your lovely letters darling and for the identity discs for Susan. Very glad to hear that you are feeling better. I have taken our pup for walks with a gun and shot a hare last night. She is very mischievous and has taken a liking to my slippers.

She is by no means house trained, and chews up anything she can. I feel she would be a handful in the home at the moment, so I shall try and train her before I bring her back to you.

Can't say when I shall be down again, so don't lock the door!

I'm popping straight off to bed now, sweetheart, and will dream about you tonight.

All my love my darling,

John

During July 1944 190 Squadron [22] dropped paratroopers and operated on eleven nights participating in small-scale secret operations.

JP drove with Emily from Portreath. She sensed his excitement. She felt lucky that he had been able to fly down again to see her that week.

'You never said much about D-day, John.' This time she wanted information about his flights. Her imagination frequently became too much for her.

'My crew were six-strong and the atmosphere at Fairford was splendid. I've also got my own aircraft and a ground crew who know the aircraft. Before D-day we'd use the full moon period for SOE and SAS operations. Highly secret!'

'I won't tell anyone you told me, go on!'

'From April onwards we dropped containers. Usually we got code letters, and made our release over the Drop Zone. We called it DZ. Later we'd get an acknowledgement that they arrived. Sometimes I wondered whether they got to the right people. We operated at lower than ten thousand feet. You'd have liked that darling. Then we'd climb to around ten thousand to cross the enemy coast. When we got to the DZ we'd be at only two or three hundred feet, usually in bright moonlight.'

'Did you often encounter flak?'

'Yes, flak was a hazard. The rear gunner dealt with that, successfully. My Stirling is familiar, and it's a versatile aircraft. I don't talk to others about each trip.'

'You do understand why I need you to tell me don't you?'

'Yes, and you are a worrier, but I'm not. By the way we get a very good meal, before we go, as well as Mars bars, sandwiches and my special issue Thermos flask filled with hot coffee. Useful when I feel the cold.'

'Have you still got your lucky mascot?'

'The scarf you knitted is always with me, and a flask, yes, just in case. By the time D-day came we'd done huge exercises and SOE drops. We also did the glider lifts.'

'What were those for?'

'Our Stirlings taxied out, then a ground crew hooked up the Horsa's tow-rope and a batman beckoned to take up the slack. Traffic lights on port side give the signal to take off. Meanwhile, the rear gunner tells his pilot when the rope is fully taut, and take-off is surprisingly easy. The glider gets airborne in about two hundred yards. Usually it works well, and at the DZ the tow-ropes are dropped.'

'It sounds a bit Heath Robinson to me.'

'We've done masses of glider-towing flights. So by the end of May all the squadrons were at peak readiness, Emily.'

'For an invasion?'

'Precisely. The trouble was that early on 5 June it was cloudy with strong winds—pretty gloomy. I was informed that the Air Vice Marshal would order the operation at night.'

'I would have felt petrified.'

'You would not have been the only one either. We all had to write letters to family in case we died.'

Emily was silent. She looked away, because she knew that letter would be kept somewhere.

'Our Stirling's were readied by ground crews and we had to be lined up correctly. The troops were also busy. They had to fit their parachutes, etc. At 2330 hours our Stirling engines burst into life. We were all away to the dropping zone at half minute intervals. There was light flak, but a Lancaster attack earlier had done an excellent job of silencing most of the enemy guns.'

'You left Fairford at 2330 on 5 June?'

'Exactly. Our Stirlings had had black-and-white-stripes put on them three days earlier. It was in moonlight and thin cloud, but good visibility to the Continent.'

'How long?'

'Three and a half hours round trip. But one squadron leader shot down, as well as two other crews. They expected heavy losses, so it was a relief not to have them. I managed to get some sleep when I got back, while the ground crews refuelled and so on, ready for early evening. I must tell you that flying over the Channel was a magical sight,' then he stopped talking as if he had an image to review.

'Go on, don't stop, what was there?'

'Our ships and aircrafts, masses and masses of them, were everywhere. The sea was covered in ships. Above them, each squadron was escorting gliders full of supplies. There were many naval barrage balloons too. Wing Commander Harrison led our squadron. Later, we had machine guns firing at us. One poor lad, a bomb aimer, but not mine, was killed. We were lucky, all eighteen Stirlings got back home.'

Emily knew that he must have felt relieved to return. What she did not understand was why he was made to write a letter in case he died. She suspected that Churchill may have thought there would be heavy casualties.

He continued, needing to tell her his part in the story, 'The next night at 1950 hours I went with my crew to the Caen area of France. We got home at 2310. Then I could write to you. Our next big trip was nine aircraft on an SOE operation to France. That's why I could not see you for so long.'

Emily stared into the distance. He expected a different response from her. John stopped the car, 'Emily you're quiet.'

'I'm just thinking how modest you all are.'

He carried on, 'You might find it interesting, because we did radar together, that we dropped packages of nickel.'

'What for?'

'It seems these were strips of silver tinsel to create deception, or false blips on enemy radar.'

They left the car and went to the beach. He held her hand. She longed to ask more, but did not dare.

JP was fearful of giving other details and causing Emily's anxiety to explode. He took her in his arms, their bare feet washed by the sea as the tide came in; they clung to one another as if their time together could suddenly vanish. He began to regret how much he had told her, and whether it had spoilt the moment.

'I miss you each day. Where next darling?' she whispered.

He thought it best not to lie. He looked into her eyes and said, 'Most of this month we'll carry on with SOE support and dropping parachutists. I think SOE have the hardest job!'

'I hope the baby will not be late.' Then she regretted what she had said, and looked away. She feared for his life.

'Darling, the signs are good on the other side of the Channel now.' He turned her face back towards him, 'You'll see, it will all end this year.'

CHAPTER TWENTY-TWO
SUMMER 1944
OLGA HEARS SECRETS

Olga and Emily sat in the kitchen. Cathy had gone home, and Olga mixed the ingredients of her cake. The windows were wide open, and crickets sang in the heat of the late morning.

'John told me secrets about his flights after we got married.'

'Emily, I understand that. Cecil used to come back to me from Burma, but he rarely spoke about his experiences. We were betrothed for years, but it wasn't until we married that he confided. I couldn't believe all the details!'

'I need to tell you, because there are days when I can think of nothing else but the dangerous missions he's on. Most have been in the last few months.'

'Do you want to tell me? I won't tell Cecil.'

'I would prefer it if Uncle does not know. I can tell you both certain things later.'

Emily sliced the apples she had retrieved from the shed.

'John was sociable, a regular Air Force squadron leader, which is different from the hostilities-only flying officers, who are in the majority both at Fairford and Defford. He liked mess life until he met me. He'd be there whenever he did not have letters or flight plans to prepare and I know he was popular, although he wouldn't admit it. He was comfortable with superiors and fellow officers, and liked a drink and a chat.'

Olga identified with her niece's dejected mood. Before the

pregnancy, Emily had often been in high spirits. Olga reminded herself that Emily was only a little older than John. They both seemed so mature; and she suspected it was due to their war experiences.

'When you were here with John, people who met him liked him. What's worrying you?'

'Since April they have done exercises towing gliders, and other simulations to drop paratroopers. On many occasions he has flown to France to drop containers, or SOE operatives. He told me that if they do not get the torch flashes from the ground in France, then they fly back with the containers and SOE personnel. Sometimes they have been fired at, which he believed meant that the Resistance people had been captured and tortured to get information about drops.'

'Yes, it may be.' Olga sensed that Emily was fearful something like that might happen to John.

'I have heard about long exercises inland, and it seems they are preparing for something big soon. I asked, but he wouldn't tell me. I knew there was something before D-day. I asked him in May, but he never told me. Yet I had the feeling then that they were planning another big push into France. He went on night operations, and some were over six hours of flying in Stirlings.'

'We all do our bit, but your John is deeply involved.' Olga felt herself start to feel anxious.

'There's a letter here, can I read it too you?'

'Yes, of course.'

'This was written on 7 April, "I carried out the exercise today and they all landed in the right place and nobody was hurt. I made a poor landing which was a bad show as it was the first time with my new crew. They all very politely said that they were used to much worse. Jolly decent of them. It usually costs a pint all round."'

'It does not sound much, but I know how he understates

things. At the end of July, when I was already here with you, he told me that they went to Kassel.'

'In Germany? '

'Yes. He said the flak was dreadful. His navigator, Reg, was shaken by the experience, and told John it was the worst he had ever felt in his four years of flying. Reg has flown here to Cornwall with him a few times already.' She paused as she thought what a kind man Reg looked, patient and polite. Reg waited in the mess in Portreath for John to return from visiting his wife, then they flew home back to Fairford.

'At least he was able to tell John what he thought,' Olga saw the fear in Emily's eyes.

'Reg took the day after they went to Kassel off. I wonder what John felt. He told me that it was not as bad as the flak over Benghazi, and made light of it.'

'When was the Benghazi flight?'

'Back in 1942 at the time he was in Alexandria, and Greece, or maybe it was Malta—I forget.' Emily piled all the chopped apples into a bowl, and threw in dried fruit as there was none of their sugar ration left. She looked at Olga with sad eyes.

'Recently, they flew at night regularly, until D-day. That's why he often seemed sleepy and tired. When he's not flying he still has to be permanently ready to go. John finds sitting around hard, although unlike all the others who also have to sit around and wait, he has plenty to do.' She thought of the letters he had to write to the families of those in his squadron who had died, or were injured.

Olga wanted to cheer her up, but knew from experience that it was the wrong thing to do; Emily usually felt better once she talked about what was worrying her. Emily needed to share her fears that day, so Olga decided she had to stop stirring mixtures; she wiped her hands and went round to sit beside her niece, and held her hands. Emily looked directly at her.

'He never goes to the funerals because there's no time, and

the family's home could be miles away. Sometimes there would be no body either. Once, he confided that the hardest moments were the wait to go on bombing raids. Often, hours pass before they get a "go ahead". He smokes his pipe, writes letters, dozes, or plans the next operation, and so on. Most people haven't a clue what goes on in the air for the RAF and their airmen!'

'That is the difficulty of war my dear. In the First World War none of us had any idea what those poor men suffered in France, not until much later. Then, nobody wanted to remember it, and people who had fought in the war preferred to keep their memories to themselves.' Olga looked out into the fields. 'It seems so long ago now.'

'Or how many have been killed on missions.' Emily raced on, 'John doesn't know whether some of the young boys he trained with are still alive. When we were on honeymoon, he told me all about the dreadful missions over Malta. Auntie, I think he makes little of it right now, so that I don't worry.' She looked ready to burst into tears.

'That's just like John!' Olga thought to herself that he had nobody apart from his wife to talk to.

'He's meticulous in his preparations before an operation. I also wanted to say that he rang to say he's coming next week, again on an exercise, if the weather holds. I'm lucky he can fly down here. He says he likes to fly home to see me. I suppose Mulberry House does feel like home to him too. I forgot to tell you, his wing commander's wife is also in Cornwall. I think their name is Harrison, and that he also comes to visit her. We are lucky, aren't we?'

'Yes, Emily, and in about four more weeks you will have your baby!'

Olga felt Emily's mood lift in her rush of words, and hugged her. 'That'll be the most wonderful moment. Cecil and I wished for a child for years. Babies are a blessing.'

Emily saw a momentary sad expression in Olga's eyes, and how she suddenly became absorbed in thoughts bigger than her own.

'Yes, we are lucky,' she said brightly trying to change the mood, and feeling that Olga's sensitivity had helped. 'Shall I make tea, then call Uncle in? Is there any cake today?'

'Yes. I'll prepare the tray. You call him. We'll sit outdoors,' Olga answered quietly.

On the way, Emily saw John's letter on the hall table. She wondered why nobody had told her when it had arrived.

RAF Station, Fairford

1 August 1944

My darling Emily,

It is exactly 1530 hours and I have just landed at base (velvet and glass). Did you ever have a letter so promptly? No one would have missed me if I had stayed all day with you. Do hope you got home alright. I didn't want you to do all that searching for me, especially without your glasses, but very sweet of you to have done it.

We were lucky that we were able to swim. Perhaps Olga would have liked to come along too. Olga would have been having her swim, while you and I were going cosily back to the aerodrome later. You could have picked her up on the way home.

My trip down was far too short, but the weather was perfect for an exercise down to see you! Do hope you managed to get some food for our puppy, Susan, and that she is being good. Susan still chews up things when she is alone, so be careful what you leave around. We shall have to see how she behaves with you for now.

I loved the journey down and I shall miss you terribly, but hope to return soon. Take care of yourself.

Love to Cecil and Olga.

All my love,

John

5 AUGUST 1944

The telephone woke everyone at Mulberry House at dawn. Emily picked up the receiver on the third ring.

'Hello?'

'Emily, it's John.'

'I thought it would be you. Are you coming again soon?' she asked enthusiastically.

'I shall be there today. Leaving here at 0630 so that means you can look for me above the house in two hours.'

'I'll look for you! Thank you.'

'Until later then, goodbye my darling.'

She felt excited and went to the kitchen to make tea. The teapot had warmed when Olga arrived.

'That was John, sorry the telephone woke you. He should be here in about two hours.'

'Good! Did he say how long he'd stay?'

'No, he was brief, but his last letter implied that he is not missed when he goes for a day. I have no idea how he arranges it, and I might try to remember to ask him this time. He's in charge, so unless the wing commander stops him, there can be no reason for him not to do an exercise to Cornwall.'

'Perhaps not much happens there on a Saturday!'

'John would find those words amusing.'

'I'll take the tray in. Change out of your nightie,' Olga told her as she put the tea cosy on the pot. Emily thought Olga's face looked tired and pale when she had come in to the kitchen that morning. Cecil returned from his tour of the garden.

'I'll need to get the greenery to Penzance this morning. Will you come for the ride Olga?'

'I would, but one of us should wait here with Emily in case she goes into labour.'

'Of course, then we'll go once she's off to Portreath for John,' Cecil said as he hugged his wife. He sensed she was pensive, and decided he'd ask her later when they were alone. After all the years together he could still feel her sadness, and he was certain he knew what it was about, but they would make time for one another later.

RAF Station, Fairford

13 August 1944

My darling Emily,

I have arrived back. Sorry I couldn't fly over today, but our take-off was delayed due to various things. As there was a strong head wind I thought I had better go straight back. I am sorry it was such a short visit yesterday.

We have done more exercises, and practice towing the gliders that we spoke about.

The investigation over the two aircraft that collided will be this week. There were no survivors. It was a terrible accident. Everyone at the station felt sombre.

The weather looks good for tomorrow and the next day, so look out for me.

Take care. You looked beautiful.

I miss you so much.

All my love,

John

JP flew on night operations on 24–25 August—twelve aircraft were dispatched to France carrying two hundred and eighteen containers and seven panniers, ten bundles, and fourteen SAS troops. They made a successful drop, and flew directly home. On the 26–27 August he led eleven aircraft to France carrying SOE personnel, two hundred and fourteen containers, and eighteen bundles. However, at the end of August bad weather and violent storms over France caused them to make diversions on return. The crews that operated at night flew through storms, and seven crews diverted to various airfields and failed to drop. They had little sleep. There were further petrol shortages.

CHAPTER TWENTY-THREE
PRELUDE TO OPERATION MARKET GARDEN

A battle plan was formulated by the British and Americans, in the hope that it would shorten the war by several months. Montgomery wished his plan and his armies would win the race for Berlin in mid-September 1944.

Mulberry House, Cornwall

12 August 1944

Darling John,

I am sitting up late writing this after you left today. Don't apologise again that you came for only a few hours. You cannot imagine how much joy it gives me to see you each time you visit, and I look up at the sky during the days that you do not come to Cornwall just in case you might have decided to fly down without a phone call, as you once did to surprise me. Holding you in my arms, even though it is you holding me facing forward (because of my big tummy) is comforting and [gives me] the loving which I need so much now. The war will be over soon, we all hope, and the gains I read about in the papers do sound positive, my darling. I suppose you know more than we do about all this!

Yes, I am eating rather a lot, because I feel hungry and there are two of us to feed. Auntie is wonderful, she knows people here who grow vegetables, and she has her own eggs, so we do not run out of food. The problem is that we cannot get extra sugar, but we have learnt to have tea without sugar, and we add things to biscuits and cakes to sweeten them, as you probably noticed. There is honey available too. You said you would come over again this week, so I shall go to sleep now and post this to catch the first post, and I hope you get it before you set off.

Tomorrow, Uncle has another concert in the music room to collect funds for the prisoners of war. I suspect he will play the Chopin that I love, and maybe the Schubert. I have not been on the piano much, but I get inspired to play when I hear him practicing each day. It is wonderful to hear the sounds coming from the other end of the garden, especially when the wind is in the right direction. Olga and I creep in occasionally, without him seeing us, and we sit quietly at the back listening to him play. He is usually completely immersed in his music, and we feel it too when he has those moments.

Write soon. Or telephone me if you are able to.

All my love,

Emily x

Emily lay in the bed that she had secretly shared with John the first time he came with her to Mulberry House, in the summer of '43. She contemplated not only how their love-making deepened their bond, but how welcoming and beautiful the antiquated house felt while he was there with her. Each part of it held memories after they had left it that year; and when she returned, certain places became attached to little memories for her. Those high ceilings in the kitchen where they giggled and made hot milk one night together while the moon shone through the large windows; the creaky places on the parquet floors—that she and Cathy polished with beeswax from Cathy's own recipe—which they both learned to avoid as they met in the night; as well as the large garden where John could disappear with her amongst the greenery, kissing and doing 'naughty' things, as John used to call it. She recalled how Cathy laughed as they were on their hands and knees one summer doing the oak parquet floor when she was only ten. Emily loved to hear stories about Cathy's childhood, and life in Cornwall in the 1920s, and she could not imagine the place without Cathy because she had become her close friend. She remembered the lovely, old, white marble mantle-piece against which John would prop himself up after dinner, when he and Cecil had had a little too much wine.

She recalled the big sofa on which she and her sister had listened to Uncle tell stories about Percy, and their escapades. There had always been a slow-burning fire in the grate on cold days. Each room held memories, which she wanted one day to share with her baby boy or girl.

Emily's room brightened as the sun rose. The big clock in the hall chimed five as another tinkled from the sitting-room below. It was too early to go downstairs. She stood barefoot at the window and looked up at a clear blue sky. Would John come again soon? There was the sound of birdsong, nothing more. No aircraft down here.

On the side of the window-frame were small pencil marks along the wall. Each mark had the name of a child and their age. The lowest read 'Emily, age nine'. The top one read 'Emily eighteen'. Olga had measured them each year they had visited. Emily remembered how they had giggled and shouted down to the others in the garden.

The roof of the music room was visible, fully covered in moss. It had seemed so far away down the garden when she was nine. Now it was merely the other side of the two acres of greenery. The dawn air was suffused with the scent of the honeysuckle which hung below her window. She would write to John again later. Would he be back today, she mused again? Yawning, she returned to her bed to read. She would rise when they would be downstairs. Sleep soon enveloped her.

She dreamt she was running down the garden, looking for the Mulberry tree. It was September, time to pick the fruits, but some squashed fruits lay on the ground and looked like blobs of blood. When she reached the tree she had forgotten what it was she had run to fetch. She began to panic. Her breathing became laboured, as she gasped for each breath. Her legs felt heavy and she could not move to run back. She heard a roar above her, but when she looked up there was nothing there. She felt tired and alone, and tried to call out, but no sound came. She woke with a jolt, feeling dazed. The dream lingered vividly all day. She told Olga what she could remember of it.

Olga's warm hand stroked hers, 'You had a bad nightmare once before here when you were a small girl. It's nothing. I'll make you a cup of tea. Now you relax, and I shall bring it.'

RAF Station, Fairford
15 August 1944

My darling Emily,

I am on duty again tonight so I am glad I had that good night's rest.

I shall also try to get some definite arrangements made about the house, so that you can be with me here once you have the baby and we can settle down locally until our next move, or until the end of hostilities.

I have received a letter from your mother who is very anxious to know the news. She thinks your brother will be called up soon, which will leave her free, so that when you have the baby she'll go down and look after you both. Cecil and Olga came along to see me off and I showed them over the Stirling which they were thrilled about and most interested. I should have done that weeks ago!

We had a nice trip back overland all the way and

descended over base in the beacon. Susan behaved herself, and slept beside me almost all the way back.

You looked wonderful. I can hardly believe how the time has passed.

All my love, dearest, I hope to see you soon.

John

The telephone rang. Nobody answered it at Mulberry House. John decided to fly to Portreath without giving them notice. He summoned Officer Reg Lawton and a crew, as the ground-crew were getting his aircraft ready. The wind and weather was in their favour, and JP was keen to get away. The Stirling flew over Mulberry House and he waggled the wings. He saw a woman wave below and minutes later his Stirling landed at Portreath. John was waiting when Cecil arrived for him.

'Good to see you, John,' Cecil shook his hand warmly.

'How's Emily?'

'She is becoming rather large to sit behind your little car's steering wheel, so I am more than happy to do the run. How was your trip down?'

'The weather was excellent. The trip was only eighty minutes.'

'Marvelous. Olga and I were delighted you took us round your aircraft last time.'

'We knew you'd like that. It was Emily's idea. I am surprised neither of us had thought of it before.'

'Emily looks good, but she is feeling tired some days, and sleeps a good deal.'

'Her mother is hoping to come down to you soon.'

'We have room for all of them!' Cecil said. As they passed a large estate John remarked, 'The hydrangeas are in flower earlier here than they are near our base in Fairford.'

'Yes, it is very beautiful at this time of year, and some of the asters in our garden are flowering, as well as one of the rare rhododendrons. We have a patch near the back of the garden that was a sea of bluebells in the spring. It has wild flowers now, and a delight to find when one reaches that end of the garden.' Cecil was distracted by a horse beside the road, and slowed right down.

'Do walk down to that part of the garden with Emily later, she loves seeing the wild flowers. We don't let her out of our sight at the moment because Olga says she could suddenly go into labour. It is a great bonus that you can fly down here.'

'It certainly is.'

'Will you have time for a round of golf?'

'I shall have to wait and see what plans Emily has. I can stay the whole day. With a bit of luck, I'll be back again in a few days.'

'News doesn't sound bad from Europe.'

'Yes, there has been good news. We've heard some bad news too, though, about US bombers, B-17s, accidentally bombing their own troops down in France last month. Only a rumour, but casualties sound high. US bombers have been successful, though, over Ploesti. It supplies the largest proportion of German oil. The USAAF 15th has bombed there again this summer. The constant missions have set large areas of Ploesti alight, I've heard. I suspect there were high US casualties, though, in their air force.'

'We could hardly have managed without the US.'

'Quite. Bomber Command launched attacks on three occasions at the end of last month on Stuttgart and Kiel. We're now practising towing gliders . . . have been for months.'

'Well, here we are,' Cecil said, as they drove up to the house. 'Best not say too much to our girls, they already worry enough about you boys.'

Emily and Olga heard the car and met them by the large Scots pine where Cecil left his jaguar. Petrol was rationed, but Cecil would run JP back to base later, and he hoped they might enjoy a round of golf. From their brief conversation he realised that JP knew a great deal about the war. It was never more than moments away from them all, and it was rare that men could speak as openly as they had that morning in his car.

Telegram: Gregory

Mulberry House, Tremena

18 August 1944

Congratulations my wonderful darling can't tell you how happy I am about David Lionel.

John

This telegram was written in pencil by the post mistress and delivered on the 18 August 1944. Their neighbours heard the news too, and came by to wish them well.

Emily had been driven the night before to the Penzance nursing home by her aunt and uncle. She had booked in for a two-week stay. John and his wing commander flew down to Cornwall.

RAF Station, Fairford, Glos.

21 August 1944

My darling Emily,

Have arrived back safe. Sorry I could not stay longer. I thought I should go straight back as there was a strong head wind.

It would surely have interrupted his feeding had I stayed. It was lovely to see my beautiful sweetheart again, and so perky. You have done very well. Between you and me, I believe he does look a bit like me; a very slight resemblance, of course.

You were looking marvellous, I was astounded. I expected to see you with your hair all down and straggly, probably weeping, and definitely shaking. I have just got a letter from your mother who is very anxious to know all the news, especially whether you made the nursing home in time and was it painful, etc. Henry still has not been called up, but she hopes to come down (sometime) to look after you and the baby.

C and Olga came to see me off again, which was really good of them. We had a nice trip back over land all the way, not much cloud, and descended easily to base.

I will endeavour to do all the necessary about the announcement and I have arranged with Olga to do the registering (of birth) at Penzance, although I expect we will both have to sign something. Now I can make a definite arrangement, I hope, about the house that we are to move to.

Do hope Bill, next door, is not making too much noise, if so throw a slipper or something at him!

Have lots of nice restful days there and get well soon. I can't wait to see you both again.

Susan is behaving herself, and going for walks with others when not with me. There are too many people here who would spoil her, and she is greedy all the time, so we must make sure she does not become a fat dog.

All my love dearest,

John

Nursing home, Penzance

25 August 1944

My dearest John,

We heard the news today that Paris was liberated.

It seems that Charles de Gaulle persuaded the Allied Commanders to take action to liberate the capital of France. After five long years. I hope this bodes well for an end to the war.

I am well, and so is our little son. I hope our puppy is behaving and that she is keeping you out of mischief. I can't look out for you, above the house, but I know that Olga and Cecil will bring you over as soon as you get to the county. We should discuss who will be his godparents next time. He is a very good baby, and sleeps after each feed. Do write if you can.

All my love, please take care.

Emily xx

Emily wanted to name her son John, but Olga and Cecil told her it would be confusing for everyone. She decided to call him Philip after JP's grandfather, or David. She hoped John would decide next time he came down to see them as she kept changing her mind. When Olga left them, Emily fed her son then she fell asleep once he had settled.

At the end of August there was bad weather over France with diversions for aircraft on their return. Crews operated at night, thus air crews found they had had too little sleep.

RAF Station, Fairford, Glos.

28 August, 1944

My darling Emily,

Lovely to have seen you once more. I'm glad everything is going so well with you and the mini one. I'm afraid I was late getting off again so couldn't come over to see you.

Incidentally, the AA Gunners on the south coast have orders to shoot at anything below one thousand feet so perhaps it is just as well. It would be a joke to see your husband being shot at from the window. I arrived back safely with puppy Susan beside me, but only to find myself on duty again. As I was diverted that night and had no sleep; I have slept ever since to catch up. I did, however, take her for a five-mile walk last night, and gave her a run right around the perimeter track in the morning. I was on a bicycle.

I may get leave on Wednesday so I'd arrive before this letter. I hope to see my naughty darling up and driving (quietly) soon. I haven't had time to see the Atkinsons as

I promised you I would. I am night flying tonight and there will be more flying again tomorrow, so I may sleep for a couple of days if I come down this week.

All my love darling,

John

P.S. Hood says that Susan should have pups first time. I shall check.

JP's Stirling aircraft continued night drops over France until 11 September 1944 when the squadrons began to prepare for the next momentous event, the Arnhem operation.

Operation Market Garden was a high-risk venture. The men who planned it hoped it might shorten the war. A secondary feature was that this operation promised to gratify Montgomery's wish that his armies might win the race for Berlin.

I am deeply touched by
your kind contribution to
my birthday presents &
grateful for your good
wishes.

Winston Churchill

John Philip gave this note from Winston Churchill to Emily for safe-keeping.

SUPREME HEADQUARTERS
ALLIED EXPEDITIONARY FORCE

Soldiers, Sailors and Airmen of the Allied Expeditionary Force!

You are about to embark upon the Great Crusade, toward which we have striven these many months. The eyes of the world are upon you. The hopes and prayers of liberty-loving people everywhere march with you. In company with our brave Allies and brothers-in-arms on other Fronts, you will bring about the destruction of the German war machine, the elimination of Nazi tyranny over the oppressed peoples of Europe, and security for ourselves in a free world.

Your task will not be an easy one. Your enemy is well trained, well equipped and battle-hardened. He will fight savagely.

But this is the year 1944! Much has happened since the Nazi triumphs of 1940-41. The United Nations have inflicted upon the Germans great defeats, in open battle, man-to-man. Our air offensive has seriously reduced their strength in the air and their capacity to wage war on the ground. Our Home Fronts have given us an overwhelming superiority in weapons and munitions of war, and placed at our disposal great reserves of trained fighting men. The tide has turned! The free men of the world are marching together to Victory!

I have full confidence in your courage, devotion to duty and skill in battle. We will accept nothing less than full Victory!

Good Luck! And let us all beseech the blessing of Almighty God upon this great and noble undertaking.

Dwight Eisenhower

General letter from Dwight Eisenhower to the British forces

CHAPTER TWENTY-FOUR
THE RACE TO BERLIN [23]
2 SEPTEMBER 1944

Cecil was driving JP to visit his son and wife in the nursing home in Penzance, and they hoped to collect Emily with baby David and bring them home to Tremena. David was exactly fifteen days old.

JP had arrived early at Portreath; Cecil had been waiting there to collect him, and during the journey to Penzance JP talked about his operations during August for his squadron without giving away too many details, although he told him they had dropped SOE operatives in France.

'How many operations have you done?' Cecil enquired.

'Since D-day?'

'Yes.'

'We have had seventeen airborne operations prepared and cancelled. Others completed.'

'Who's in charge of operations?'

'A chap we call Boy Browning, Deputy Commander, etc. There are rumours he disagrees with someone higher up who has a new battle plan for this month. Boy believes those plans are bad, and not properly evaluated.'

'Hmm. If two personalities clash about tactics it could lead to problems, couldn't it?'

'Montgomery has his own peculiarly optimistic input,' JP said as they turned a steep corner.

Cecil glanced at him, but did not like his look. There were no cars on the road and Cecil asked, 'John, how do you get to know these details?'

'Talk in the mess, mostly. Still, one hears things. Trouble is, now that it's September, we've had to deal with fog, sudden storms and high winds.'

'What about reduced daylight?'

'Yes, that too, and the transport of supplies has got harder, so we can't airlift much.'

'What do the Resistance know about the Germans in that part of Holland?'

JP wondered whether he should tell Cecil much more. He was worried about the chatter he had heard a few nights before in the mess. Two panzer divisions were somewhere in the Arnhem area. Major Urquhart was fearful, and had been voicing objections about the forthcoming operation.

He abruptly changed his mind and spoke frankly about his own misgivings. 'The Major is horrified by the assumption that the Germans would not put up much effective resistance.'

'What did he say?'

'During the planning conferences he told them that there are too many parts of the scheme which do not allow for things going wrong along the way.'

'John, give me some idea.'

'If paratroopers capture the bridges, XXX Corps' tanks could drive up a narrow corridor, and walk into Germany. But they have to cover sixty-four miles, in a short time, and things on the way could go wrong. The Major is alarmed that there is a general desire by others to get the airborne into action, and that they weren't worried about all the unexpected risks. The other camp compare it to the collapse of the Germans in 1918, and that the same should happen this time . . . but some of us, well quite a few of us, think they could be wrong about the Germans rolling over that easily . . . if it was the Italians, maybe!'

'The war could be over by winter if the operation succeeds?'

'Precisely, Cecil. But he does not believe the Germans are going to roll over and surrender. It is based on too many assumptions.'

'So have they started any combat plans?'

'Yes. I will tell you more later. We had better be cheerful. Emily will pick up on my thoughts. She is very perceptive.' John waved to a nurse in the grounds as they drove in. He remembered her kindly serving extra food; she had later brought him sandwiches when he had joked about being hungry after a long flight.

Emily waited in her room with David Lionel in her arms. Her small bag was packed. He woke when he heard his father's voice, and seemed to look toward him. JP took his son, after giving his wife a peck on each cheek. Cecil hugged her warmly. Emily suddenly started to cry. The men looked embarrassed.

'Nurse told me I might get weepy,' Emily confessed, more to calm their astonishment. 'I did not believe them, and I have no idea why I am crying. Maybe now that I am leaving here it feels as if I have all the responsibility of a young baby, and nobody to ask if anything goes wrong.' A huge sob followed, and she tried to smother it with her handkerchief.

Olga had prepared a hearty lunch for them, which was interrupted by Emily having to breast feed David. The men went outside to smoke their pipes; and the women talked as Olga tidied away the roast and Emily burped her son. Emily noticed Olga had lost a substantial amount of weight. Suddenly, the back door banged as the wind caught it.

'I couldn't wait until tomorrow to see him,' Cathy ran into the dining room with her arms outstretched.

'You can hold him. I'd love a rest!' Emily handed her son to Cathy.

'Oh, he's so like his father,' Cathy said. 'I have not held a baby in my arms for such a long time.' She gurgled and cooed while they finished clearing the table.

'Have some apple crumble with us, won't you, Cathy?' Olga asked.

'Yes, please, yours is always delicious.'

The men returned looking sombre. 'What happened out there, you two look as if you saw some evils pirits?' Emily said to her husband.

Cecil replied too quickly. 'No, just another naughty young man trying to steal some plants while we were smoking; we managed to shoo him away.'

Emily raised her eyebrows at JP who smiled sheepishly.

Third of September 1944, Brussels is liberated; 4 September, Antwerp is liberated; 8 September, German V2 bombs strike London.

RAF Station, Fairford

8 September 1944

My darling sweetheart,

Nice ride back from Cornwall, although a bit cloudy near the end. Susan didn't enjoy it much, and fell asleep on my knee for most of the way. Lots of fellows here enquiring about you and David, which was kind of them.

I got up early this morning and went out with the gun and Susan, and shot two huge rabbits and four partridge in an hour. I'm going to have a good supper one day this week. I had a hearty breakfast afterwards. It would have been wonderful to have you here with me for this beautiful September morning.

I had a lovely holiday and I was so happy to be with you and David. Did I imagine that he sleeps better now? I hope I wasn't responsible for your getting too tired, my darling.

I cannot understand why Mother hasn't written, but maybe the letter is lost.

Susan sends you a big lick. Take care of yourself, darling, and keep warm. I hope to see you again as soon as possible. There is too much going on here, but I will write soon once I know what our plans are. I'll telephone you if I can come down for the day.

All my love to you both,

John

Emily read and re-read his letter as she walked in the garden alone. Olga saw her from the upstairs window. She'd felt unwell and returned to bed after breakfast. Cecil worked on the far side of the garden. Olga felt the heaviness of sleep envelop her, just like when she was young and had been hard at work, except this morning she also felt a pain in her back. Emily's voice carried up, but Olga could not decipher the words.

Emily brought Olga her dinner in bed. She'd put a pretty pink flower on the tray.

'Auntie, how do you feel?' Emily noticed there was more colour in her face.

'Yes, I do feel refreshed. I don't understand why I felt so tired earlier. Nearly half the month has gone, where does each week go? Still, it brings us closer to the end of the war, I hope.'

'That's what May says to John when she sees him.'

12 SEPTEMBER 1944

John worked at his desk. Susan was under it, her body curled up by his legs. He felt the warmth of her, and when he moved she rose and started wagging her tail, hopefully.

'You won't get a walk yet,' he patted her. 'Lie down, I have to work.' He turned to his papers, then looked out at the weather and wondered what it would be like in Cornwall. His thoughts turned back to the battle plans . . . but that did not last and his mind was briefly back in Tremena.

Where is Emily and what is my son doing? If only I could be there. Maybe soon. Too many people arguing here about plans, procedures, and ifs. The Polish contingency are important to us, but some up high do not realise it. Sosabowski has made comments about the importance of Arnhem to the Germans. A gateway to Germany, I think he said, yet our commanders think there are only low calibre enemy troops there. Why are the planners not looking at the smaller details? So much of what we have done is high-risk, but this battle plan seems worse . . . I think Monty wants to reach Berlin with his armies before anyone else. Is he in a race? Antwerp should be opened up, and the Schelde estuary cleared, or the Germans will escape into northern Holland . . . then reach Arnhem just when we get there. We must drop our troops close to their target—within easy reach of the bridge that they are meant to seize. The DZ seems too far away for the paratroopers and glider-borne troops to achieve what is expected of them in two days. When we had a briefing two days ago nobody responded when Major Urquhart asked, 'Any questions?' Are they confused?

I must write to Emily. It looks unlikely I can get time to go down. I feel like her blue eyes are on me now. I cannot forget how she looked at me when the holiday was over. I tried not to let her know, yet I felt her gaze on each part of my face, as if she was memorising each wrinkle, line and mark on me. She ran her fingers through my hair and held my face in both her hands. When she kissed me at Portreath, she tasted of the plums we had eaten earlier. She looked sad. I know she has no reason to be.

What did she say to me?

She stood by the car and waved until our plane was out of sight, I saw her figure getting tinier, a thin black line, and then disappear.

Nine aircraft flew to France with a total of two hundred and sixteen containers and eighteen panniers. Five aircraft were successful. Squadron leader J. P. Gregory and three other crews had no reception, and returned with their loads.

RAF Station, Fairford
14 September 1944

My darling Emily,

Many thanks for your two nice letters—although I have never heard such rot about your being miserable. You have been a perfect mum. We are very lucky that we have each other. I miss you too.

The Atkinsons are moving out of the house in about ten days. Furniture is going to be moved in for us immediately. The snag is that I don't think I shall be able to occupy the house for reasons I can't explain. I shall have to start looking for another in a totally different part of the country. However, it may serve for a few days as I shall have to bring you and the car up sometime. I have bought the Baby Belling which has knocked me back £12 this month.

So sorry about your sleepless nights, it must get easier soon; also about early morning nappies, perhaps that will pass as he gets bigger!

Thanks for enclosing a letter from Mother.

Things have been pretty chaotic here from the moment I touched down, and the wind holds many things. Everything seems to be happening as I suspected, which is unfortunate in its way, but fortunate that I suspected it.

I have just eaten a lovely orange so this will probably smell of orange.

Susan has been behaving herself well, although it is most difficult to find a suitable lead for tying her up as she has bitten through her lead and several ropes. She wanders about the camp quite freely now. I haven't any idea where she is at the moment.

I phoned up Micky yesterday, but I heard he is missing after an op.

I heard that Smithy has been killed . . . Edward is doing alright though.

I had a very demanding op. the night before last, couldn't keep awake on the way back, it was lucky that George [24] was working well.

No more news, darling. When I am alone I think about being back with you at Mulberry House; our walks in the garden, or holding each other by the sea shore, and our long nights together the first time I came to Cornwall.

All my love to you both, and to Cecil and Olga.

John

(I have a fairly good joke to tell Olga from one of my crew).

15 SEPTEMBER 1944

There was an assumption that the Americans could carry out night operations. The Americans were not ready. It fell through, and a new plan was drawn up called 'Market'. It remained centred on the capture of three bridges, and two more US airborne divisions were added to the force. The operation would be in daylight, despite its greater vulnerability. Fair weather was essential. As there were insufficient aircraft available for one assault, the operation would take place over two days, with a third day for re-supply. Heavy losses were expected during the first lift.

Meanwhile the enemy was concentrating their defences along the routes planned for the transport aircraft. In the RAF officers' mess they talked about being confined to camp for two to three days. The men ate, drank, played cards, smoked, and waited for the next operations.

'This was the hardest time,' the navigator Reg Lawton said years later.

Mulberry House, Cornwall

14 September 1944

Darling John,

I have only had one letter from you since you left. I do miss you, especially after our days together. You seemed calm and relaxed, as you exchanged jokes with Olga. Cecil said he enjoyed playing golf with you. It felt strange to wake up with you beside me again, and now I dream of that each night, but the disappointment floods into me when I wake up. Last night I dreamt I saw you at the end of the beach, and I ran towards you, but I could not get to you. You were wearing your flying goggles, and swimming trunks! That should make you laugh.

Olga is not well, and the former robust woman is not in evidence. I have taken breakfast up to her several times. We sit together talking while she eats, then she has another rest, until lunch. If it's not a cool day we both sit together knitting and listening to music in the garden room. We hear the news on the wireless when Uncle comes in. David is very good, and mostly eats and sleeps. We have an easy, comfortable routine, and I wait for the post. I hope Susan is behaving herself. I'd like her back here soon, to take her for walks, and get my figure back.

All my love always.

Emily xx

I think of you every hour.

Forty-eight hours before Operation Market Garden, General Eisenhower approved Montgomery's plan, but a single piece of intelligence about two German Panzer divisions in Holland gave him serious doubts; especially as the two of them had been arguing again about the operation. Montgomery said he was not concerned to hear about Panzer divisions, and he decided not to cancel the largest airborne operation of the Second World War.

16 September 1944

JP picked up his mail. A letter from his wife, and one from his mother, May.

Briefing: JP was in a sixty-foot (twenty-metre) building illuminated by fluorescent lamps. A low platform lay across one end. A back wall was covered with maps. Coloured tapes showed the assault routes. Windows were covered with blackout curtains. Rows of trestle tables and chairs occupied most of the room. Some of the officers were looking at maps. JP felt tense, but he seemed calm to his men.

As the briefing of the Market Garden plan unfolded the men realised the enormity of the operation. An officer gave a summary of known troops in Holland. He didn't reveal that two divisions of Germans were there. Market Garden was a two-stage, complicated battle plan.

The first stage involved a huge airborne drop on northern Holland. To be timed to coincide with the invasion of southern Holland by land forces of the British Second Army.

The second stage involved paratroopers and glider-borne forces of First Airborne Division, dropped by the RAF into Holland, to capture and hold the great road bridge at Arnhem, while the tanks of Second Army's XXX Corps were to race across Holland to consolidate any of their gains.

Success depended on:

1. An absence of serious enemy resistance, in the Arnhem area.

2. The capture of the Arnhem Bridge before the Germans had time to blow it up or bring up reinforcements. The bridge, which was key to the entire operation, had to be captured and then held at all costs until ground forces fought their way through, as quickly as possible, to join the airborne troops.

3. Successive waves of RAF airborne reinforcements from England, to back up the RAF's initial drops.

4. Finally, the arrival at Arnhem of XXX Corps, within forty-eight hours of the drop.

17 SEPTEMBER 1944

Sunday was a bright morning. The first wave of aircraft carrying parachutists took off.

Thirty-five thousand men, together with equipment, jeeps and guns, were to be lifted by transport aircraft and two and a half thousand gliders from twenty-four airfields.

Leading the operation were 190—JP's squadron—620 Squadrons carrying, between them, twelve loads of pathfinding troops to be landed close by the bridges at Arnhem and Nijmegen. At Fairford, take-off was shortly after 1000 hours. JP's 190 Squadron had six aircraft airlifting ninety-seven pathfinder troops, and another nineteen towing gliders in which there were one hundred and thirty troops, seventeen Jeeps, seven lightweight motorcycles, a heavy motorcycle, seventeen trailers, seven guns and a bicycle.

With the task over Holland completed, their tow ropes dropped, JP's Stirling climbed away and made for home at 180 mph. By mid-afternoon they were back at base with a few scratches from flak.

The airfields were fog-clad, which caused alarm. A five-hour delay for re-supply was enforced, but then with cloud and hazy conditions, JP's Stirlings took off from Fairford again. The route taken was the same as on 17 September. Flak had increased.

Communication with troops and units on the ground in Holland was impossible. The radio sets carried by the invasion force proved useless as the technology had failed them. Unless within earshot of one another, no one knew what anyone else was doing.

Montgomery and Eisenhower were still arguing.

Some planes crashed or exploded on the ground in Holland when they were shot at.

JP's squadron lost an aircraft.

'We're home soon!' his navigator, Lawton, said excitedly as they approached the coastline. The bomb aimer McEwan talked with Cullen. JP was silent until they landed. He returned to base with flak damage to his aircraft.

'Let's get something to eat. Ground crew, can you fix those holes before tomorrow?' JP asked.

'Of course, sir.'

RAF Station, Fairford

18 September 1944

My darling Emily,

I believe we are half way through, and what we are doing could shorten the war, but Monty has taken risks.

I have just eaten a hearty meal, and my crew too seem happier when they have something in their belly. One of them keeps us entertained when we are flying, but I don't add to the crews' conversation. Mostly you are in my thoughts, and each day I think of your routine, and what we might me doing if I was in Cornwall with you.

I had a strange dream last night. There was this huge steam engine, and I was driving the train. It was a beautiful machine, but I lost concentration and pressed the wrong pedal, then the train toppled over. We were unhurt and it made hissing sounds. When I woke up it was Susan who had been snoring. Yes, I did laugh about your dream.

I send you my love and can't wait to hug and hold you again, and to feel your warmth.

John

19 September 1944

Several Stirlings had been lost or damaged. JP took off from Fairford with his crew carrying containers and panniers to the drop zone. The enemy were waiting. They shot the British paratroopers as they parachuted in.[25]

CHAPTER TWENTY-FIVE
NEWS FROM THE FRONT

Three loud knocks on the front door of Mulberry House.

Cecil opened the door. A young boy was standing waiting on the front step.

'Does Mrs Gregory live here?' he asked.

'Yes, she does,' Cecil replied.

The boy handed him a telegram and said, 'I'm sorry, sir.' Then he returned to his bicycle to ride back down the hill. The telegram was addressed to Emily.

Cecil hesitated, fearing the worst news. He had seen Emily walking in the garden with Olga and four-week-old David. Cecil went to the back of the house, where he found them, eventually, near the old mulberry tree. He gave her the telegram. She stared at the little brown envelope and held it in both hands, then tore it open and read the words which were written in pencil.

'No!' Emily gasped, as she passed it to her aunt.

Olga and Cecil read it together. The whole village would know, because Cathy worked at the post office that morning.

Post Office Telegram 11.20 pm G.R./T OHMS

20 Sept. 1944

Priority

Mrs E. Gregory, Mulberry House, Tremena.

Regret to inform you that your husband 40819 Sq. Ldr.

J.P. Gregory is missing as the result of air operations on 19 September 1944 letter follows any further information received will be immediately conveyed to you pending notification from air ministry. No information should be given to the press.

O/C No. 190 Sqd. Fairford Glos.

Cecil and Olga felt helpless seeing Emily's grief, but she quickly started to plan.

'I had better arrange to go back home to Essex. I'll need to fetch our puppy, Susan, from Fairford. Father will come with me, but it is a long journey from Cornwall with David.'

'I will travel with you my dear,' Olga volunteered. 'I couldn't think of you doing that journey on your own. We can stop at relatives on the way, and if David needs anything while you are driving I can attend to him.'

Emily began to organize herself, 'I need to keep busy,' she told her uncle.

'I'll get a picnic basket filled with all we need for the journey,' Olga said. 'When would you like to set off?'

Cecil interrupted, 'It is best if you plan it carefully and go tomorrow. Don't rush.'

'I'll let Father know.'

'You stay here, and I'll go and send them a telegram,' Cecil said.

'Don't tell them he's missing. Write that I am coming home on Sunday.'

23 SEPTEMBER 1944

Olga, Emily and David arrived late at Highcombe. Her parents saw her red, swollen eyes, but did not ask questions. Emily took out the telegram and handed it to her father.

It took two weeks before she received further news.

RAF Station, Fairford, Gloucester

8 October 1944

Dear Mrs Gregory

The enclosed letter was found among your husband's personal effects with a request that it be forwarded to you in the event of his being reported 'missing'.

Yours faithfully,

Group Captain, Commanding

RAF Station, Fairford

A blue envelope was enclosed with a 2½*d*. postage stamp addressed to:

Mrs John P. Gregory

Highcombe, Sewardstonebury, Nr. Chingford, Essex

5 June 1944

My darling Emily,

I find it very difficult to write this letter because I know I am going to see you soon. If I am a bit late I'm sure I'll be alright on the other side, but if the worst happens, which I know it won't, I shall always be with you, my darling, and I do pray you will learn to forget as Jonny David doesn't want to have a sad Mum. I can't write anymore because my imagination runs away with me.

I love you more than anything on earth.

With every bit of my love,

John P.

PS. Darling it goes without saying that my worldly possessions are all yours. Give my love to all and thanks for everything.

Emily suddenly remembered the conversation she had with John two months before, when he told her that they had all been told to write letters home before D-day. So this was what he had written. She felt a sharp pain in her solar plexus and put her palm there as though to ease the ache. Emily wanted to believe he was missing, because the same thing had happened to Pam. She felt the urge to write to her friend and to talk to her, because she thought Pam would understand, more than anyone near her now. She decided to make contact with her first. She would write later to people who might pull strings and get information for her, like Graeme and Uncle Michael.

'Father, I'll need to write a few letters while David is asleep.' She raced up to her room to get to work.

She took out Graeme's letter of 20 September 1944 and re-read it.

No. 190 Squadron, Royal Air Force, Fairford, Gloucester

20 September, 1944

Dear Mrs Gregory,

It is with very deep regret that I am writing to you to confirm the telegram that has already been sent to you about John, who did not return from an operation on 19 September 1944.

We all took-off together, and John and I were side by side throughout much of the trip there.

It was not very pleasant at the target end however, and several aircraft were hit by flak, and had to make emergency landings. From circumstantial reports it would appear that John was one of them, and if this should prove true, he and the crew should stand a chance of getting away without much trouble. In view of the military situation, I cannot say if they would have landed in allied- or enemy-held territory, and we must, therefore, await further details, which in the latter event should in due course come through the International Red Cross society.

Lacking, as I am, in any definite details, I cannot with any surety raise your hopes more than the other next-of-kin, but I feel confident in John's ability to pull the cat out of the bag if humanly possible.

In accordance with Air Ministry Orders, his personal effects assembled at this station are being forwarded to the Standing Committee of Adjustment, Central Depository, RAF Colnbrook, Slough, Bucks., who will communicate with you direct at the earliest possible moment. I have taken the liberty of looking after Susan who shares with me a very great affection for John, and will do so just as long as you wish, so please do not worry yourself about her.

John and I were the best of friends, as you know, and the whole squadron and station feel his absence far above words. I know and appreciate the dreadful suspense through which you are going, and wish I could add more to relieve it.

Please do not hesitate to write to me if I can be of any assistance whatever, and I shall, of course, let you know anything I hear at once.

Yours very sincerely,

Graeme Elammior

The next letter from the Air Ministry lifted her spirits. She discussed it with her parents.

'Surely, Father, if three of the crew have returned home safely, it must bode well?'

'Yes, I agree. Try to be patient, we are sure to hear some news soon.' He handed the letter back to her.

'May I see that letter?' her mother asked.

Telephone No: Gerrard 9234

Air Ministry (Casualty Branch), 73–77 Oxford Street,

London W1

30 September 1944

Madam,

I am commanded by the Air Council to express to you their great regret on learning that your husband, Squadron Leader John Philip Gregory, DFC, Royal Air Force, is missing as the result of air operations on 19 September 1944, when a Stirling aircraft in which he was flying as pilot set out for action and was not heard from again. Three of the occupants of the aircraft have since returned to safety, but no news of your husband and the three others has yet been received.

This does not necessarily mean that your husband is killed or wounded, and if he is a prisoner of war he should be able to communicate with you in due course. Meanwhile enquiries are being made through the International Red Cross Committee, and as soon as any definite news is received you will be at once informed.

If any information regarding your husband is received by you from any source you are requested to be kind enough to communicate it immediately to the Air Ministry.

The Air Council desire me to convey to you their sympathy in your present anxiety.

I am, madam,

Your obedient servant,

J. C. Smith

Emily had no income. She preferred to be independent and wrote making enquiries about her husband's salary.

In October the Air Ministry wrote to her again.

Telephone: Sloane 3467

Air Ministry, 2 Seville Street, Knightsbridge, London SW1

20 October 1944

Registered

Madam,

With reference to your letters dated 29 September and 10 October 1944 together with application dated 10 October 1944, I am directed to inform you that instructions have today been given to Lloyd's Bank Limited (Cox's and King's Branch) Royal Air Force Agents, Tralee Hotel, St Michael's Road, Bournemouth, Hants., to pay to you with effect from 20 September 1944, a temporary allowance comprising the married rate of allowance and two-sevenths of the pay in issue to your husband on the previous day.

The payment, at the rate of £5 3s. 8d. (five pounds, three shillings and eight pence) a week, will be made in advance on the first day of each calendar month and the sums now due in respect of September and October 1944 will be paid forthwith.

The allowance will continue in issue for a minimum period of three months unless it should be established that your husband is alive, in which case issue of his Royal Air Force emoluments would be resumed. If, however, your husband is still missing at the end of this minimum period, the allowance will continue at the same rate to 20 March 1945 (that is twenty-six weeks from the date of notification that he was missing) unless during the extended period further information is received regarding him when you will be notified of any amendment which may in consequence be necessary.

If on 21 March 1945 your husband is still missing, the rate of temporary allowance from that date will be amended to £18 0s. 0d. (eighteen pounds) a calendar month.

This monthly rate of allowance is one-twelfth of the

annual pension of £180 plus an allowance of £36 a year in respect of your child and represents the amount that would be payable if it were known that your husband had died in circumstances entitling you to pension. Payment at this rate will continue so long as your husband remains missing.

The certificate forwarded with the form of application is returned to you herewith.

I am directed to inform you that enquiries are being made regarding your child's birth certificate and a further communication will be sent to you.

I am, Madam,

Your obedient Servant,

Ian Parker,

For Director of Accounts.

EMILY'S VOICE

I had been in need of love. When I found John it had given me the source of warmth and care that fulfilled me. Suddenly, it was snatched away, and the anxiety returned. I became fearful of the black emptiness, and a hollow emotional future. When I was asked, 'How are you Emily?' I felt barely able to hold myself together. Had I tried to answer, I may have collapsed into tears; only my nights alone gave me the freedom to allow these tears to flow uncontrollably.

In the dark, I imagined everything from his captivity to his death, and back to serious injury. An injury, isolated from the world, and John waiting for rescue; or death alone in his cockpit. It was still a question unanswered, and one that blighted my mind in many ways.

I often returned to those last moments at Portreath before he left for the battle at Arnhem, how we clung together, our minutes ebbing away. Yet it had happened to me before, and he had returned. In the moment of John leaving—an instant which clutched at my emotions—I had felt his embrace, and then the sensation of being cut away even before our last separation. I had scrutinized his face, felt his hair through my fingers. Feeling my tears dammed behind my eyelids, I had wondered why I felt that way. The intimacy held behind thin walls of skin.

I was like a somnambulist after the telegram. Reflection became too painful. Yet it was the remembering that also gave me hope. They had stolen a life from me, which made me into a fighter. I knew I was not alone, and so many other women must have been feeling like me, each of us suffered if not loss then anxiety, fear . . . I wrote letters, and I got many back. Then a letter from John's navigator, Reg, arrived the first day of December. I read it again, before replying.

32 York Avenue, Great Crosby, Liverpool 23

30 November 1944

Dear Mrs Gregory,

You will have been wondering why you have not received a reply to your letter. The reason is that I am no longer with the old squadron and I have been at Inverness for the last two weeks and your letter has only just reached me. I am now at home for two or three days awaiting a new posting. I haven't the least idea where this will be, but if it should be anywhere near London I will come and see you if there is anything further you would like to discuss, or if there is anything I haven't made clear. Please let me know if you would like me to come, after you have read this letter, for, on my way to Inverness I called to see Mrs MacEwen, the rear gunner's wife, and although what I could tell her was not of any real help, unfortunately, at least I was able to answer a few questions that had been puzzling her.

You will have been wondering, too, why I did not write to you as soon as I got back to England. I saw the adjutant of the squadron and asked him for your address. He asked me what I wanted it for and I said I was sure you would like to hear from me some of the details of what happened. He replied that I had already told my story to the authorities and that I should leave it to them to do any communicating with you, as they would do, of course, as soon as anything new came in. So I had to leave it at that.

On Sunday 17 September we flew to Arnhem to drop paratroops in the invasion of Holland. It was an easy trip, practically no opposition. The next day the crews drew lots for who was to fly and we drew a blank. On the nineteenth we went again and all was fairly quiet until we were right over our target where there was a lot of flak. Even then I thought we were getting through nicely, but suddenly John gave the order, 'Prepare to abandon aircraft.' Followed immediately by, 'Abandon aircraft.'

I clipped on my parachute and followed the passenger, Squadron Leader Bantoft, down the steps into the bomb-aimers cabin where all three of us got the escape hatch open and went out, the bomb-aimer last, I was second. As I passed John on my way to the hatch he was sitting calmly at the controls, and as the plane at that moment went into a steep climb, I thought that he was pulling her up to give us height to jump, but I found out later that this was not so.

As you already know I made a safe landing and managed to make my way to our lines. The next day the area I was in developed into the 'Arnhem Pocket' where I was for six days before being evacuated over the river to Nijmegen with the rest of the troops.

In these six days I spoke to many of the soldiers about the fate of our plane and they all told the same story. I could identify our plane to them by telling them it was the one which went into a very steep climb after being hit and they all recognised the one. They said they saw four men jump by parachute and that the plane then fell, but no one saw it hit the ground, for the simple reason that these men were dug in in thickish woodland and their view was very restricted. They were almost certain that there was no fire for they did not see any smoke. It was impossible, of course, for me to try and find the wreck for it was now in, or behind, the German lines.

The first night I was on the ground I met Squadron Leader Bantoft and the next day I met F/O Cullen, our bomb-aimer. F/O Cullen was with me from then on. When I met him he told me that he had just been to see F/Sgt Byrne, our engineer, who was not far away in a house being treated for a broken leg which he sustained on hitting the ground. His story was that he was in the rear of the plane helping to push out our parachute supplies when a shell hit us and burst in the rear of the fuselage, killing two soldiers who were with us to push out these supplies. The wireless operator baled out through this hatch and he (Byrne) followed him. The house in which Byrne was being treated was almost immediately captured by the Germans and so he is now a prisoner of war. Squadron Leader Bantoft told me that the control column was useless in John's hands which, of course, was the reason we were told to bale out, and so it seems to me that this shell which hit us severed the wires in the rear of the plane which controlled the rudder, etc.

That is all I know of the facts. While I was floating down I did not see the plane, I was watching the ground all the time. We were at a thousand feet when we were hit (at 3.50 p.m.) which is a low height for parachute jumping, but I am sure there was time for John to get out after me. Perhaps he stayed to try and crash land, but it is no use my speculating, you see I know so little that it was not until the next day that I found out why we had baled out.

I do not know Squadron Leader Bantoft's address. He was someone from Air Ministry I think. F/O Cullen is on the old squadron at Great Dunmow. Nothing has been heard of the wireless operator.

Considering the circumstances, I had a pleasant evening with Mrs MacEwen and her family. She is keeping cheerful and optimistic. She is pinning her hopes on the plane having made a landing of sorts and that he has been taken prisoner. I sincerely hope that this proves to be the case and that you soon receive word of John. The crew always knew how lucky we had been in getting such a pilot for a skipper. We enjoyed those few trips down to Portreath that, by the way, was the nearest I came to meeting you when you waved to us as we 'shot-up' your car on the road home from Portreath that day.

I gather from your letter that you are in touch with the squadron, for you knew they had moved to Great Dunmow, so you may know already that Wing Commander Harrison, who wrote our 'missing' notifications, was himself shot down at Arnhem on the twenty-third and is believed killed.

The place where our plane is lying is about two and a half to three miles west of Arnhem, about two hundred to three hundred yards north of the railway line which runs from Arnhem to Utrecht, so it is still in the fighting area and so I imagine that no effort is made to clear up such an area until the fighting has moved on.

I think that is all, I only wish that I could be of more help to you.

I hope that you and the little baby are well.

Yours sincerely,

Reg Lawton

By the time I received another letter from John's uncle, I had read and re-read Lawton's letter.

Subsequently, I received a reply from John's uncle Michael in Newcastle.

> 5 Manor Gardens, Longbentow, Newcastle.
>
> 1 December 1944

My Dear Emilie [sic],

How can I write this letter and convey to you my feelings which I trust you will be able to understand? I can only say, my dear, I am sorry I sent you that wire—to give what I thought was fresh news—and buoyed you up with hopes regarding dear John. Can I say this, however, Emilie, I did not know the exact position. I only knew my best boy—I love him as a son and a brother—was missing. That was the brief news I received from my sister—John's mother—and I therefore set to work to try and find what [had] happened. The enclosed letter from Lord Westwood will tell you I did my best.

You see Billie Westwood is one of my best friends— John knows him well—the three of us having played golf together. Maybe I should have worded the wire differently, but can only say I [was] more excited than a schoolboy on receiving it, thinking at least the news was good, not knowing, of course, you already knew this.

Emilie, my dear, I cannot put on paper how much John means to me—love for a man to a man is so different from a love of a man to a woman—but if there is anything I can do for both you and young David, would you please call on me. No doubt John has told you about Marjorie— my wife—and myself as he used to always try and come and stay with us. Marjorie has the feeling that John is OK, although naturally she is like yourself very worried.

I do not know you very well, my dear, having only seen you once at the wedding, but I know that John could not go wrong in his choice, and being a bit of a psychologist myself, I knew when I saw you his choice was OK.

How is young David keeping, and how old is he? Do please write and let me know. I have a redheaded daughter—she will be fourteen years on Xmas day. We all hope to come to town shortly and we should very much like to see you and David. Well, Emilie, we—all of us—can only hope and pray everything is all right and that John will come back to us all, and when I see him I'll give him a piece of my mind [about] letting Jerry beat him, after all, I taught him.

In conclusion, dear, give my best regards to your family and keep your chin up.

Yours etc.

Uncle Michael Watling

I had difficulty remembering what happened that day after the telegram arrived telling me John was 'missing'. Did I tell my Uncle Cecil? People were kind knowing how hurt I was—how sad we all were. My life suddenly seemed aimless, but Lionel David kept me on my feet; he was hungry and needed my milk, and to produce enough breast milk I needed to eat and drink liquids. I had never felt less hungry in my whole life, and that day I felt sick putting anything into my mouth. When Olga asked me to stay, I knew I could not. I had to go back to my parents. From there I would try to discover John's whereabouts.

I recalled again our last night together, walking in the fields at dusk, and seeing the fireflies flickering beside us and in the distance when it became dark. John had been in high spirits after his long holiday with us. He had arrived grim-faced and nervous, his eyes fatigued, and body-weary, yet when he came to leave me he seemed calm and happy.

Each evening after the sun had set, we would sit with Uncle Cecil and Auntie Olga as the sky turned to a glittering darkness, and we would be served some deep red wine or a local brew. We had shared walks in fields dotted with an explosion of red poppies like fireworks in late summer.

John, Olga and Cecil had played golf competitively, although in good humour, while I had watched or taken David with me along the lanes, enjoying the blue and white cornflowers beside the paths in the wilder edges of the hedgerows, and I had picked early ripe blackberries to add to the apples that Olga saved from their orchard. People had all the time in the world to talk, and we had been cushioned from the evils of the London bombs and sulphurous smoke.

Sometimes we would wake early as our son was hungry. The hazy morning sunlight gave us moments of shimmering beauty, especially when it was misty and we could hear the murmurs of insects and birdsong.

I would be on my way alone now until we met again.

Two weeks after I wrote to Reg, his reply came, in neat and careful handwriting.

> RAF Station, Scone, Near Perth, Scotland
> 13 December 1944
>
> Dear Mrs Gregory,
>
> Thank you for your letter which has been forwarded on to me up here.
>
> I am afraid I cannot say whether F/Sgt Byrne has been officially reported a prisoner of war yet. I do not know how one does find out, except by reading through the lists of names as they are published in, for instance, *The Times*. The local branch of the Red Cross would be able to advise you.
>
> If you are thinking of writing to Byrne for any information he may have, I should advise you not to, for such questions would not get past the censor.
>
> With regard to your other question, the soldiers seemed to agree that the plane fell off sideways on to a wing tip

after sticking its nose up (as I described) but no-one saw it fall far as it became hidden by trees when it was still a long way from the ground.

As you see, I have been posted a long way from London so I am afraid I shall not be able to come and see you. I am sorry, for I should have liked to very much. Please let me know as soon as you receive any word of John.

Best wishes and the compliments of the season.

Yours sincerely,

Reg Lawton

Emily found work in a school attached to the local stables.

In January 1945 she was allowed to bring her son with her because other widowed women at the school all helped one another with the fatherless children.

A letter arrived in February 1945. It was forwarded from Cornwall, as the Air Ministry still seemed to have her old address.

Telephone No: Gerrard 9234

Air Ministry, (Casualty Branch), 73–77 Oxford Street,

London W1

15 February 1945

Madam,

I am directed to inform you, with deep regret, that all efforts to trace your husband, Squadron Leader J. P. Gregory, DFC, have proved unavailing.

In view of the absence of news for so long a period, it is felt that you should be informed of this department's grave anxiety for his safety, but action to presume that he has lost his life will not be taken until evidence of his death is received, or until such time has elapsed that it is considered there can be no longer any likelihood of his survival.

Such action will then be for official purposes only and

will not be taken until this department has communicated with you further.

I am to assure you that all possible enquiries are continuing.

I am, Madam,

Your obedient servant,

F. Carlinson

For Director of Personal Services.

CHAPTER TWENTY-SIX
BATTLE OF ARNHEM (MG) [26]

The unfolding of Market Garden revealed all the symptoms of military incompetence. However, 'for sheer initiative, quickness of mind, fortitude and selfless heroism, the conduct of those who actually fought the battle has never been surpassed.' [27]

AUTUMN 1944
EMILY'S VOICE

My memories of John were saturated by our nights together. Our heightened sensual emotions, images of our evenings by the fire in the winter, or walking out in the countryside with Susan, as well as bathing on the beaches in Cornwall. There sat Cecil, who often watched us on the beach, with his pipe in his mouth, and Olga on a rug usually reading and framed by the dark rocks all around her in the sand.

I had walked with Olga the day after the news about John; I remember the dark grey thunderstorms were rolling in from the horizon, and the ocean at our feet was an intense murmur of roaring sand beneath the waves: like the feelings inside of me. Warm-hearted Olga sensed my pain. Her eyes were fatigued, and her cheeks sunken. We were quietly going through the day, but I was waiting for an imagined future.

The night before we left, the three of us were silent at dinner. Olga and I drove back to Essex in John's little car with David asleep in his basket. I felt her calm thoughtful care glide over and around me. Then, after a day, the morning sunlight saw us on the edge of London with its smoking chimneys. Each mile passing beneath the tyres was another taking me and David away from the place where I had always been happiest.

Another telegram arrived eight months after Olga had left us in Essex.

> May 1945, 11.15 London CTO OHMS
> Priority CC. J. P. Gregory
> Mulberry House, Tremena Cornwall.
> From Air Ministry, 73 Oxford Street, W1
>
> Ref. OX 215
> Deeply regret to inform you that your husband, Sqd. Leader John P. Gregory D.F.C. 40818, is now reported to have lost his life as the result of air operations on 19 September 1944. The Air Council express their profound sympathy, his mother is being informed. Letter follows shortly.
> Under Sec. of State.

Emily did not read the letter.

Field Marshal Montgomery's subsequent description of Market Garden as 90 per cent success, a sentiment which drew from Prince Bernhard of the Netherlands the comment, 'My country can never again afford the luxury of a Montgomery success.'

Defeat was absolute and terrible.

Short on everything but courage, the men of the First Airborne Division held on until their numbers had been reduced from 10,005 to less than a quarter of that figure.

Total allied losses in killed, wounded and missing exceeded

17,000 some 5,000 more than those who became casualties on D-day.

Dutch civilian casualties were estimated at between 500 and 10,000.

Emily wrote three years later:

I had left my parents and worked as a stable hand and a nursery teacher, so that David could live with me at work. In the summer of 1946 I had gone to help Cecil in Cornwall, but it had not been as before and Olga was unwell. Then we heard that she had cancer. I was once again in deep mourning, and not comforted by the letter my Uncle Cecil wrote to me, fearing that he too might follow her.

> Mulberry House, Tremena, Nr. Hale, Cornwall.
>
> 20 July 1948
>
> My dear Emilie [sic],
>
> Thank you for your kind and consoling letter.
>
> I cannot believe, even now, that darling Olga has gone out of my life forever. As I walk around this empty house, every nook is eloquent of her presence—her knitting here, her handbag there, the things on her dressing table, just as she left them, etc., etc.
>
> She was reverently taken out of this house, leaving it for the last time in her coffin, on my birthday, the seventh, of all days, to rest in the parish church overnight in readiness for the funeral the next morning at 10 o'clock, when she was laid to rest in St Erth cemetery. We put it at that time, so that few should know, as she would have wished, for she hated mourning and fuss, and giving trouble to others. Yet many came and there were nearly fifty wreaths. So much loved was she.
>
> The complete change from the sunshine of her

companionship, to utter loneliness, makes me hope that I shall not have to live very much longer to endure it.

My love to you from your sorrowful

Uncle Cecil.

When Olga died, Cecil commissioned a beautiful stained glass window in her memory which can still be seen in the church where they both worshipped.

Amongst my father, Ben's, letters after he died, I found my Uncle Cecil's letter to my father, which was left clearly for me to find one day. This helped me to understand the puzzle of Mulberry House.

I had been desolate after Uncle Cecil's death and was also confounded by his Will. I think my father wanted me to see this letter because he had felt powerless to influence his own brother, Cecil, at that time.

Mulberry House, Cornwall

29 July 1948

My dear Ben,

It is a dreadful thing, when, nearing the close of one's life (for I am now in my seventy-second year) for one's wife to be taken—especially such a one as Olga—who, by all expectations of life, would have outlived me by twenty-five years or so.

Instead, she is in her grave some thirty years before her natural time, and the scene in consequence has utterly changed from one of the sunshine of her companionship to extreme loneliness.

I cannot believe, even now, that she has really gone out of my life for ever as I wander around this empty silent house. Every nook is eloquent of her presence and her work, which has made the place so beautiful.

Her things—her work-box here, her handbag there,

her knitting and embroidery—just as she left them, poor darling.

The utter finality seems impossible to grasp. I asked Margaret to go up to you and Mary to tell you about the funeral, and I am glad to hear she did this soon after her arrival home. I just managed to hold myself in hand, and walk upright through the terrible ordeal. It was all very simple, as she would have wished. I asked the vicar to make the service as short and simple as possible and timed it for 10am, so that few should know about it. The poor darling hated mourning, and giving trouble to others. She was taken from the house for the last time the night before (my birthday of all days) to rest in church overnight, in readiness for the funeral the next morning.

Outside on the hearse there were some fifty of the most beautiful wreaths . . . she was loved by rich and poor.

Thank you for your comforting letter.

The thought of leaving here for a change would do me no good at the present time. I may become more reconciled later on to the shattering blow. At present I'm not normal. If ever I get so again, I might be able to stand up to a return to an empty house.

Besides, there is so much to be done. There is Olga's Will and affairs to be settled. Then there is my Will to be remade—of course I had left this place and all it contains to her. All is now altered.

This brings me to one of the main points of this letter to you. It is in confidence to you and Mary. I do not want what I am going to say to go beyond you two during my lifetime. I know I can rely upon you both to respect that confidence. It is this:

I have decided to leave this house and contents and the Pittosporum plantation to Alicia and her husband. I feel I should like the place to remain with and in the family. It is a house of unusual charm and character, and one not easily obtained these days—Olga loved it and we have both been very happy here.

I shall make a proviso that Emily receives £150 a year clear of any deductions from Pittosporum proceeds. I have given a good deal of thought to the foregoing and am not unmindful of others.

But you see, you must have a man (and a good strong one at that) and wife to run the plantation here. Emilie has no husband (poor girl). My other brother's boys have no horticultural tastes.

A general sale—including the bits of antique furniture Olga collected and other furniture, Persian rugs etc. she got, and all the beautiful wedding presents we received—is unthinkable.

Alicia and Gerald I know want to settle in Cornwall on retirement. I have already written to them informing them of my intentions to save any further efforts on their part as to seeking a place near here.

I have had so many letters to write lately, that I forgot if I have fully and adequately written to Mary to thank her for her kind and consoling letters. Please give her my love and thank her indeed. Anyway, she will read this too, for it is a joint letter to you both.

Any time, any of you can come down, I shall always be glad. I shall have somebody to talk to.

There is nothing more I can say at the moment.

With much love to you both.

Yours ever,

Cecil

P.S. Please acknowledge receipt of this. C.

ENDNOTES

[1] (p.34) London 1920–24. Economic stability had been decimated by the First World War. During the war, some of the men did not have decent clothes or uniforms. There had not been enough blankets. With no welfare, families helped one another. The Salvation Army supported people, but they too became overwhelmed. Rations for some foot soldiers at the closing stages of war were mean; there were also many men who could not eat, because they had no work. The poorer men kept their old army clothes so they could keep warm. They also traded some items for food. Bravery and survival had given them dignity and self-esteem, but it did not last. Many discovered that there would be no acclaim or accolades. Some tried, in vain, to return to their old jobs. Others quickly discovered that they were repaid by their home country with poverty and homelessness. Unemployment was widespread . . . their country's response for their sacrifices in the war. Some though, were fortunate because they had their family.

[2] (p.35) The wretchedness of the First World War had passed. Fighting had been their work, now they fought to find work, anything at all, so they could eat, survive and retain their dignity.

[3] (p.41) He became one of nearly two million ex-servicemen. They had risked their lives for the nation. He hoped the nation would look after its men when he returned to England.

[4] (p.51) In 1926 the General Strike in England in support of the coal miners lasted for nine days. There were one million

unemployed in England, and two million unemployed in Germany.

5 (p.51) Emily first saw this elegant four-mast sailing ship in the summer of 1936 near Salcombe in Devon. The circumstances of the sighting of the ship became unexpectedly dramatic in a very short period of time during June. Emily had been on her way to Cornwall.

The history of the ship *Herzogin Cecilie* was that she was launched in April 1902 at Bremerhaven in Germany. She had been built for the north German Lloyd Steamship Company who used her as a cadet training ship. The crew of sixty-five cadets were not given any labour-saving devices, they were trained by four officers and a captain to use their strength rather than mechanical deck winches. Ben Hale, a navy cadet, was trained for a period on the vessel.

The *Herzogin Cecilie* in full sail, with her four tall wooden masts, would have been a breathtaking sight. She was approx 334 feet long, with a 46 feet beam. The total cost to build her was said to have been in the region of £125,000.

For a period of time the *Herzogin Cecilie* was also called *Duchess Cecilie*. The name came from the figurehead which was of the Duchess Cecilie, daughter of the Duke of Oldenburgh. This ship was used to carrying cargo and training future young deck officers up until the outbreak of the First World War. Then from 1914–18 this beautiful ship lay hidden from those war years in Chile. At the end of the war *Duchess Cecilie* was handed to the French, even though the Germans were energetically asking for her return. However, although the French had been given this ship under the terms of the Versailles retributive terms, they judged that the days of sail ships were slowly ending. The ship was left moored at Ostend. One Captain Gustaf Erikson was on the lookout for suitable sailing vessels, and when informed by his aide-de-camp that a ship matching his requirements lay in Ostend, and was for sale, he made an inspection and offered £12,000 for her. When the price was accepted, she subsequently joined his Erikson Fleet. This was a substantial ship and became quite a successful purchase for Erikson, despite having to renovate parts of her deck. He became the proud owner. At the time of her purchase she carried 45,000 square feet of sail, made up of 35 sails, and her foresail alone measured around 87 by 33 feet. As he planned to use her for cargo, Gustav Erikson removed all unnecessary cabins to gain extra space. While she had been built to carry a total crew of eighty-five, he planned to send her to sea with a crew of only twenty-five under the command of one captain. On one occasion in 1934, the *Duchess Cecilie* had raced at 18 knots ahead of a steamer, while on a trip carrying cargo. While the steamer had been forced to bank up her boilers, to increase speed, Captain Erikson had beaten the steamer by merely using all 45,000 square feet of sail which made her speed along with only two men at the helm. She looked a splendid sight, and passengers in the steamship leaning over to watch the race saw the magnificent ship gradually sailing away from view, at a speed they could only dream about on the steamship.

Tragically for the *Duchess Cecilie,* her best run was to also be her last, when she was bound for home from Port Victoria via Falmouth after a voyage of eighty-six days.

In April the ship made sail for Ipswich where Captain Sven Erikson was to load some grain. In fog, off past the Eddystone lighthouse, and near Soar Mill Cove, she hit rocks and came to rest only five hundred yards from the cliffs. By June 1936 the media had taken up the progress reports and the fight to save the ship which had laid so close to shore.

A decision was made to tow her to Starehole Bay, and this was where she was seen not only by Emily, but by many people who came to view the progress of her salvage. She was beached for safety at the bay, stern first. However the rotting cargo of wheat was causing major problems, and was being offloaded. Volunteers were coming from all walks of life to help take off the cargo, and work carried on until around 18 July when a gale sprang up from the southeast. Starehole Bay faced due east and was open to a heavy swell that was being pushed by the wind. There were only one thousand tons of wheat left on board, but the *Duchess Cecilie* started to work deeper into the sand. Below the tens of feet of sand was an unknown layer of hard rock. Throughout the gale large waves pounded the ship and came crashing into the bay, washing right over her. Later the sounds of the pounding of the surf, was joined by a sound like the firing of a large pistol, which echoed around the bay and off the cliffs. For those who knew about ships, it was the dying sound of the cast iron rivets snapping under the strain of the hull breaking up. Many sailors lived in the surrounding hills and valleys, and word quickly spread that the *Duchess Cecilie* was dying in the bay. People in pubs and shops talked of the latest news, although with more sadness, than optimism.

The once beautiful vessel remained in Starhole Bay for nearly another year reminding whoever came to see her of the treacherous coastline around Devon, but also as a curiosity for holidaymakers. It is said, that it is still possible to see her, from the cliffs surrounding Starehole Bay, above the National Trust property Overbecks. Only the outline of the memorable ship lying beneath the clear waters can be seen. There is a bronze model of the ship in the local museum. Previously, the model used to be in a pub overlooking the bay. Once the history of the *Duchess Cecilie* became less known amongst the younger generations, the ships' model was then moved to the museum.

[6] (p.104) In 1928 women over the age of twenty-one were finally given the right to vote on the same terms as men.

[7] (p.106) During 1936 Winston Churchill had been consistently urging the government to be wary of German

sentiments. He was also critical that England was not prepared militarily; especially in the air. During Hitler's rise to power, Churchill had persistently advocated vigilance. Few wanted to hear his warnings and criticisms of Hitler, or even that Germany posed a danger to all of Europe. Most of Parliament and the population took little notice of him, and seemed blind to the threat from Germany. Churchill wanted his country to be strong to ward off another world war. In January 1936, following the death of his father, George V, the Prince of Wales became King Edward VIII. He was never crowned.

December 1936 saw the abdication of King Edward VIII. Winston Churchill was involved in advising the King before the abdication, but Churchill was hissed and booed into silence in the House of Commons when he took up Edward VIII's cause.

[8] (p.114) All diplomatic efforts to stop German aggression had been in vain. The British people talked about the possibility of war. Secret preparations were processed in 1938 for another war.

[9] (p.119) The British were not prepared for a world war which therefore led to continuing problems. Although they successfully defended their positions in Malta by a whisker, re-arming it for its role as an offensive base proved more problematic. Convoys were in great danger. It was decided that a big operation should be mounted bringing in one convoy direct from the United Kingdom via Gibralter, and another one from Alexandria. Strategic bombing would take place in support of the proposed operations.

[10] (p.127) A week after his appointment as Prime Minister, he was at the microphone again talking to his people on the radio. The words were heard by JP and others on his RAF base in Egypt, Emily and Alicia in London, Cecil and Olga, Cathy, and everyone who had a radio—even people far outside the

British Isles. By then the whole world was beginning to take an interest in the plight at the centre of the British Empire. Sailing craft and motor boats, small and large, were descending towards the Dunkirk beaches from every direction from coastal towns all over Britain. They had set forth to rescue their thousands of soldiers from the French beaches.

[11] (p.127) Dowding had experienced the disastrous RAF losses in the Norwegian campaign, as well as in France, between April and June 1940. The loss of more than one thousand of his aircraft was as close as he dared get to a catastrophe. The front line fighters who had been killed there were a sad consequence of those air battles, and Dowding met with the Cabinet on 15 May to persuade them to limit this wastage. He had urged them to reconsider because the RAF would be needed for the air battle over Britain in the months ahead. What the RAF later accomplished at Dunkirk left them even more vulnerable. Their lack of aircraft was acknowledged.

[12] (p.128) Churchill, W. S., *Their Finest Hour, The Second World War*, Vol II, (Cassell, 1951). Winston Churchill speaking in the House of Commons, did much to counter the criticism by attributing a glorious victory at Dunkirk to the RAF, as well as to the general public. But it was in vain.

[13] (p.128) Rommel knew from information gathered by the Germans that the British were building up their strength in Egypt. Rommel was keen for a final assault that would take him to Cairo. Britain's lack of preparation for a world war led to continuing problems; although they successfully defended their positions in Malta, re-arming them for a role as an offensive base was proving more problematic. Convoys were in great danger. It was decided that a big operation should be mounted bringing in one convoy direct from the United Kingdom via Gibralter,

and another one from Alexandria. Strategic bombing would take place in support of the proposed operations.

[14] (p.140) After Dunkirk, Bomber Command were involved in strategic bombings of targets in Germany. Shipping and enemy ports were often the targets. The German Luftwaffe were strongly attacking coastal convoys and naval installations and airfields all over southeast England. Aerial dogfights, which were frequently witnessed by civilians all over the countryside, continued. On the ground it was commonplace to hear aircraft overhead, and looking up one saw formations of British and German aircraft, or aircraft dog fights with the Germans.

The RAF airmen were trained to scramble and get airborne within a few minutes. Usually the planes would be out on patrols trying to spot the Germans who intended to attack the airfields. All over the coast were lookout points.

In places elementary radar was already operational.

[15] (p.144) Hitler was convinced Britain's plight was precarious, if not impossible, and from 2 July 1940 he ordered contingency plans for an invasion, once the RAF and their airfields had been destroyed. The German military and naval advisers proposed intense naval and air attacks on British ports and centres of distribution; their intention was to annihilate RAF Fighter Command as a prelude to the invasion, and to terrorize certain populations. Britain had no intention of surrendering. In summer of 1940, overhead in the skies over England, aircraft were heard almost daily even if they could not be seen.

[16] (p.145) That day, on the cliffs above Portland, Winston Churchill, along with two generals, happened to see the fighting above. With Churchill surveying coastal defences was an unknown corps commander, Bernard Montgomery. Both had watched the aerial combat.

[17] (p.149) He subsequently became chairman of BEA-British European Airways.

[18] (p.150) While Italy was still neutral, the British shipped aircraft reinforcements through the Mediterranean. When Italy entered the war on 11 June 1940 the RAF had fewer aircraft than the Italians who could fly bomber reinforcements direct from Libya to Eritrea, and frequently did so, crossing the Sudan by night. Italy subsequently joined the Germans. The British were frequently delayed with lengthy gaps for vital spares for RAF aircrafts.

[19] (p.172) SOE, Special Operations Executive, were sometimes called Churchill's Secret Army and were composed of courageous men and women during the Second World War. It was formed in 1940 to conduct sabotage, espionage and reconnaissance in occupied Europe. They were dropped behind enemy lines, in frequently dangerous zones. The organisation employed over 13,000 people of which 3,200 were women. Churchill ordered SOE to 'set Europe ablaze'. A very high percentage of these brave men and women died, if they were found they were tortured and shot, or sent to concentration camps. Some in the higher echelons of British military society had the attitude that espionage and sabotage, in the Second World War, was not appropriate. For example, Lord Portal scotched a plan by SOE to ambush a particularly troublesome Luftwaffe bomber-crew. Portal's reason was that he could not associate himself with 'assassins'. There seemed to be a 'fatal preference for honourable ignorance, rather than useful knowledge gleaned by devious means, not confined to the soldiers in the field, but as an attitude of mind, permeated the highest levels of military intelligence,' said Dr Norman Dixon

The RAF used Lysander aircraft and later Stirlings to drop SOE agents and supplies over occupied France.

One of their most famous successes was on D-day when the

second German SS Panzer division began to travel north. SOE agents syphoned off all the axle oil from the rail transport cars and replaced it with abrasive grease—all of the rail cars seized up.

In 1945, Eisenhower wrote that the disruption caused by SOE played a considerable part in the Allied victory.

[20] (p.180) On the 25 July 1943, Benito Mussolini's Fascist government was overthrown in Italy.

In German-occupied Denmark, German-sponsored terrorists blew up Danish theatres and other places that the Danes used for entertainment. Explosions and sabotage erupted. On the 29 August the Danish fleet scuttled itself, and the Germans began further reprisals. Jews had been ordered to wear an identifying badge, but then thousands of Danes wore them too, to protect their Jews. Jews and others were shot in the street.

[21] (p.200) Gregory–Hale. On 15 January 1944, quietly at St Michael's, Chester Square, by Canon F. H. Gillingham, uncle of the bride, Sqdn. Ldr. J. P. Gregory DFC, only son of Mrs Powell and the late Captain Lionel Philip Gregory, RFC of Hampstead, to Emily Hale WRNS, youngest daughter of Captain B. J. Hale CBE, RD, RNR and Mrs Hale of Highcombe, Stewardstone, Essex.

Daily Telegraph, Wednesday 19 January 1944

[22] (p.206) No. 190 Squadron was formed in Newmarket on 24 October 1917 as a night training unit. In 1918 it moved to Upwood where it was disbanded in January 1919. On 1 March 1943, during the Second World War, No. 190 reformed with Catalinas and flew anti-submarine patrols over the North Atlantic until disbanded on 31 December 1943.

On 3 January 1944, No. 190 Squadron reformed at Leicester East as an airborne forces squadron equipped with Stirlings. Flying began in March with glider-towing exercises and supply-dropping missions over France in April. Then, on D-day, they began sending twenty-three aircraft with paratroopers to the initial dropping zone, following up during the day with eighteen more towing gliders.

During the first two days of the airborne landings at Arnhem, in September 1944, No. 190 Squadron flew forty-six sorties; all but six were towing gliders.

[23] (p.229) January 1944, Soviet troops advanced and pursued retreating Nazi troops. D-day, on 6 June 1944, saw British and allied troops landed on beaches in Normandy and mainland Europe. On 27 June, US forces advanced from Normandy and captured Cherbourg. In France, Caen was liberated by British and Canadian troops on 9 July 1944. On 15 August, the allies invaded the south of France . . . and on 24 August the Germans surrendered in Paris.

[24] (p.236) George was the name given to the autopilot.

[25] (p.241) British goals were known to enemy troops at the start of the operation as the Germans had seized maps from captured paratroopers that disclosed the intended targets.

[26] (p.259) In the summer of 1944, Soviet Russia overran the sites of three concentration camps, Sobibor, Treblinka and Belzac. In September 1944, in Holland and Greece, millions of people had been starving. On 27 January 1945 the Soviet Army entered Auschwitz.

[27] (p.259) Dr Norman F. Dixon, MBE.

ABOUT THE AUTHOR

Vivien Gilliard started her career as a Montessori school teacher, while raising two children.

This lead to an interest in child development and attachment issues, and in 1984 she gained a Psychology (Hons) degree at Brunel University. She worked in the careers service at Brunel, then took an MSc at Surrey University, which led to working in the NHS.

A visit to Oosterbeek, Holland, in 1999 reignited her interest in the impact of war on young families—and sometimes on the following generations—which had been largely overlooked at the end of World War One.

Shakespeare called it the 'blast of war,' *Henry V,* III, l.